ICE DRAGON

THE DRAGON MISFITS BOOK 1

D.K. HOLMBERG

ASH
PUBLISHING

M ovement caught his attention. Jason swung his
bow around, peering out through his left eye as
he took aim, solidifying and readjusting his stance now
that he'd moved. He hoped the crunch of snow as he
squared off wouldn't disturb the rabbit. The rumbling in
his stomach was likely to do that anyway.

Holding his posture, he focused on the rabbit. He took
a deep breath in preparation for releasing the arrow, but
an explosion behind him startled the creature and he held
off, letting go of the draw but still keeping the arrow
nocked for the time being. The rabbit went scurrying
across the snow, moving far more rapidly than Jason
could. Cursing under his breath, he hurried forward,
looking to see if he could find any way to follow, but it
had disappeared.

All that hunting, and for nothing.

He'd spent the better part of the morning out here

looking for the fire-blasted creature, and now the festivities in the village would be the reason he failed.

Crouching where the rabbit had rested, Jason shoved a gloved hand in the snow, moving it around to see why the rabbit had stopped here. Maybe there was something he could gather, that would offer him something in exchange for missing his kill, but there was nothing.

Wind picked up, gusting across the slope of the mountain. This high up, there wasn't anything to block the wind. No trees—not like there were much further down the mountainside. Only the blank glaze of white all around.

A few distant peaks were visible, but they were all far enough below that he saw them as reflected stretches of white. This mountain rose the highest, a dangerous land, though one where his people had lived for generations.

With the wind gusting, everything became a blanket of white, making it difficult for him to see anything. Jason had to wait for the wind to die down and the snow to clear. When it did, he made out the distant neighboring peak reflecting the pale sunlight. Other than the steep drop-off, nothing else was visible from here.

He shifted his snow-white coat, trying to protect himself from the wind. It still bit through, managing to overwhelm his ability to stay warm. Most of the time, Jason had to dress with more layers than he preferred in order to maintain body heat. If he only had a dragonskin cloak, he wouldn't need quite as many layers, but they were rare and only for those with money, something he definitely did not possess.

As he stood, he thought he saw a flicker of movement. It was farther down the slope, near the stream that would eventually lead to a hidden cave. Jason waited for another sign but didn't see anything.

Always move with light feet. Don't let them see you.

The guidance his father had given him years ago, the beginning of his hunting training, stayed with him.

Starting forward, he was careful. *Light feet.*

At first, he thought maybe it was the rabbit. There *was* something there. It blended into the snow, and as he stared, it moved quickly—almost impossibly so.

By the time he'd reached the stream, there was nothing.

Just his imagination.

That and the cold. That was ever present.

Another explosion sounded behind him, and once again he glanced toward the village. He didn't see the point of the festivities the same as others did, and wasn't at all interested in returning just yet. He had game to catch, food to bring back to his mother and sister. Still, with the morning having been wasted like this, there was no point in staying out here.

Looking out over the snow-covered slopes, he looked for anything out of the ordinary. *Keep your gaze moving. Look for the unexpected.*

Only, on this side of the mountain, there *wasn't* anything unexpected.

Clutching his jacket, he started back. With each step, his boots crunched the snow. The cold managed to seep up through them, and though he had long ago learned to ignore it, it was still unpleasant. As he walked, he continued to search for anything that might reveal the presence of other animals, but he came across nothing.

The area around the village had all been overhunted, and it was unlikely he would find anything of use here. That didn't keep him from trying. He spent most of his days hunting, looking for small game, rabbits and squirrels and anything he might be able to easily capture, forced to use his bow rather than to set traps. Any time he tried setting a trap, someone from the village took what he'd caught. It annoyed him, especially as they had much more success going down the backslope toward the city of Varmin.

Another explosion boomed and he frowned, staring up the slope. The mountain village was an hour from here, far enough of a walk that it would take him considerable time to return, and yet, he still heard the sounds of the explosions, the festivities of those within the village.

Maybe it *was* time to get back. The longer he was gone, the less time he would have before the evening festivities started in full. If he didn't make any sort of trade, he and his family wouldn't eat. His rumbling stomach reminded him of how long it had been since he'd eaten anything at all, and though there were the festivities, he doubted anyone would be more welcoming than usual.

Jason started back up the slope of the mountain,

winding around as he went, following the hard-packed path. He was able to move quickly. The thick soles of his boots didn't grip the snow so much as keep him atop it, not sinking. If the snow were lighter, he'd need snowshoes, but rarely were they necessary this high up the mountainside. Were he to travel south, toward Varmin along the back slope, snowshoes might be necessary to climb back up. As he didn't have snowshoes, it was a good thing he didn't venture that far often. The hunting *could* be better, but it involved him being gone for more days at a time than he felt comfortable with.

The path wound along the mountain, working up through the outcroppings of rock, heading toward the village. Every so often, Jason would pause, listening, hoping he might find something to eat before needing to fully return, but so far, there was nothing.

By the time he reached the village, he was tired. The rumbling in his stomach had eased over the last bit of the climb. Jason had enough experience with overwhelming hunger to know the cessation of the rumbling in his stomach was problematic. It had been too long since he'd had much to eat. They had broth, and while it was better than nothing, it still didn't do much for his ability to feel satiated.

Pausing at the outskirts of the village, he looked around. Snow covered most of the buildings, keeping the roofs obscured. It was the way the mayor wanted it, knowing the best bet to keep themselves hidden was by obscuring their presence here. The easiest way to do that was by leaving the snow covering the buildings and not clearing it out of the streets. It was part of the reason none of the buildings in the village were painted anything other than a plain white; it was a better way to remain concealed. The only difference today was that a fire burned in the center of the village in the festival square.

After having spent as much time as he had outside, and with the chill that worked through him, he wanted nothing more than a sense of warmth and was drawn toward the fire. It was still early, and because of that, there weren't nearly as many people at the square as there would be later, but there were still plenty. He stayed at the edge, yet even from here, the sense of warmth was a welcome reprieve.

"Look at that. Dreshen came to the celebration."

Jason turned slowly, recognizing the voice. Reltash was the same age as Jason, and they had been friends when they were little, but that was before Jason's father died. He was more muscular than Jason, and had a jaw that looked chiseled from ice. His black hair seemed made of dragon-skin, as if he were naturally immune to the cold.

"Everyone is welcome in the celebration," Jason said, looking past him where others already danced.

"I just figured that considering what happened to your father, you wouldn't necessarily want to celebrate."

Jason glared at the other man. He ignored Ingrid and Bradley, on either side of Reltash. They followed Reltash and would do whatever he instructed them to do. They liked to play at independence, but Jason had enough experience with them to know that independence for them meant following the other man, doing what he wanted, and typically, that involved picking on him. He was an easy target for many reasons.

"You don't know anything about what happened to my father," Jason said.

Few people did. That was the problem.

"I think everyone in the village knows what happened to your father, Dreshen."

He started forward, shouldering past Jason. Reltash was nearly two hands taller than Jason and considerably larger, a typical size for those within the village. Jason was slight compared to most, and when he'd been younger, that had given others plenty of reason to think they could pick on him.

Avoid fighting, but don't let them see you as less than you are.

Jason pushed that piece of advice away. It did no good here.

They made their way toward the fire, standing near it, far closer than what Jason would have been able to withstand. That was another thing that was different about him, though in reality, there were quite a few things about him that were different.

Reltash and the other two joined in the dancing, quickly moving in a circle, their coordination for the celebratory dances better than what Jason would have been able to do. He didn't have the same rhythm that they did.

"I hope you can ignore them."

Jason turned and smiled at Tessa. She was one of the few who was kind to him, and yet, eventually Jason knew that would change. There was a limit to kindness within the village out here, as remote as they were and dependent on each other. Strength was prized, and Jason had proven that he wasn't nearly as strong as so many others.

"I ignore them as well as I can," he said.

Tessa had the pale complexion of so many within the village, and a thick dragonskin hat covered her head, obscuring her golden hair, leaving only her round face visible. The stitching along the border of the hat marked her family crest, that of one of the first of the dragon hunters, though the last of the dragon hunters had been decades ago. It did nothing to diminish her family's position in the village.

"I do share their surprise," Tessa said.

"Why?"

She shrugged, meeting his eyes. She had two blue eyes, fitting in far better than he did with his mismatched blue and silver eyes. "Considering what happened with your father…"

"That was long enough ago." A year. That had to be long enough now. His family demanded it be. "I've moved on."

"That's good." Tessa rested a gloved hand on his arm. "I'm always thankful for your father on the festival."

"Most people don't see it like that."

"Most people don't know what he did for me," Tessa said.

She smiled at him again and Jason tried to smile back, but he didn't feel it the way he should. Tessa was being kind to him, the same way she was always kind to him, but he couldn't help but feel as if it were a pitying sort of kindness. He didn't want anyone's pity. His father had died protecting her. He had been strong. A hunter to the end. The kind of man Jason would never be.

"The way he blocked the burst of flame..."

A dragon. That was what had killed him.

"I sometimes wonder what it looked like, but I never got a clear glimpse. Your father sent me running before I had the chance to do so. Had he not, I probably would have died with him. When I came across the hunters—"

"I know."

She sighed. "I shouldn't remind you. I'm sure it's harder at this time."

It hadn't been. Tessa reminding him made it so it was. "He'd be proud he saved you."

That was the truth, too. His father *would* have been proud that he'd managed to save her.

He would have been prouder had they caught the dragon.

There had been no sign of it. Nothing other than the charred remains of his father and the stories Tessa brought back. After years without a single dragon sighting, one would suddenly appear and take his father from him?

"I'm glad you came," she said.

"I am too. Better here than imagining things down the slope."

"What sort of things?"

Jason shrugged. "It's probably nothing. My imagination. The snow. All of it made me think there was something where there was not." He grinned at her. "Maybe it was a dragon."

"Jason Dreshen! Don't say that!"

He sighed. "You're right. I shouldn't joke. Not about that."

"You should not."

She watched him for a moment before hurrying off, joining the others near the fire. It was the advantage their dragonskin jackets offered. Not only were they more immune to the heat, something he most certainly was not, but the dragonskin seemed to absorb the heat, holding on to it and offering a warmth that remained for much of the year. It was the other reason that dragonskin was so prized.

It was similar to tellum, the ore mined near them. A small amount of the ore produced significant heat. Those with money were able to weave it into their clothes, and many of the wealthy of the village—and there *were* some— used it instead of dragonskin.

Another explosion went off, this one not far from him.

The cannons were designed to be a part of the celebration, and in the evening, colorful explosions would light the sky, both as a way of celebrating and as a way of taunting the dragons that once had plagued their homeland. It had been almost a century since dragons had attacked the village, long enough that for most, the threat was a distant sort of danger.

That wasn't the case for Jason. His knowledge and understanding of the dragons and the threat they posed was far different than most. He had lost more than most his age, no longer having his father around the way that others—including Reltash—did.

As he watched, the cannon was loaded again. Morris, an older, gray-haired, solid man, worked at filling the cannon with explosive powder. It was considered an honor to work the cannon, and many trained for years to have that honor.

Several men surrounding Morris were laughing as he worked, watching over his shoulder, and Jason was brought back to his father. He'd been the cannon master at that time, a role he'd tried teaching Jason, something that Jason had thought he would eventually be able to do. Now even that dream was lost to him, like so many other things.

Chanting began, and the circle around the fire parted, allowing several of the village elders to make their way through, carrying a wooden totem. Wood was rare, and a piece this size would have to be dragged up the mountainside all the way from beyond Varmin. This year's totem was far more decorated than previous years: The painting was elaborate, depicting scenes of battle, dragons flying around it, and at the center, a man they only knew by the name Zarath, who held his hands in the air. Zarath was the dragon master, the one who controlled the dragons attacking the village, and because of Zarath, everyone had suffered.

They carried the totem to the fire. Once there, it was stood on end, and the chanting continued. Jason remained at the edge of the circle, wishing as he did each year that he would be able to get closer to the fire, but without dragonskin clothing, he was forever forced to remain watching from a distance.

"We open the celebration of our freedom with the demonstration." Mayor Jans held his hands up in the air. They had been dusted with ash, making his normally pale skin nearly as dark as the dragonskin jacket he wore. "We celebrate our safety. We celebrate our freedom. We celebrate our people!"

With each statement, the chanting intensified, at first just a steady murmur. Each statement was punctuated by another slap, the intensity to it rising louder and louder, and Jason found himself murmuring the chant under his breath. There had been a time when he could get closer to the flames, but he had never had his own leathers, having borrowed those from the city. That was an advantage of his father serving as the cannon master.

"Today we sacrifice this symbol of violence. Today we once again recognize the struggles our people faced. We celebrate those who sacrificed. We celebrate those we lost, even recently. The dragons are not gone and we cannot forget. We celebrate... And we remember. Those lost to the dragons will be remembered. We hold them in our hearts."

The chanting grew louder and louder. The cannon exploded and Morris began loading more powder, working quickly. As he often did, Jason found himself watching the cannon as much as anything else.

"Oh great Dayvos. Watch over us again this year, help us ensure that we remain safe, that we continue to thrive. We ask for your protection as you have granted each year. We offer the sacrifice to you."

The mayor lifted the totem, and with the others around him, he heaved it onto the fire.

It was covered in the powder the cannon master used, and because of that, the totem began to crackle, quickly engulfed in flames. They burned a bright red, turning blue, and as they did heat began to spiral into the sky, thick with a dark cloud of smoke.

Jason stared at the fire rather than looking up toward the clouds the way so many did. He watched as the totem was engulfed in flames, and felt a grim satisfaction in the destruction. The flames had consumed so much for his people, and even more for himself. Because of that, he wanted nothing more than to see the totem—and Zarath—consumed.

It didn't take long for the flames to devour the totem, engulfing it completely. Jason watched, a hint of a smile curling his lips, his hands balled into fists. He could feel the heat coming off the totem, and if he weren't dressed in his bearskin coat, he might have attempted to go closer, but as it was, he remained standing at a distance. It was better to keep himself protected. Safe. Any closer and he would risk burning along with the sculpture.

The chanting shifted and gradually became a song. Jason sang along, letting the words fill him, a celebratory thanks for safety that they all called out to their god. When it was done, the chanting eased and the dancing began again.

Jason turned away. He needed to find something for his family, a way for them to subsist for another few days —at least until Jason managed to procure something more. The hunting had been difficult this winter, though it was never easy in these lands. At least, not for him. He couldn't leave his family as long as it would take to venture toward better hunting grounds. Instead, Jason had to depend upon luck, hope he could find squirrels and rabbits, and pray he came across larger game like some of the fox or deer that occasionally wandered up the mountain slope. Most of the time, he didn't encounter any of that. Most of the time, he was lucky to find a rabbit every few days. There *had* been something by the stream. Maybe tomorrow he'd go back, though by tomorrow, whatever he'd seen today would be gone.

He depended upon his ability to trade for necessary food, but it wouldn't be long before they were out of items he could trade. Eventually, they *would* run out, and then what would he do?

Either the tellum mines or the iron mines in Varmin. That would be his only option.

Only, he didn't want to go to the mines. That meant leaving the village, the only place he'd ever known. And his father hadn't wanted him to work in the mines. Doing so meant abandoning his sister and mother. That was one thing he'd promised his father he'd never do, and he intended to honor it—even if it meant he starved.

Jason wouldn't allow himself to think like that. He also wouldn't allow himself to think that his family was going to suffer because of his failings. And he wouldn't allow himself to even consider the possibility he would not succeed. His father would have been disappointed in that sort of thinking, which was why he refused to accept it.

As he started away from the festival, another explosion thundered behind him.

He glanced over his shoulder, listening to the chanting, the laughter, the happiness. He felt none of it. He wasn't resentful others did, but he simply didn't have the time. There was much more for him to do.

2

Jason stopped in front of the small shop. Snowmelt dripped from the roof, and the ground in front of the door was slick with ice. By nightfall, everything would freeze, turning to a dangerous glaze. Each morning, the shop owners would need to break up the ice, typically by mixing it with more snow, using that as their way to ensure that no one got hurt walking into their store.

It was part of the reason boots like those Reltash wore would be so prized. Jason's boots were less so. Partly that was due to the fact that his boots didn't have much grip, but partly because they were made of bearskin. While warm, they weren't nearly as high quality as those made from dragonskin. They were his, though, and he'd never felt the need to barter with people from Varmin—though in part that was his complete lack of anything worthwhile to barter.

Stepping into the shop, it took a moment for his eyes to adjust to the dim light.

"I'll be right with you," a voice from the back of the shop said.

Jason remained in the doorway as his eyesight continued to adjust. As it cleared, he looked around the inside of the shop, surveying everything here. Master Erich had some of the best meats in the village, and he had often taken pity on Jason, though he kept worrying about the time when Master Erich would no longer have the same kindness.

The inside of the shop smelled wonderful, and it set Jason's stomach rumbling, his mouth watering, and he knew better than to allow it to appeal to him like that. There was no promise of anything by coming into the shop. Master Erich certainly didn't owe him anything. The counter contained a thin layer of tellum, enough that it heated the entirety of the shop. It was comfortable in a way Jason never was.

"What can I… Oh. Jason."

Jason smiled. Master Erich was an older man, thin despite his towering size, and blood spattered his apron. His hair was balding, making his high forehead even more pronounced. "Master Erich. I was hoping you might have scraps you might be willing to part with."

Most of the time he asked for scraps, though he hoped for more. He tried not to get his hopes too high, knowing that Master Erich had to earn a wage the same as anyone within the village. Just because he was kind didn't mean he should be taken advantage of.

"I'm sorry, Jason. With the festival…"

Jason understood. With the festival, everything would have been turned into treats. It was unlikely there would be any food remaining. Not only the people of the village celebrated during the festival, but those ᴧwho lived outside the village, on the outskirts, would come here, partake in the celebration, and use it as an opportunity to trade.

He should have known better.

"If you come back in a few days, I'm sure I'll have something."

Jason nodded. "I understand. You know, I could help. I'm sure there's something I could do to make it easier on you during the festival."

Master Erich shook his head. "Normally I would accept any help, especially yours, but my brother and his children have come to the village for the festival, and… Well, I have more than enough hands to assist."

"Of course."

If only he had a few coins, something to trade, but all he had was his empty stomach. And his bow, but he needed that for the off chance that he might eventually catch something again. It might be that he would end up in the mines regardless of what he intended.

He headed back out and wandered to the edge of the village, ignoring the singing and chanting at the festival plaza. There was nothing within him that felt at all interested in celebrating, at least not right now. What he wanted was food.

He paused at the edge of the village, staring outward. In the distance, movement caught his attention and he squinted. He always looked out with his left eye—the silver one—as he was able to see more clearly out of that eye. His vision came with a hint of colors, not just those which he could see out of his blue eye, but almost as if he were able to make out distinctions in warmth and coolness. His father had been the only one aware of that and had cautioned Jason to keep it to himself, worried that were anyone else to find out, they would banish him from the village.

Dragon sight.

That was what it was called, and thankfully, he didn't have any other features of those who favored the dragons, but his silver eye—and the strange connection it gave him to seeing—was enough.

In the distance, the line of people coming toward the village drew his attention. They were dressed only slightly better than him. Many of the people who lived outside the village on the back slope of the mountain didn't have much money, either. Only those who came up from Varmin—and from even further down the mountainside, though they rarely ventured this far—owned anything fancier. Furs and sheepskin, all finely made, some of them even with embroidery along them, a luxury in the village.

He was tempted to head out of the village once again. Maybe with everyone coming toward it, something would be scared up for him. The problem was in the danger of staying outside the village at this time of day. The winds would shift and the cold would pick up, placing him at a real risk of exposure to the elements.

Not only that, but snowfall tended to occur at night. It could come down quickly, and without the necessary equipment, he could be trapped out in the snow. He had enough experience navigating the mountain that he doubted he would be truly lost, but he didn't want to risk it.

He watched for a little longer, staring into the distance, regarding the people as they approached. He didn't recognize any of them, though Jason didn't know most people who lived in the backcountry. Many of them only came in for festival time, though there were some who came for trade, visiting people like Master Erich, staying for a night or two in the small inn near the center of town.

Pulling his gaze away, he headed back into the village, wandering along the side streets until he reached his home. They were on the downslope, a place considered less safe than higher up the peak, which made it less desirable. Then again, it had also been less expensive. After his father's death, they'd been forced to move, and his mother had brought them here to this place, a home that was more affordable but colder.

He pushed open the door, missing the warmth that once had filled their home.

"Don't leave it open," his sister snapped from the far side of the room.

She was wrapped in two blankets. Jason closed the door quickly behind him, but some of the draft managed to get in, gusting behind him, letting the cold air swirl all around them.

"I thought you'd be at the festival."

Kayla pulled the blankets around her, tucking even her wavy brown hair inside. She was thin—far too thin. Were he to see his reflection, he'd probably say the same about himself. "It's too cold."

Jason grinned. "It's always too cold."

"Not always. This one is particularly cold."

"You can get near the fire."

"I tried, but…"

She turned away, and Jason knew better than to push her. She suffered just as much as he did, if not more. Kayla had a bit of a harder time because she was home with their mother. At least he was able to leave, go hunting. He didn't have her patience, and she didn't have his stealth. It worked for now.

"You didn't miss anything, anyway."

She started crying, and she headed toward the back of the room.

Jason hurried over to his sister and slipped his arm around her shoulders.

"It's just…"

He pulled her close, hugging her and realizing just how thin she'd become. He needed success hunting to help both of them. They couldn't rely on the kindness of others in the village for much longer. Either that, or they would have to leave. With their mother as sick as she'd been, that would be difficult.

Kayla leaned her head on his shoulder, almost the same height as he. Though he was short for the village, Kayla was average height. "It's so hard at the festival time," she said.

He squeezed her again, hugging her tight. "I know."

She stopped for a moment, and when she pulled her head away from his shoulder, tears continuing to stream down her face, she shook her head. "The festival is supposed to be a time of celebration. I hate it that we can't celebrate."

"We can. Eventually, it will get easier." That was what he told himself.

"That's what they always tell me, but it doesn't seem like it's getting any easier. And with Mother..."

Jason glanced toward the back of the room. Their mother was probably still in bed, the same way she'd been over the last year. When she did finally get up, she rarely said anything, which made it hard for both Jason and Kayla to deal with. It would be easier for them if their mother would manage her grief, and the fact that she couldn't made it so that he and Kayla had a hard time moving on.

"How is she today?"

"She got out of bed to pee."

"I suppose that's better."

"You suppose? I'm the one who has to wash the sheets when she doesn't."

Jason peeled himself away from his sister and made his way to the small hearth. He grabbed a shovelful of dried dung and threw it into the hearth. Wood was scarce and too much work to haul up from lower down the mountain, which meant dung was all they really had to use, something that made it difficult to stay warm. They had to conserve how much they used as well, trying not to burn through it too quickly, but there were times when they needed heat.

At least during the festival, he didn't need to burn quite as much. They could get as close as they could tolerate to the fire, warming themselves that way. They might not have the same benefit as those who had dragon-skin jackets or cloaks or even hats, or as those who had dragon bone sculptures carved from the remains of dragons and still holding onto that ancient heat, but they were able to stay warmer than they did most times.

"Why don't you go and fill up the pot with snow."

"You caught something?"

The hope in her voice nearly broke his heart.

"I will tomorrow. I saw something, so I know I'll have success."

Kayla watched him and hurried to one of the cabinets, grabbing a pot and carrying it outside without saying another word. While he was working in the hearth, trying to get the dung lit, he heard a shuffling.

"What did you catch?"

Jason stared at the dried coals as they slowly crackled

to life. Eventually, they would burn brightly, but quickly. Always too quickly. "We have broth."

"What's in the broth?"

Jason straightened, turning to his mother and wiping his hands on his pants. "The same as we had the last two days."

His mother's face was pale—even paler than most in the village—and dark circles around her eyes gave her a haunted appearance. Her hair was disheveled, though it had been that way for quite some time.

"Your father would have—"

Jason stiffened at the start of the comment. It wasn't the first time his mother had made comments like that, and knowing her, it wouldn't be the last. "I know Father would have been successful by now. Maybe you need to go farther tomorrow. Or with the others."

Jason stared at her for a moment before turning away. He headed outside and passed Kayla packing snow into the pot. She did so without gloves, and her hands were already turning red. What was she thinking, coming out here like that? Why would she risk herself to the elements? She knew better.

"Where are you going?"

"Off for a while," he said.

He pulled his jacket around his shoulders, trying to ignore the swirling wind. Snow was already starting to fall, flakes thick and heavy now, but soon enough, he expected they would become sharp needles that threatened to carve his skin.

He wandered away from the house, at first heading away from the village before deciding better of it. His sister still needed him, even if his mother wasn't willing to bring herself back together. If his mother had managed to keep going—the way that Jason and Kayla had—they might have a way to pay for more than just scraps. A healer's time was valued.

The sound of laughter drew him, and he turned back toward the village and the festival. The voices belonged to Reltash and a group of others the same age as Jason. They were laughing and singing, performing the festival march as they traipsed through the streets, and he turned away before they caught sight of him.

Jason ducked alongside the nearest building, staying low to the ground. One of the advantages of his snow-white bearskin jacket and boots was that he blended into the snow better than the others did with their dragonskin. With those, they practically stood out, drawing attention. Then again, with his silver eye, he was able to see them moving in a different way. There were shades of orange and red around them, brighter now that they had stood so close to the fire, and he focused on that, watching them as they moved along the street. None of them turned in his direction, which he was thankful for. If they had, Jason wasn't sure what he would've said—or what they would have done.

When they were gone, he glanced over his shoulder, debating whether he would return home. Kayla could handle making the broth without him, and was probably better at it than he was. With their meager supplies, she managed to season it far better than he ever could.

Another explosion fired once more, and as the light was beginning to fade, its detonation called to him. He could feel it thundering in his chest, and he remembered the way the powder felt as it was mixed into the cannon, the colorings sprinkled on top. It was all too easy to recall what had gone into the mixture, the way the explosions would ring out, and the smile on his father's face as he remarked upon the nature of each firing.

Before he knew it, Jason was drawn back toward the festival plaza. The fire danced against the growing darkness and he stood frozen for a moment, watching it. There was something rhythmic and soothing about it, and yet he had no desire to get too close to it. Not like so many others did.

At this time of night, the festival began to change. There was less of the ceremony and more of the true celebrating. Foods he couldn't afford were brought out by butchers and bakers and anyone who thought they could offer something along the street for others to purchase. He crept forward, watching, and found himself pushed into the growing throng of people.

He couldn't see well, his height a disadvantage here, and as he was pushed forward, he found himself drawn toward the cannon.

It fired again and he looked up. Red sizzled in the sky, a circle forming. It looked something like a fireball, though his father would have done a better job. Not that

Morris was bad at his job. His father had worked with him, training him in the years before his passing.

"Jason?"

Tessa approached from across the festival plaza, carrying a sweet bread wrapped in burlap, and was starting to bring it to her lips. A smile formed, and she slipped close to him.

"I wasn't expecting to see you out this late."

The cannon fired again, and he glanced over. "I wasn't going to, but..."

This time, green erupted in the night sky, sparkles streaming all over, the colors bright, mixed with a hint of blue. It created a shimmering pattern that seemed to undulate in the sky.

"I liked your father's better."

He nodded. "Morris isn't bad. I think with enough practice, he could be a good cannon master."

Another explosion rang out, this time yellow and purple. The mixture was strange, a combination of colors that his father never would've chosen. He could tell that Morris was working quickly now, hurriedly repacking the cannon.

"Still."

They stood in silence, people pushing up behind them, forcing him forward, ever closer to the cannon. Eventually, he caught a glimpse of it, just the barest sight, nothing more than that. He tried to stay back, knowing that if he were to get too close, Morris would invite him over. Jason had no interest in getting near the cannon. It would be too hard.

"Are you hungry?"

"What was that?"

Tessa offered him the bread. "Hungry. Are you? I know you don't always eat as well as you should."

"I do fine," he said. "There was something today near the stream. I'm sure I'll find something soon."

Tessa laughed softly, touching him on the arm. "That's not a criticism, Jason Dreshen. It's a comment on how hard it is to catch food around here."

"I do fine," he repeated. His stomach took that moment to betray him, rumbling loudly.

Tessa chuckled, forcing the sweet bread into his hand. "Take this."

"You don't need to do that. I told you that I would find—"

Tessa shook her head. "I know I don't need to, but I want to. Take it. I can get more."

He held on to the sweet bread, staring at it. A loaf like that could last his family a week. By that time, it would be stale but no less sweet.

"Thanks."

She laughed again. "You don't have to be so stubborn. I'm happy to help."

"I didn't realize I was being stubborn."

"Well—"

The cannon fired again, and a scream followed it. Jason jerked his head toward the cannon and started forward before thinking about what he was doing.

When he reached it, he found Morris lying alongside the cannon. His dragonskin coat smoldered. He didn't appear to be moving.

Where was his help?

A cannon master didn't work alone, and when it came to the nighttime festivities, it didn't make sense for the cannon master to not have assistants.

"Morris?" He dropped down onto his knees next to the man, but the heat from his jacket made it difficult to get too close. Morris had spent the better part of the day near the fire, and his dragonskin jacket had absorbed much of that heat.

"Let me," Tessa said, sliding in next to him. She pressed her head down to Morris's chest. Jason almost cautioned her against it, but with her dragonskin hat, she wasn't in any real danger. She could withstand the heat of Morris's coat, much like she could withstand the residual effect of the explosion along his chest.

"Heart's still beating," she said. Tessa met his eyes and Jason looked around, searching for anyone who could help. Everyone was so caught up in the festivities that they hadn't paid any attention to the fact that the cannon had stopped firing.

"We need to bring him to my mother."

"Are you sure?" There was another question lingering in it, one few were willing to ask aloud.

"Who else could we take him to?" Jason asked.

Tessa nodded, reaching for Morris's arms. "You grab his legs."

Jason was thankful for his gloves and clutched Morris's legs, trying to ignore the heat radiating from the dragonskin boots. He would have a hard time dragging him, so they needed someone else who had dragonskin clothing to help.

"Jason?"

He shook his head and started off, dragging Morris more than he carried him. Thankfully, they went across the snow, though the jacket had the effect of melting the snow as they passed over it. Tessa was strong and managed to keep Morris lifted a little bit, though not so much that he didn't drag.

Jason fought his way through the crowd, worried his mother wouldn't be well enough to help. She hadn't been well enough in a long time.

As they elbowed their way through, he crashed into a man who was about his height. He glanced at Jason before his gaze darted down to Tessa. "Let me help," the man said, his voice a gravelly sort of growl.

Jason didn't have the strength to argue. Even if he did, there wasn't an argument that he would've been able to voice. Nor did he necessarily want to. Having someone else help carry Morris would be better. They could get him to his home faster that way.

"Where are we going?" the man asked.

"Healer," he managed to say.

"What happened?"

"Explosion," he said.

The man glanced past Jason, his gaze drifting toward where the cannon would be found. He said nothing, and together with Jason, Tessa and the stranger managed to lift Morris, keeping him above the snow. As they carried him, they bumped into a few others, though not so many that they were slowed. They drifted away from the sounds of the festivities, and Jason glanced over at Tessa, wondering why she would be spending her time with him like this.

He was tempted to tell her to go, but he didn't really want her to leave. He was appreciative of the fact that she was here, that she was willing to help, and he worried that if he sent her off, she would actually go, so he said nothing.

By the time they reached his home, a small trail of smoke drifted from the chimney. Jason spotted a hint of red against the outline of darkness and worried his sister might have put too much dung into the fireplace. If she had, there wouldn't be enough remaining for the rest of the week. He could try to search for other sources of heat, but within the village, it was incredibly valuable. Everything that could burn was held on to.

He shouldered open the door, dragging Morris with him. The stranger said nothing, moving along with him.

Once they got into the room, a hint of warmth greeted him. It was too much.

"Jason? Did you... What is this?" Kayla asked.

"Where is Mother?"

Kayla glanced at the stranger and then at Tessa before her gaze darted to the back room. "She already went to bed."

"We need to get her up."

"Jason… Are you sure that's a good idea?"

He nodded to Morris. "The cannon backfired."

The only thing Jason could figure was that Morris had been standing too close to the cannon. One of the things his father had taught him about the explosives was that if he stood too close, and if he didn't have a long enough fuse, there was some danger in a backfire. His father was always one for safety, to the point where he'd forced Jason to stay back a significant distance while he was watching. Even doing that hadn't always made him happy. His father would have preferred Jason to have watched from behind a dragonskin cloak, though they didn't have many that he could use.

"Can you just go and wake her?"

"I can try." Kayla scurried off, and it gave him an opportunity to look at the man.

He wasn't so much taller than Jason, something that was fairly uncommon in the village. Most people were a hand or two taller than him, and incredibly muscular. This man was lean, almost as if he were underfed, no different than Jason. He was dressed in a strange gray fur. It wasn't bearskin, and it certainly wasn't dragonskin, but it wasn't an animal that he recognized. The hood of his cloak was pulled up, concealing most of his face other than the hint of a shadowy beard.

"Thanks for your help. I think we can handle it from here."

"I can stay," the stranger said.

Jason glanced over at Tessa, and she shrugged.

"I'm Jason Dreshen. This is Tessa Olive."

The man nodded, but he didn't offer his name.

A shuffling near the door to the back room caught his attention, and Jason turned to see his mother smoothing her hair back from her face, her sleepy gaze sweeping around the room. "Jason? Did you find any food?"

He shook his head. "It's Morris, Mother. The cannon backfired, and—"

"I can't help him."

"You can. You just have to—"

His mother looked up, and the darkness that he'd known since his father's death flared in her eyes. "I can't help them."

She turned away, shuffling back into the room.

"What was that about?" the stranger asked.

"That's my mother."

"I take it that she's a healer."

"She was," he said.

"What happened?"

"My father died about a year ago. She couldn't save him."

The stranger met his gaze for a moment before nodding. "Why don't we see what I can do." The man leaned forward, crouching next to Morris. He began to peel away Morris's dragonskin coat, and when it was off, he handed it to Jason. "Take this outside."

"Once it's off, he loses the benefit of the stored heat."

The stranger looked up. The shadows in the distance of his eyes were unreadable. "I'm sure he won't mind when he recovers."

Jason started toward the door but Tessa shook her head, grabbing the coat from him. He was thankful for it. The coat was already starting to burn his hands. Even through his gloves, the heat was intense. It was a strange thing about dragonskin. Having just a little bit granted the wearer protection from its heat. As Jason had none, he wasn't protected at all from the heat coming off the jacket. Considering the way the man had peeled the jacket off Morris, he must have some protection of his own.

"Can you help him?" Jason asked.

The man nodded, pushing back the hood of his cloak. He had dark, disheveled hair, and in the dim light of the inside of the house, Jason was able to make out the gray flowing through his beard.

"I have some experience with helping those who've been injured, but I'm not sure whether it will be effective on him."

He reached into his pocket, as if looking for something that might help him, and when he pulled his hand out, Jason realized that he held a small circular stone. He pressed it on Morris's chest and began to mumble softly, his words little more than a whisper and too faint for Jason to make out.

The heat within the room began to build and Jason turned his attention to the hearth. The dung glowed too brightly, far more brightly than it should. What had Kayla been thinking, lighting the hearth like that? Why had she ruined so much of their supplies? She knew better, even if she *had* been cold.

"I'll be right back," he said to the stranger and hurried over to the hearth, taking the shovel and shifting the coals around. They began to fade, the bright light dimming, and Jason leaned back on his heels. At least they hadn't burned through all of the coals. Just enough that they had wasted some.

Turning back to the stranger, he found the man pushing something back into his pocket. Jason watched, thinking he might be able to figure out what it was, but the man kept his back to him, making it difficult to make anything out.

"How is he?"

"He should pull through," the stranger said. "The jacket he was wearing conveys both a blessing and a curse."

Jason blinked. It was the first time he'd ever heard anyone describe a dragonskin jacket as a curse. If he were so lucky to have one, he would certainly not view it that way.

"Why a curse?"

The stranger got to his feet, wiping his hands together. "He'll need water. And I suspect he'll be hungry."

"We don't have much in the way of food," Jason said.

"Then find someone who does," the stranger said.

The stranger reached the door and started out it at the same time as Tessa was coming back in. They bumped into each other, and she looked up, starting to apologize, before catching herself. Her eyes widened and she stepped to the side.

When the stranger was gone, Jason frowned at her. "What was that about?"

"Did you see his eyes?"

Jason frowned and shook his head. "He was wearing his cloak most of the time," he said. And even when he wasn't, he was looking away so that Jason didn't have the opportunity to look in the man's eyes.

"They were like yours."

"Blue and silver?"

She glanced toward the door. Wind whistled in and Jason hurried over, closing it quickly before all the heat rushed out. With as much dung as they'd burned, he didn't want to allow the heat to fully escape. Now that they had heated the home to this temperature, they might as well take advantage of it.

"Not blue and silver. Silver."

Dragon sight? He had always believed himself unique, and at least around the village and the surrounding areas, he was so.

"Maybe you saw it wrong."

"Maybe," she said.

"You can go back to the festival. I can stay with Morris."

"I can stay with you."

Jason smiled and shook his head. "I'm fine. Really. Besides, if Morris comes back around, I'll make sure he gets back to the cannon."

She glanced toward the door before nodding. "Don't stay in all night."

"Even if I do, I'm sure you'll have fun."

"Jason—"

He squeezed her arm. "Thanks for your help."

When she was gone, Kayla emerged from the back room. "How is he?"

"The stranger seemed to help. I don't know what he did, but he said Morris should be fine. He told me to give him water and food."

Kayla looked up at him. "Food? How are we supposed to give him food when we don't even have food for ourselves?"

Jason pulled the sweet bread from his pocket and handed it over. "We have this."

"Where did you get this? Did you steal it?"

"I didn't steal it. Tessa gave it to me."

Kayla started in on it, eating quickly, having no hesitation, not the way that Jason had. "Thank you."

"For what?"

"For sharing it."

He cocked his head to the side. "Of course I'd share it. You're my sister."

3

A soft cough caught Jason's attention. He stirred, having slept poorly, and turned to look. The coals in the hearth glowed softly, barely any heat emanating off them.

"Where am I?"

He got to his feet and hurried over to Morris. "You're in the Dreshen home."

Morris clutched his hands to his chest, blinking. "The cannon."

Jason nodded and leaned close to Morris, helping the man sit up. He was about ten years older than Jason, solid —much like Jason's father—and his thick beard had been singed by the explosion.

"What happened?" Jason asked.

"I don't know. I was packing the powder into the cannon and it backfired."

"My father said that could happen."

Morris took a deep breath, wincing as he did and clutching his hands over his chest. "That's what he told me, too. I followed all of his instructions, Jason. It shouldn't have backfired like that."

Jason smiled. "He always told me that despite our plans, things sometimes go awry."

"I suppose," he said.

"You don't think so?"

"I... I don't know." Morris looked around. "Is your mother here? I'd like to thank her for helping me."

Jason glanced at the door leading to the back room. "She's asleep. And it wasn't my mother who helped. There was a stranger, a visitor to the village, who helped you."

Morris took a deep breath. "I should thank him, too."

"If we can find him."

"You don't know who he is?"

Jason shook his head. "I don't know anything about him. He offered his aid and then disappeared."

Getting to his feet, Morris looked around. "Where's my jacket?" There was a bit of urgency in his voice, and Jason understood it. The dragonskin coat was valuable, and he didn't even think it was Morris's. It was probably borrowed from the village, the benefit of being the cannon master.

"We took it outside."

"Why outside?"

Jason shrugged. "The stranger wanted it outside. I don't really know." Had they left it inside, they would have had some extra heat, so it would've been beneficial.

Without it, it had grown considerably colder inside than it had been.

"I take it you brought me here?"

"Me and Tessa Olive. We thought my mother would help."

Morris was silent for a moment. "I'm sorry, Jason." When Jason didn't immediately say anything, he took that as an invitation to speak more. "I'm sorry about what happened. I'm sorry I took over for your father. I'm sorry that—"

Jason shook his head. "You did well."

"But the cannon was silent."

"I'm sure you can get it fired again."

Morris clutched his chest, wincing again. "I'm not really sure I want to, to be honest."

Jason glanced toward the back of the home. It was late, but the festival would still be ongoing. "I could help."

"I'd like that."

Jason gathered his coat, leggings, and boots, slipping into them, and when he was ready, Morris followed him out of the home. They found the jacket hanging from a hook outside, melting the snow around it.

The snow would return overnight, leaving no evidence of the coat ever having been there and no sign that the snow had been disturbed.

Morris slipped on the coat and buttoned it quickly before turning to him. "This should have been yours."

"I wasn't going to be ready to take over the cannon for quite a while," he said.

"Still."

Jason could only shrug.

Morris looked around. "I forget how far out you are."

"It's not so bad," Jason said, nudging past him as he started back toward the festival plaza. Morris followed, saying nothing, and Jason was thankful that the man didn't speak. There wasn't anything that he could say, anyway. The closer they walked, the more the festival fire began to draw him. As they neared, he waved briefly to Kayla where she stood at the edge of the fire, thankful she'd come out, if only for warmth. He didn't see any sign of Tessa, though she was likely with others. She'd done more than her part helping him get Morris to safety, and she didn't need to be dragged into staying just because of him.

They weaved along the outside of the crowd, and Jason was thankful Morris didn't try to get too close to the fire. He wouldn't have been able to follow him, but then, Jason would've managed to reach the cannon regardless.

By the time they arrived at the cannon, they found it untouched. The bucket of powder near it remained.

"It's a good thing we didn't lose that," Morris said. "It's difficult enough to get supplies up here, and that powder is one of the hardest for us to find. Even in Varmin, they don't have much powder."

Morris leaned over the bucket and began to scoop more out.

Jason turned to the cannon, looking it over. He hadn't examined it after the accident, but now that he was here, he studied it, running his hands along the surface. It was cold now, the metal having chilled. Perhaps that was part of the problem. A warm cannon often fired better, at least according to his father. The metal would expand and contract with the heat and cold, and it was more reliable when it was heated.

Unless Morris had done something wrong.

This was Morris's first time firing the cannon, at least without any help. His father had done so for years and had been mentored for four years prior to taking over, a luxury Morris had not had. In that way, Jason probably had as much experience with the cannon as Morris.

Not that he expected Morris to acknowledge that claim. He wouldn't have expected anyone to have come to him looking for help, and as he ran his hands along the surface, he remembered the way his father had instructed him. He searched now for anything that would be off.

"Search for irregularities," his father had said, his hands pressing over Jason's as he ran them along the length of the cannon. *Always make sure that your tool is safe before you use it.*

Jason could remember the way his father's hands had felt upon his, the warmth of them, callouses making them rough.

"Only when you're confident there's nothing irregular about it can you move on to the next step."

"What's the next step?"

"Examine the barrel."

He turned to the barrel of the cannon, peeking inside. With his silver eye, he was able to see the contours of the interior in a different way than even his father had. When his father had instructed him in looking along the barrel, he had done so, searching for any signs of irregularity along the metal, and hadn't seen them during that first lesson.

Would he see anything now?

As he peered inside, he couldn't be certain, but there was something that seemed off.

Morris reached him, a scoop of powder in hand.

"Hold on," Jason said.

"What is it?"

"Inside the barrel," he said.

He reached an arm inside and felt for the contour of the metal, tracing his hand along it. He started toward the front, sweeping it back. The residue from the powder smeared beneath his hand and he pushed past it, focusing beyond that, looking for anything else.

As he reached back, he found it. At first, he thought it was a crack, but that wasn't it at all. There was something else. A harder lump.

Jason pulled his arm out, reached for his belt knife, and stuffed it down into the barrel, scraping along the edge. He didn't think the knife was harder than the cannon, and as he scratched at the strange lump, he felt it finally give way.

Stretching as far as he could, he reached all the way into the cannon, pulling that lump out. It was solid, and seemed to be coated with residue. Almost as if it were a lump of powder, but that didn't seem to be the case.

"What is that?" Morris asked.

Jason shrugged. "I don't really know. My father told me to examine the cannon both outside and in before firing it."

Morris nodded. "He told me the same."

Jason studied the other man and realized Morris probably hadn't done the necessary examination as he should have.

He wasn't going to say anything about that. It wasn't his role. He wasn't the cannon master. Then again, Morris wasn't the same cannon master his father had been.

"Make sure there's nothing else inside, and you should be good to continue firing," he said.

"Thanks for your help," Morris answered.

Jason stood off to the side, watching as Morris packed the cannon. While he was doing that, Jason examined the lump he'd pulled from the inside. It was coated with residue, and he stuffed it into his jacket pocket to look at later. Sometimes the powder could do strange things, and with enough moisture, he suspected it could lump like that, though efforts were made to ensure that didn't happen.

Then again, his father had been the one to make those efforts. He didn't know if Morris was doing the same things that his father would've done. It was possible that Morris wasn't nearly as prepared as Jason's father would have been.

When Morris was done packing the powder, he ran a fuse out and motioned for Jason to move out of the way. He complied, standing off to the side. Morris added another sprinkling of powder—the colorant—and tipped the cannon up, aiming it toward the sky.

Turning back to Jason, he winked.

"A little something special," he said.

"How special?"

"You'll see."

He reached the end of the fuse, pulled out a splint, and tapped it together, sparking a light. The fuse ignited and the flame raced along it, reaching the inside of the cannon.

Jason covered his ears.

He looked up, waiting for the explosion.

None came.

Morris frowned.

"What did I do?"

Jason shook his head. "I—"

The cannon thundered.

Sparks burst from the end. They crackled, sending a fireball shooting into the sky. It was orange and yellow, and it gradually flickered over to a blue hue.

The crowd behind them cheered, some clapping their hands, but Jason only frowned. He understood what Morris had been getting at. The fireball was large—much larger than they normally were. It meant that Morris had packed more powder than he probably should have.

Could that have been his problem? Maybe he had been

packing too much powder in all along. In doing so, it would lead to a strange explosion like what he'd just experienced.

"It looks like you've got things figured out," Jason said.

Morris grinned, heading toward the barrel and grabbing another scoop of powder. Several others drifted out of the crowd, heading toward them, and Jason backed away. He wasn't going to stay here while Morris worked, not with some of the others who wanted to watch.

"That was the best explosion yet," someone said.

"Even bigger than we're used to."

"Sometimes you have to go big," Morris said. He started coughing, and Jason glanced over, noticing how he winced and clutched his chest.

The fool was going to end up injured again if he wasn't careful. If he continued to fire the cannon like that, using too much powder, it might explode on him. Worse, if he didn't examine it before and after each firing, others were going to get hurt.

That wasn't Jason's problem. He wasn't the cannon master.

With Morris now serving as the cannon master, it was possible—even probable—he never would be.

He headed away and drifted down the side of the slope. The back side of the mountain led into a rocky bowl, and on the other side of it, the mountain sloped down to another village. It was small, barely more than a collection of a few houses that had a fairly easy time reaching this village for the festivities. They didn't set off on their own. Beyond that was the nearest city, Varmin, over three days away.

The hunting should be better in that direction, but the upper portion was usually picked over by the people from his village and the one below, forcing hunters to descend further. It was part of the reason he chose to go around the front face of the mountain. It was snowier, but there was the chance that others wouldn't have been there. Even were he invited with the hunting parties, he wasn't sure he'd go along.

A dark shape caught his attention and he paused.

An enormous ballista was anchored to the mountain. In the darkness of the night, it was difficult to make out much about the ballista other than the gleaming end of it. As long as Jason had been in the village, he'd never seen it fired. No one had, as far as he knew. It was a remnant of a time before, a remnant from when the dragons still attacked. The ballista had been their only defense.

Similar weapons circled the entirety of the peak, surrounding the village. There were seven of them, anchored deeply, kept clean from snow, someone else's job to ensure they were ready to fire. All of them were loaded with the precious trees, long, slender trunks sharpened, tipped with enormous metal barbs, and prepared to fire at a moment's notice.

Thankfully, that moment had never come in all the time he'd been here. Jason wasn't sure what he would do if it did. Certainly he wouldn't be ready to fight, and he doubted he would be prepared for the possibility he would need to deal with a dragon attacking. No one would be ready for that.

The cannon fired again, another thunderous sound, and he glanced back. One of the others with Morris let out a whoop of laughter, and Jason could only shake his head. They were making a mistake. Morris had to know it. His father would've trained him better than that, but the other man still didn't seem to care. More likely than not, Morris wasn't even bothering to check whether the cannon was safe in between uses. It had been his own fault the cannon had misfired.

He was drawn to the ballistae and headed toward the nearest one. When he reached it, he ran his hand along the trunk, feeling the smooth surface of it. Time had weathered the wood, but it was smooth, stout, and still impressive.

It was hard to imagine what it would have been like to see it fired. They used a similar powder as with the cannon, firing the ballistae a great distance, far enough that they could take out a dragon from the town itself.

"I bet they wouldn't even know," a nearby voice said.

Jason dropped to the ground, using his white coat and pants to blend into the snow. At least in the darkness and with the snow, he would be relatively obscured.

"As soon as you fire it, someone's going to know."

"Sure. They'll know then, but we'll be long gone."

Jason lifted his head, trying to see. Who would it be?

It sounded like Reltash, but firing one of the ballistae wasn't something he would do. They didn't have any replacement bolts. They would weaken the town. Even Reltash wouldn't be foolish enough to do that.

"Just go and get some powder from the barrel," someone else said.

This time, he was certain it was Ingrid. He recognized the voice, though why would she be dumb enough to try something like that?

If he stayed here, they would know he'd heard them talking about firing off the ballistae.

The cannon fired again.

"See? He's not gone at all."

"Fine. Maybe he's not gone. We can wait until he settles down, and then we can go for some of the powder."

"We shouldn't," one of the voices said.

"Would you be quiet? What does it matter? There are six more. Why shouldn't we have a little fun?"

That was definitely Reltash.

He didn't want to be here when they attempted to fire one of the ballistae. Not only was it a mistake, but it would bring the anger of the town elders and the mayor.

The voices started to head away from him, and he breathed out a sigh of relief.

Would they actually try to do that?

Normally, he would've said no, but with that group, he wasn't sure. Reltash likely thought himself protected from any consequences. His father ranked high enough in the city, was wealthy enough that he wouldn't have to worry, though he wouldn't be able to buy a replacement bolt. The trees were long gone from this part of the mountain.

Nothing like that grew nearby. Anything they could procure to replace any loosed bolts would be far down the slope, and it would be nearly impossible to bring back up the mountainside.

Crawling along the snow, Jason tried to stay invisible. He headed down the slope for a little while before turning back up. He wound his way back into the village, and as he reentered the crowd, he bumped into someone.

"Dreshen. I didn't think you'd be at the festival," Reltash said.

Jason's heart hammered. Would he know Jason had been near enough to hear what they were planning? "No? Probably because I was busy helping Morris with the cannon."

"Helping? Like you used to help your daddy?"

Jason resisted the urge to snap at him. "Right. I used to help him. And at least I know how to use powder and not blow myself up."

Reltash glared at him. "What's that supposed to mean?"

"What do you think it means?"

The other man glowered at him. "You'd better be careful with that powder, Dreshen. Even Morris had a little trouble tonight."

"What do you know about what happened?"

Reltash only grinned at him.

Jason took a deep breath and pushed past him, but he couldn't ignore the sense that Reltash glared at him, his stare lingering on Jason's back.

4

J ason stared at the snowy hillside. He held his bow at the ready, fully drawn so that his hand just barely touched his face. He wasn't sure if what he detected was real or not, but there seemed to be a hint of movement on the other side of the ridge that he could just barely make out through his silver eye.

It was at times like these that he appreciated his eye. If nothing else, he wanted to find a rabbit. A squirrel, or anything. His stomach rumbled. The hunk of sweet bread he'd eaten had only taken the edge off his hunger, nothing more than that, and he needed to find something to sustain them over the next couple of days.

Creeping forward, he used the natural camouflage of his bearskin clothing, letting it blend into the snow. A fresh blanket covered the ground, and because of that, it didn't crunch under his boots. It gave a little more traction as well, making movement easier. He'd seen no sign of prints but felt confident that he would come across something.

Hunting requires patience and deliberation and finally quick action.

He reached the ridge line. As he looked down, his breath caught.

A herd of deer.

He'd never been so lucky to see an entire herd before. He knew they were out there, and there were some who were lucky enough to have come across them, but Jason was not one of them. In all the times he'd been hunting, he'd never seen that many deer. It was rare to come across a single deer, let alone six, like he did now. If he were able to bring down even a single one, he'd have food for a month. It had been a long time since he'd managed to catch one. The last time was when his father had still been alive.

He held his hand steady, afraid to move at all. If he did, he feared the animals would notice, and if they did...

Checking his arrow, he held it steady. He focused on the deer, making sure his aim was true. Which one would he pick? For the first time, he had a choice. In this case, he had to go for the largest, didn't he?

The largest would likely be the strongest. It would be more likely to fight and to run.

If he went with the largest dear, he would run the risk of it running off, even if it were injured. He had no false belief he'd be able to keep up with an injured deer bounding away.

Shifting his aim, he focused on a medium-sized one.

If he were quick, he could pull another arrow from the quiver, and—

The deer started to move.

...quick action.

He had to act now.

Jason fired.

As soon as he did, he reached for another arrow, nocking it in a smooth motion. His father had taught him archery, and his father had been skilled, though Jason liked to think he was even more skilled than his father. Most of that came from the dragon sight.

The first arrow struck and he fired again, catching the deer a second time in the neck. The creature fell.

The others were startled, and they ran.

He stalked over toward the deer, and when he reached it, he said a quiet prayer to Dayvos before flashing his knife across the creature's throat. He waited for it to bleed out and started to drag it back to the village.

He'd been successful.

There were more deer, and if he were lucky, he might even be able to track them.

An emotion he hadn't felt in quite some time surged in his cold chest. Hope.

With the venison, they'd not only eat for a while, but he could even trade it for other items. They might even be able to get some grains. Considering how rare those were, he couldn't imagine that luxury.

The trek back to the village took a long time. He

buried the deer behind the stone cottage he shared with his sister and mother, packing it underneath the snow and ice, sealing it as tightly as he could. It was better to preserve it that way, and would give them an opportunity to butcher it at his leisure. The neighboring cottages were far enough apart that he hoped no one saw what he'd brought to the village. Theft was rare here, but it *did* happen.

He hurried into the home. Kayla was there, working in the kitchen, and she looked over. "You're back already?" she asked.

"Venison."

She dropped the bowl she was cleaning. "What?"

He couldn't help the grin spreading across his face. "Venison."

"You got one?" she whispered.

"I got one. I buried it behind the house. Better yet, there was a herd of them."

She blinked. "A herd?"

"Listen, Kayla. With that many deer... I'm going back."

"Are you sure that's wise?"

Wise didn't matter. What mattered was that he took care of his sister. His mother. With that herd, he could do more than he'd done for them so far. "I know it's getting late already, but if I don't go, their tracks will be covered. If I can get another one..."

After taking a deep breath, she nodded. "Go. Show me where you buried it."

He grinned, hurrying out of the house, and Kayla

followed him, not dressed for the cold but for the first time, he didn't care. He understood why she wouldn't care, either.

He pointed to where he had buried the animal and she moved some of the snow away. Her breath caught when she got to the smooth fur.

"How long has it been?"

"Too long," he said. "Do you think you can make something with that for tonight?"

"I *know* that I can," she said.

He stood, rubbing his stomach. It was too bad he didn't have time to eat anything now, but he was thankful for the sweet bread Tessa had provided. Without that, he might've been too hungry and weakened to drag the deer all the way back here.

She hugged him. "Thank you. This might even make Mother feel better."

Jason started back out, away from the village, trailing after the path he'd made when he'd dragged the deer through the snow. Every so often, droplets of blood marked where he'd come from, giving him an easy way to navigate, and he reached the small section beyond the ridgeline where he'd first spotted the herd.

Jason glanced up at the sky. It was getting late and the wind was starting to pick up, but in his excitement, and filled with hope, he didn't allow that to slow him this time. Instead, he raced forward, reaching the place where he'd bled out the deer, and followed the prints of the rest of the herd through the snow. With as many deer as there were, it was easy enough to follow. Had there been only one, the tracks might have drifted over more quickly, but with five deer remaining, he was able to find where they'd gone. If he waited, the prints would be gone by morning. Not only would the wind lead to drifting, covering them with banks of snow, but the fresh snow that almost always came each night would cover them just as well.

He had to move quickly. He checked his bow, then his quiver, patting them to make sure he had the necessary supplies, and hurried across the snow as he searched for the path the deer had taken.

He worried what would happen if he failed to find them.

Nothing. He'd already gotten one, so this hunting trip was a success regardless of anything else. Even if he didn't find another, he would still have gotten his family food for the next month. That was enough. It had to be.

He followed the tracks, hurrying across the snow, and for the first time, he didn't wish for dragonskin boots. His bearskin boots were heavy enough for here. Besides, with as light and fluffy as the snow happened to be, he was able to stay practically on top of it as he hurried forward.

He maneuvered quickly across the snow, making his way through the thick blanket. The further he went, the more he began to sink into the snow itself. The wind started to pick up, whistling around him, and he clutched his jacket. Days like this, it would be better to have warmer clothing. Then again, it would have been better for him not to have risked coming out at a time like this.

Hunting in the middle of the day, when the sun was still shining, was far safer than coming out like this as the weather turned and cold began to blow around him.

The tracks shifted direction and Jason followed them. They meandered around the slope of the mountain and he continued to follow them, noting the way they looped around. They picked up the pace, almost as if they had been chased here.

Jason didn't see anything else that would suggest the deer had been chased by anything. What had inspired the deer to change their course?

He paused, searching the horizon, using his silver eye to peer out and look for anything that might suggest a change in temperature, the shifting warmth that would indicate where he could find the deer, but he didn't find them. Nothing but white around him. A few rocky outcroppings. Snow swirling around him. No movement.

It meant he would have to continue following the tracks. The farther they went, the harder he knew it would be. He traced the tracks, moving as quickly as he could, and paused every so often, looking into the distance, searching for signs of either movement or shifting colors that would suggest that he would find them.

The sun began to set, dropping below the neighboring mountaintop.

Eventually, it would be too dark to continue tracking the deer. If he had any heat signatures, anything he could uncover with his silver eye, then he might be able to use that to follow them, but without anything, he had no idea which direction the deer could have gone.

It was time to head back.

There was no shame in returning. The only thing that disappointed him was the fact he'd allowed himself to feel the optimism, the belief he might finally have a break for their family, but not coming across the rest of the herd didn't mean they would suffer. They had meat for the month. In that time, Jason could continue to hunt. He could continue to collect other animals, and perhaps they would even get ahead.

He debated what to do, considering whether he should return or continue to follow the tracks.

As the wind whistled around, he knew it would become increasingly difficult to do so. Soon, the snow would cover the tracks completely.

Either way, he would lose the ability to follow the deer, and then he would wander.

It was not difficult to find his way toward the village. It was directly up the slope of the mountain, and Jason had hunted enough times outside of the city that he was able to return without needing the guidance of the village itself to lead him.

His father wouldn't have turned away.

Then again, his father often went out with larger hunting parties—and off the back slope, and because of that, they were able to hunt more easily than Jason was able to do.

He breathed out and turned back upslope.

He wasn't giving up.

As he went, with the daylight fading, he noticed a soft rumble.

He frowned. In the mountains, a rumble like that could be dangerous. It could indicate an avalanche had been triggered, and though they'd people within the village who were trained to ensure the avalanches were controlled, sometimes they were triggered regardless. He knew better than to get caught out in an avalanche like that, aware that if he were to get trapped, he could get swept down the mountain—or worse, covered by the snow.

Rather than staying here and waiting, he began to hurry.

As he did, he looked up the slope, focusing, searching for any sign of snow shifting, the telltale signature of an avalanche, but he didn't see anything.

Instead, there came another rumbling.

It almost sounded as if the cannon were being fired, but that couldn't be it, could it? The festival was over—at least mostly—and there was no need to continue firing the explosives, regardless of whether or not there were some remaining. They would last until the following year, until the next festival, and there was no shame in holding on to them until then.

When it came again, he realized that it wasn't an explosion.

At least, it wasn't an explosion like he had thought.

It was a ballista bolt.

Reltash.

That stupid man.

After hearing their plan the night before, he knew that was what it had to be.

When was the last time the bolts had been fired like that?

It had been years. Long enough that Jason had never even seen them fired, though he had known they would have been.

He trudged up the side of the mountain. Darkness fell, swallowing him.

Jason continued to work his way up the side of the mountain. It was difficult to tell how much farther he had to go. He had made a mistake pushing as far as he had, thinking he had time to track the deer. What had he been thinking? They were far enough downslope by the time he'd gotten there that he had only put himself in danger.

Now he'd be caught out here in the night. With the wind picking up, the cold swirling around him, he didn't know if he would be able to get back to his house.

As he went, he thought he should have reached the village by now. Where was it?

Another rumble, and he looked up.

This time, he was certain it was the sound of an avalanche. If the ground started to shift, he'd need to try to angle downslope, anything to ensure he moved out of the snow flow. He didn't see anything.

Even his strange eyesight wouldn't help him here. He might be able to detect movement, but without the heat gradient, there would be no way for him to notice anything. If it was an avalanche, it would obscure his ability to find anything.

Trudging up the side of the mountain, he wrapped his arms around himself, trying to keep warm. With the wind whipping around, he was growing increasingly cold, and the longer he went, the more he feared he would end up frozen out here in the night. Others had frozen, not making it back to the village before the terrible winds picked up. Without the assistance of a dragonskin jacket, he might not be dressed warmly enough to survive.

Snow began to drift, and he felt it shifting beneath his feet as the rumbling returned.

This time, there was no question. An avalanche.

He wasn't going to be able to outrun it. The snow moved too quickly.

Jason had lived on this mountain his entire life. He'd encountered a few avalanches before, but they still terrified him. Most of them were small, little more than a shelf of snow breaking off and forcing him down. Others were larger—the kind where people died.

He had no idea which this was. With the rumbling, he feared a larger avalanche.

Which meant he'd have to try to either move away from the main part of the snow sliding down, or be prepared for it to bury him.

He turned, making a split-second decision, and started angling down the slope.

His feet carried him as quickly as he could go across

the snow. As he went, the rumbling continued to build, louder and louder, and he hazarded a glance behind him, but in the dim darkness, he wasn't able to make anything out.

Jason turned his attention back down the slope and continued to run off to the side.

Was he going to be fast enough to outrun the avalanche?

5

J ason lost track of how long he'd been running. Half the time, he'd been sliding, his footing slipping; but each time he paused, he could swear he heard the avalanche return, the unstable snow shifting beneath him, screaming at him that he didn't have anyplace secure quite yet.

It meant he had to keep running, but he wasn't sure that he was able to do so. The longer he went, the more tired he became. How long had it been?

It seemed as if he had been running for an hour, possibly longer. The longer he went, the less likely he'd be able to make it someplace safe.

Already he'd gone farther downslope than he ever had before. Even when he'd been out with his father, he hadn't hunted this far down the slope. Doing so was dangerous because it brought him away from the village, to the point where he wouldn't be able to return in the same day.

There was nothing in this direction. No villages. No cities. Nothing.

At this point, all he could think about was finding someplace to stay warm.

The wind continued to tear at him, freezing him, and if he didn't find a place soon, he would end up out in the cold, suffering, and he might not make it through the night.

He needed shelter, but what kind of shelter could he find?

The snow itself could provide some. If it came down to it, he could burrow a hole into the snow and use that to insulate himself. Then again, he wasn't sure he was dressed warmly enough for that. His feet were already cold despite the fact he had dressed as warmly as he could.

Jason hurried onward, trying not to think of what would happen if he didn't find a safe place. He was tired, not thinking clearly. As he wound down the slope, he could swear he saw a flickering light, almost as if there were something down there.

Maybe an animal.

He had been going far enough that it was possible he would have run into the herd of deer again.

They shouldn't have been up the slope that far in the first place. There wouldn't have been anything for them. No food to graze on. No shelter from the cold and the wind. For them to have wandered that high had to mean they were scared into going up there.

What would have chased the deer?

Something else.

Something *worse*.

Dragons once hunted these lands. They called them their own.

His father's words came back to him again, but he didn't think it was a dragon. They wouldn't be spotted in the mountains. At least, he wouldn't have thought they'd be spotted the mountains, but then he'd heard the ballista fired.

How had he gone from finding a deer and being so thrilled with that to where he was now? He couldn't believe he would suffer like this, that he would end up in this situation, but he had to find a way to survive. He had to find a way to return, if only for Kayla and his mother. Kayla wouldn't be able to survive without him. His mother wouldn't either. At least they had the meat. It would give them enough time and reprieve to last a little longer.

As he went, he was increasingly certain there was something down there, though he wasn't able to tell what it was. It wasn't moving, and the strangeness stood out against the night. He covered his blue eye, using only the silver one to see. Sometimes he had to do that in order to find the contrast. The only problem was that it affected his depth perception when he covered his other eye.

As he stared, focusing through that eye, he could swear he saw contrast. Colors.

It wasn't imagined.

A fire?

That seemed impossible to believe. Why would there be a fire along the slope?

He didn't think there was another village here. There were homes scattered along the slope, but they were incredibly infrequent. He'd not encountered any of them, either. Most of the homes were found in the backcountry. It wasn't quite as rugged, and the snow didn't fall as often or as thick as it did on this slope.

Maybe that was what he had come across. If he had, then it was possible he would find someone who could help, and he might be able to survive the night. As long as he didn't have to do it out in the open, he thought he would be able to pull through.

As he hurried, he stared into the distance, watching the colors, searching for anything that would tell him what he was seeing and whether or not it was real.

The closer he came, the more certain he was that it was a fire.

Jason slowed his steps, approaching more carefully. A fire out in the open like this suggested someone had something to burn. Seeing as how he hadn't encountered anything yet, no signs of trees or brush or anything that could be useful for a fire, he had to wonder who was out here and what they were burning.

He allowed himself to be drawn toward the fire. Almost too late, he realized he was focused only on the fire and not on the possibility there would be someone around it.

Jason hesitated, remaining motionless. He didn't want

to draw any attention to himself, and he slowly sank to the ground. At least his bearskin jacket and pants would conceal him, but the movement might have already drawn attention. He stared into the distance, looking for anything that might suggest there was someone out there, but he didn't find anything.

If they were wearing dragonskin, he might not even see them. That was one of the strange advantages to it. Even with his dragon sight, he wasn't able to determine the heat differential between the dragonskin and the snow. It was a strange thing, almost as if the dragonskin jacket absorbed the cold of the snow, deflecting it outward, making the wearer almost invisible.

Use the mountains. The snow. Blend into it. The bearskin offers advantages dragonskin does not.

Jason smiled at the memory. It had been his father's way of trying to convince him the bearskin was somehow more valuable. As they'd caught it together, perhaps it was.

He crawled forward. At least the snow was soft, and moving like this allowed him to go soundlessly, so that nothing out there would be able to hear him. With the wind whistling around, his passing would be obscured, so if anyone was trailing him, they would soon lose his tracks.

There was no further sound of the avalanche. All signs of that had faded, the rumbling gone, and he no longer felt the snow stirring beneath his feet the way he had before.

Thankfully, that much was over, but what would happen if it started again?

He would have to keep running.

Another gust of wind swirled around him, and he shivered. It was cold, and this close to the snow, he wasn't finding any residual warmth.

The fire drew him, enticing him, and he wanted nothing more than to be close to it, to allow the heat to fill him, to surround him, and yet, he hesitated.

Until he knew who was here, he didn't know that it was safe to approach too quickly. Could they be from the festival? It would be a strange direction for someone to travel afterward, especially at night. Most of the people who came to the village for the festival remained for longer stretches than this.

Unless they weren't with the festival.

He continued crawling, and when he was near the fringe border of the fire, he relaxed. At least here, he could start to feel the warmth. There was the fire, but there was no one else here.

As Jason allowed himself to relax, a hand grabbed him. "What are you doing here?"

It was a gruff voice, but it was strangely familiar.

"I saw the fire," he said, trying to jerk free.

Everything within him was on edge. His heart raced. A sheen of sweat worked on his back, freezing almost immediately. It did nothing to help with how cold he was. Even if he wanted to run, he wasn't sure he'd be able to.

His body was achy and stiff, and he was tired from being out all day.

The hand released him and Jason staggered back, looking up at the figure. They were dressed in heavy furs, with a hood covering the face, making it difficult to see anything. More than that, the furs managed to mask him from using his dragon sight, preventing him from seeing anything at all.

Were the furs some kind of dragonskin?

It didn't seem that way. When he'd been closer, he'd felt none of the heat off of the fur in the same way he would detect with dragonskin.

What was it, then?

Better yet, *who* was this? Why was he out here in the night like this, camped on the mountain slope out in the open?

"You can sit by the fire."

"Who are you?"

The figure ignored him, turning away and heading downslope.

Jason tried to see where he was going, but the light from the fire made it difficult to see anything, and he was cold. Rather than trying to stare after the man, he hurried closer to the fire, letting the warmth fill him.

It was bright, and it danced higher into the sky than he would've expected. More than that, as he studied the flames, he realized he couldn't tell that anything was burning, but somehow there was warmth and heat coming off the fire.

Fire like this would be beneficial in the village. If there was some way of creating flames like this without burning anything, his mother and sister could remain warm.

He couldn't find a source.

That wasn't quite true. At the center of the fire, there seemed to be a small circular object. It looked something like stone, and there was something about that stone that was familiar.

He'd seen a stone like that before from the stranger in the village.

That was why he'd seemed familiar, but what would he be doing out here?

Last he'd seen him, he'd been in the village, celebrating the festivities. Jason didn't know if any of the visitors had departed already. It was possible he'd already left, but traveling this direction was unusual. Few—if any—festivalgoers came this way. Most went along the back slope of the mountain toward Varmin.

He needed to reach the stranger.

At the same time, he didn't want to leave the flame. He didn't want to leave the warmth, and desired nothing more than to stay where he was, to enjoy the heat that he hadn't experienced in quite some time.

He held his hands out, letting the warmth fill him.

He would wait. The stranger would have to return to the fire.

Jason sank down to the ground, the warmth and the comfort of the flames filling him. He looked around, but he came across nothing to explain where the man had gone.

More than that, he came across nothing that suggested he was ever even here.

A distant rumbling sound came again and he tensed. Focusing on the slope, he waited, worried the snow would begin to shift again. If it did, he'd end up cascading down the mountainside. At least he was warm enough.

Jason found himself curling up on the snow. He stayed just at the edge of the fire, letting its warmth press upon his face, his hands, his entire body. He basked in it.

And drifted to sleep.

6

C oming awake with a start, Jason looked around.
Dreams had come to him, along with memories of hunting with his father. In that dream, he had been tracking a larger animal. His father hadn't bothered hiding his excitement in trailing after the creature, the first time in months they had encountered a deer.

"What if we lose his track?" Jason had asked.

His father looked down at him. He was a large man, though not as large as many in the village. He smiled at Jason, a hint of a sparkle behind his blue eyes. "As long as we move quickly, we aren't going to lose the deer. We need to be more concerned about a dragon snatching it from us."

His father had started off, leaving Jason staring after him. "There aren't any dragons left."

"Not here," his father had said.

"Where are they, then?"

"Gone. Thankfully."

"But we still have the ballista."

"They serve as a means of protecting ourselves from the dragons. Not anything we need. Not anymore. The dragon hunters have been gone for generations."

"What was it like?"

His father glanced over as Jason raced after him. "To be a dragon hunter?"

Jason had nodded. "They have always seemed so terrifying."

A strange, almost bittersweet expression crossed his father's face. "I don't know. Our family came to the mountains…"

His father never got the chance to finish.

They caught sight of a deer.

He tapped on Jason's shoulder, signaling him to lower.

He crouched, raising his bow, and fired.

His aim was off.

His father's was not.

The arrow streaked true, and he followed with another.

"I won't be able to hunt as well as you."

"Eventually you will. You have the sight. That gives you advantages that others don't have."

"What sort of advantages? All it seems to do is draw attention to me in the village."

His father ruffled his hair as they started toward the fallen deer. "Be proud of what you are. You are part of a distinguished heritage of those with dragon sight."

Jason blinked open his eyes from the dream, noticing streaks of heat all around him.

Even in the dream, he missed his father.

Why that dream, though?

Maybe it had something to do with the dragon sight, or maybe it had something to do with where he now found himself. He needed to embrace his dragon sight.

This far down the slope, the neighboring mountains loomed closer. The snow reflected the growing sunlight, a blaze of white making it difficult for him to see anything. He squinted, studying the distance where dawn already began to break, the sky lightening.

Jason sat up, breathing in, and noticed that the air was crisp and cool. The winds had died, and he was not nearly as cold as he had been before.

At first, he thought everything had been part of the dream and that the fire had been only his imagination, but as he rolled over, he saw it was still there, burning brightly. It had changed very little, and surprisingly, the snow around it hadn't melted all that much.

More surprising was the fact that the strange stone at the center of it remained.

Jason blinked, trying to clear his mind, and found it was more difficult than he would've expected. He was lucky to have survived.

The stranger.

Where was he?

Jason had been certain he'd encountered the stranger,

but why would he have allowed Jason to come sit by his fire?

Better yet, how did he have a fire like this?

"You're awake."

Jason spun and saw the stranger coming from back up the slope. "I'm awake." He studied him a moment. Heavy furs covered the man. They were a mixture of grays and whites, stitched together, and they left him with a ragged appearance. The massive hood covering his head was even thicker than what he remembered from the village. "Who are you? What are you doing here?"

"It's time for you to head back. If you get going now, you should be able to reach your village by sunset."

The stranger stepped past him, reaching into the flame itself, and grabbed the stone. As he did, the flame went out.

Magic.

There are magics in the world. Pray you never see them.

Jason had never known why his father would have told him that. Seeing magic that way made him want to see *more* magic, not less.

"Who are you?"

The stranger ignored him, standing and stuffing his hand into his pocket. With it went the stone, disappearing, leaving Jason wondering who this man was and why he had helped.

"You won't have much time. I suspect we're going to see more snow today, though it's going to start downslope first before working its way up. If you get going now, you should be able to—"

"How did you make the fire?" His gaze went to the man's pocket, and he was tempted to try to reach for it, but even though he and the man were of a similar size, he didn't think he would be able to overpower him.

More than that, there was the comment Tessa had made. The man had silver eyes, much like him.

The man cocked his head, studying him. As he stared at Jason, he had a sense the man regarded his eyes—particularly his silver eye—closely. There was something strange about the way he watched him, and it seemed as if the stranger recognized what the silver eye meant. "You'd better get going. You don't want to get caught out another night."

"I can make it back. I've lived on this mountain my entire life."

"Have you?"

Jason frowned at him. "Yes."

"How long is that? How old are you?"

"Seventeen."

The stranger glanced over his shoulder, looking up the slope of the mountain. He took a deep breath before letting it out slowly. His breath puffed out in a plume. "Seventeen," he whispered. A sense of heat built from him. "It's called a dragon pearl."

He'd never heard of a dragon pearl before, but there were many things people attributed to the dragons he wasn't sure were real. "You can make fire with a dragon pearl?"

"You can do many things with a dragon pearl."

"Such as healing Morris?"

The stranger turned toward him. It was almost as if Jason could see through the hood, though as he looked at him, he wasn't sure that he could. Maybe that was nothing more than his imagination since all he could make out were the stranger's eyes.

"As I said, you can do many things with a dragon pearl."

"Are you going to share your name?"

"Do you think that asking me over and over again will get you closer to the answer?"

Jason just shrugged.

"My name is Therin Dargish."

"Are you from Varmin?" That didn't seem right. If he was from that city, he would have been traveling down the backslope, not the front face of the mountain. "Why haven't I seen you at the festival before?"

"Because I've never visited the festival before."

"Why did you come this year?"

Therin cocked his head, studying him. "You're wasting valuable time."

"Only if you don't answer."

The other man shook his head. "I came looking for answers."

"What sort of answers?"

"The sort I didn't find."

Therin started down the face of the mountain. Jason hesitated before racing after him. He wasn't about to let this man get away from him before he had more answers of his own. He had so many things that he wanted to know, not the least of which was why Therin had come to the village and what he had hoped to find.

More than that, he wanted to know more about the dragon pearl, if only so he could see if there was some way to have one himself within the village. He could imagine using it, creating fire the same way Therin had and heating the entirety of their house. With something like that, they wouldn't have to rely upon dung collection, and he wouldn't have to worry about his mother and sister freezing while he was gone.

"The longer you follow me, the longer it's going to take you to return."

"The longer you don't answer, the more likely it is that I'm going to have to stay with you."

Therin turned in his direction, and Jason still couldn't see through the hood of his jacket, unable to make out anything about his features. The only time he'd seen him had been in his home, and that had been darkened.

"I saw how much you worry about your people. You're not staying with me."

That much was true. If he stayed with Therin, he *would* end up trapped here another night. Without a fire, he might not be able to get back.

Therin continued to make his way down the slope, moving quickly. He walked easily over the soft snow, and each step he took seemed to drift over immediately, almost as if the snow covered him, obscuring his tracks.

Jason glanced behind him, looking to see if the same thing happened to him, but he couldn't see that it did.

Why would he be the only one making footprints while Therin did not?

"Are you some sort of sorcerer?"

There are different types of magic. Inherent and borrowed. Both are dangerous.

Jason suspected the inherent magical users were sorcerers. The others... he didn't know what the others were. Either way, they didn't have anyone like that in the village. The closest they came was the dragonskin jackets, and even with that, that was more a nature of the dragons themselves rather than anything magical. All understood the dragons had fantastical abilities, and while they were terrifying creatures, they were powerful.

"A sorcerer?"

"With the fire. Your footsteps. The way you were able to help Morris. All of that seems to me that you're some sort of magic user. A sorcerer."

"Is that what you think I am?"

Jason shrugged again. "I'll be honest, I don't really know. I've never seen anything like it."

"That's because you said you haven't left your village."

"Is what you can do common?"

"Common enough."

Therin continue to make his way along the side of the slope, practically gliding above the surface of the snow, while Jason had to trudge through it, each step more diffi-cult than the last. The longer they walked, the harder it was to keep up, and he worried he wasn't going to be able to keep pace with Therin.

Then again, perhaps the other man didn't want him to.

He'd already suggested he return to the village, and the longer he went, the more difficult it was going to be for him to make it back easily. He did need to get back. Spending his time out here, continuing to this end of the side of the mountain, meant he was either going to be stuck another day outside of the village, or he was going to have to stay with Therin.

There was another possibility, but it involved finding one of the outlying homes. They were scattered, difficult to come across. The people who lived in them preferred the isolation. Jason wondered if Therin weren't taking some way that would navigate around, avoiding other homes.

Therin stopped, turning to face him. "Keep following me and you won't be able to get back."

"I can get back. It only takes a day to climb the mountain."

"The longer we go, it will take you more than a day."

He was right, and though Jason didn't want to admit it, he also didn't know what would happen if he continued. This was already farther than he'd ever wandered, and returning would take every bit of strength he had. He could hurry, but being hungry and tired meant it would be less likely he'd be able to reach the village easily.

"What did you come to the village looking for?"

Therin looked at him for a long moment. "Something that no longer exists."

The other man continued along the side of the mountain and Jason watched, unable to shake the sense that his feet never sunk into the snow.

He could return. For that matter, he *needed* to return, but he had time. Having found the deer bought him time. It gave him nearly a month before his family would run out of food. Even that was probably not completely accurate. Without him, they wouldn't need nearly as much food.

"Is it dragons?"

Therin slowed. "What was that?"

"The dragons. Is that why you came to the village?"

"What about the dragons?"

"There was a firing of the ballista last night."

Therin pushed back the hood of his cloak. As he did, Jason was able to make out the deep silver of his eyes. It was much like what Tessa had said, and it surprised him. He'd never been around anyone else with the dragon sight, and seeing someone like that, seeing the twin silver eyes, unsettled him in a surprising way.

Was that the way he made others feel?

"What did you say?" Therin asked.

He shook away the unsettled feeling. "The ballista fired last night."

"Are you sure?"

"I thought it was an avalanche at first, but…"

Therin looked up the slope of the mountain, a deep frown on his face. "When did you hear this?"

"I don't know. I was tracking a herd of deer—"

"A herd?"

Jason nodded. "I'd gotten one and was hoping to get another"—or two, if he were completely honest—"when I thought I heard the ballista bolt fire."

"Are you sure it wasn't part of the festivities and not the ballista?"

Jason shrugged. "It could have been. Morris was firing the cannon, but his injury would make him less inclined to fire quite as many as he normally would."

Therin turned his silver gaze on him. Jason thought he felt something from him, but it had to be his imagination. "You should return and check on your people."

"Come with me. You were looking for information, and—"

"Your village doesn't have what I'm looking for."

"What are you looking for?"

A hint of darkness flashed in Therin's eyes. "Nothing for you to worry about."

Jason needed to return. He'd been gone long enough as it was. He could continue to follow the other man, but doing so would only push him farther away from the village, and it was possible he wouldn't even be able to get back. Even if he turned around now, it would take him the better part of the day to make his way back, and he would be exposed to the elements by the time he returned.

The idea that he might learn of magic almost

compelled him to remain, but it was the thought of his sister home alone with his mother that motivated him. He'd been gone long enough—overnight, even—and needed to return before Kayla started to worry.

"Safe travels," he said.

He turned away and started back up the slope. He went quickly, pausing to watch where Therin went, but the other man disappeared quickly.

Jason hurried up the slope. He trudged through the snow, racing along, and as he went, he tried not to think of how far of a climb he had. It was considerable. He was far enough away that it would take the better part of the day to even get to familiar ground.

He tried not to think about Therin and the strangeness of the man, the magic he obviously possessed, the way he had of lighting fires.

Magic can change lives. Ruin them.

When had his father said those things to him? They were memories of advice his father had given him, snippets of conversations that drifted to him while wandering the mountainside, but he didn't remember him telling him that.

Magic, though.

Even if he didn't have it, knowing that it existed...

It did nothing for him. Even if it existed—and now that he had seen it from Therin, he believed it did—it didn't change anything for him. When he returned to the village, he would still be poor. He might have a deer, and he might have some way of staying fed for a while, but how long would that last? Hunting for food had become increasingly challenging, and he would constantly be searching, looking for some way to find the next meal. Eventually there had to be a point where they wouldn't be able to get another meal.

Jason pushed those thoughts out of his head. There was no point in them, either.

As the day passed, his stomach rumbled. He did his best to ignore it, trying not to think about it. Focusing on the hunger did nothing more than remind him of how much he suffered. Instead, he chose to think about what it would be like when he returned to the village, to the deer meat he would be greeted with, and the opportunity to finally be satiated.

The longer he trudged up the slope, the harder it was. He was tired and growing increasingly exhausted.

What *had* Therin been looking for?

Whatever it was had drawn him into the village, but was it the village itself or was it the timing of his arrival there? Could it be that he'd come for the festival, thinking he might uncover something that would provide him with the answers he was seeking?

Jason paused, looking downslope. How long had he been going? It felt as if he'd been climbing for hours, and the shifting sun made it difficult to tell. Clouds obscured his vision, leaving a hazy view over everything. He looked back to discover his footsteps were slowly getting covered over, making it look as if he'd only been walking for a dozen steps.

He wasn't going to be able to make it back to the village. He was going to have to find a place to hunker down until the evening storm blew past.

As he climbed, his gaze darted around as he looked for someplace to hide from the elements. Mostly he wanted to get away from the wind, get out of the cold. He could melt the snow, have something to drink, and he could satiate his stomach.

There *was* a place, a cave, but it was difficult to reach. Finding a shelter inside it would be even harder, but it might be the only place he could go. Jason trudged along the mountainside, following the stream leading to the cave, until he caught sight of the opening.

He had neared the mouth of the cave when a glittering caught his attention. Lifting it up, he held it to the fading sunlight. A strange rock.

It was cold, bitterly so, probably from being out here so long. Still, there was something about the way the light reflected off it that appealed to him. As he slipped it into his pocket, movement caught his attention and he spun.

It was the same strange movement he'd seen when he'd been by the stream before. Whatever it was blended into the snow, making it difficult to see.

Jason started forward, ready for whatever might be there.

He couldn't tell what it was.

Maybe it was nothing.

The movement pulled his gaze again. Quick. Too quick.

Tensing, he continued to stare.

Then he saw it. A small rabbit moved along the slope, but not *quite* where he expected to see it. That had to be what he'd noticed, though.

Jason reached for an arrow slowly. Any sudden movement would startle the rabbit. At least this way, he could return with another prize. When he reached for the arrow, he pulled his bow off his shoulder and slowly nocked it.

Bringing it back, he focused, looking out through his silver eye, and used that to help him target the rabbit. He loosened the arrow. It went flying... And missed.

The arrow streaked past the rabbit, and the rabbit went hopping quickly off.

Jason scrambled after his arrow and debated chasing the rabbit before thinking better of it. There was no point in hurrying after the creature. It wasn't as if he had nothing to eat. Then again, if he was stranded out here for the night, he *would* have nothing to eat.

Looking up the slope, he tried to figure out how much time he had before nightfall. The shifting winds suggested it had already reached afternoon. With the cold coming, he needed to make a decision, and he hesitated before creeping off in the direction he'd seen the rabbit go.

As he made his way forward, he caught sight of it.

The rabbit hadn't gone all that far. Either the arrow hadn't startled it nearly as much as he had expected, or something else had caught its attention.

Jason drew the bow, bringing the string to rest against

his nose. He breathed in before relaxing his hold on the string and loosing the arrow.

This one flew true.

He struck the rabbit, which hopped once before falling.

Jason hurried forward, ready to claim the creature, but another surge of movement drew his attention.

It came from down the slope.

Figures were moving toward him.

There were three of them. All of them were dressed in dark jackets—dragonskin—and they were moving quickly.

Jason frowned, dropping to the ground, the rabbit forgotten.

He stared, but none of the men were familiar to him. That meant that none of them were from the village, but where were they from?

7

T he men continued to approach, and he stayed low and close to the ground, using the snow and his clothing to keep him concealed. Jason was afraid to even breathe, worried they would see him somehow. He could head back to the cave, but that would only draw their attention.

He tried to burrow into the snow, getting low.

It would be one thing if he knew who they were and why they were here, but there was nothing about them he recognized other than the fact they wore dragonskin clothing.

Shifting the snow so that it covered him, he tried to be as concealed as possible, but had to do so carefully. The bearskin covered him, but it was dirty, not nearly as pure white as the rest of the snow. If it were later in the day, the bearskin would provide better camouflage than now.

Footsteps crunched the snow near him.

Jason kept his head down, trying to keep obscured but worrying they would see him anyway. Steadying his breathing, he remained as motionless as possible.

The footsteps grew quieter.

Maybe they were moving away. He couldn't tell, and he refused to move until he was certain they were gone.

He focused on staying as quiet as he could, worried that any sound might draw their attention. He laid in place, unmoving.

There wasn't even any speaking. They were moving near him but saying nothing. That unsettled him.

Another crunch came, more sounds of footsteps, and Jason remained completely frozen in place. Cold pressed along him, seeping through his jacket and his pants, even managing to work up his boots. He thought he was mostly covered, but what if he had not managed to do so?

Something grabbed him.

Jason was jerked free of the snow, thrown backward, and a man wearing a dragonskin cloak pointed a sword at him. He had a clean-shaven face, darker skin than those in the village, and short hair. His angular jaw matched his nose, and deep silver eyes stared at him.

"What are you doing here?" The man had a gravelly voice that reminded him of Therin, but other than his eyes and his voice, nothing else about the two was similar.

Jason hesitated. He wasn't about to reveal the presence of the village to these men. There was something... *off...* about them. "There was an avalanche."

The man grunted, but he didn't put his sword away,

holding it aimed at Jason's chest.

The other two men approached. They looked similar, and he flicked his gaze to each man, noting that they shared the same eye color.

"Where did you find him?"

"He thought to conceal himself in the snow."

"Get rid of him, and we need to keep moving."

"Look at him, Parson."

The other man—Parson, Jason suspected—leaned slightly forward. He was a bit larger than the other two, and he had flecks of gray in his hair. His jaw was square more than pointed, and his eyes were deep silver. Heat seemed to radiate off him, emanating from his dragonskin clothing.

"What am I supposed to see?"

"Look at his eyes."

Parson sniffed. "Just one."

"One. He could be useful."

"Maybe. Bind him, and we'll bring him with us."

Jason started to tense, backing away. What did they mean that they were going to take him with them?

The man who had grabbed him approached, and in a flourish of movement, he sheathed his sword and reached into his pocket, pulling something out from within it. It took a moment to realize it was a length of slender rope.

"Don't fight," the man said.

"What are you—"

Jason didn't have the chance to finish. The man's hand swept across his face in a hard slap, sending Jason down into the snow. The man was on top of him in a moment, wrapping his wrists together tightly enough that Jason didn't think he could pull them apart.

The rope was slender, but it was strong.

"I told you not to fight."

The man grabbed his wrists, jerking him to his feet.

Jason couldn't move. They had him bound.

Because of his eyes.

Not his eyes. His *eye*.

The dragon sight eye.

The man took a length of the slender rope, hooking it to his wrist, and looped it into his belt.

He was forced to follow. At first, Jason thought they were going to head toward the village, but that didn't seem to be the direction they were going. They swept around, as if looping around the outside of the mountain, and never ascended any higher.

If they were out here, dressed for the weather, it surprised him that they wouldn't go for the village. Unless they weren't here to find the village. They had come for something else, but what?

"Who are you?"

The man spun and with a slap across his face, Jason tumbled.

The man didn't say anything more, just jerked on the rope.

He was forced back to his feet and scrambled after the man, trying to keep up. His head spun, pain throbbing in his jaw.

If he could get to his knife, he could cut through the rope.

He'd have to do it when they wouldn't be paying attention, although he didn't know if he would have that opportunity. But if one opened up, he'd need to be ready to run.

They hadn't even checked to see if he had any weapons. They had pounced on him, tying him, and seemed unmindful that he would be able to even try to escape.

Maybe he wouldn't be able to.

He tried to move a step ahead so his arms left a little slack on the rope, then reached beneath his jacket and pulled on his knife. He managed to slip the blade from the sheath and then held it carefully. He wasn't ready to escape quite yet, not wanting to draw attention to the fact that he had it, but soon.

Instead, he just squeezed it.

What about his bow? He still had that, but without having room to use his arms, there was no way to fire it. It troubled him that they hadn't even bothered to take the bow off him. It was almost as if they weren't concerned about him having the weapon. Why wouldn't they be?

Unless they had some other way of dealing with him.

He thought of Therin. He had the same color eyes as these men, which left Jason wondering if perhaps they all had the same abilities. What if they were all together?

If that were the case, then Jason didn't want to draw

them to the village. He didn't want to expose anyone to that sort of danger, not even people he didn't care about.

At least with the knife, he had a chance of freeing himself.

They paused, and Parson and the other man headed off for a moment, disappearing. The one with the rope remained, holding on to it and holding on to Jason.

"At least tell me who you are," Jason said. When he escaped—and he *would* escape, as this was his mountain after all—he would need to alert the village that there were strangers attacking along the slope.

Strangers with magic.

He spun toward him and Jason tensed, waiting for the strike, but it didn't come.

"You shouldn't be out here," the man said. "Where is your master?"

"My what?"

The man frowned. "You don't have a master?"

He watched Jason for a moment, leaning forward, sniffing.

As before, Jason had the distinct sense of heat coming off the man, a strange sensation that was different even than what he expected from the dragonskin clothing he wore.

The man turned, and Jason swept his gaze around and decided he had to act. Now.

The others weren't here, leaving only this man in front of him. He didn't know if he'd be able to get very far, but he wasn't going to remain captured.

Jason slashed at the rope.

It came loose and he jerked his hands, getting them free, and went running.

He'd gone only a few steps before he heard the man shout at him. He ignored him, continuing to run, choosing to head downslope. Going upslope would be too much of a challenge.

He stayed low, keeping his head bent, and slammed his dagger back into its sheath, spinning around to check if the man was following. So far, he was not.

There was movement behind him, but it was difficult to make out.

Refusing to slow, he unslung his bow, grabbing for an arrow.

He wasn't about to be caught again, and if he was, he wasn't going to be dragged away.

Nocking the arrow, he readied for the possibility that he was going to have to fire on these men. He would only get a shot or two off, and if he missed, he had little doubt they would come racing at him.

And that was if they weren't magic users.

What if they used some sort of fire magic on him?

He'd seen what Therin had been able to do. While it might have managed to heal Morris, it had also lit a flame. If they used something similar like that on him, would he be consumed by flames?

Jason tried not to think about what would happen. He tried not to think about what the fire would do, the way it would consume him, and he tried not to think about how much it would hurt.

He didn't even know if they were magic users.

He slipped.

Landing on his back, he realized he was lucky.

Something exploded near where he'd been.

Snow went flying all around and he continued to slide down the slope of the mountain. Jason rolled, trying to turn so he could see what was coming, but he couldn't tell.

A shape raced toward him.

It was moving faster than should have been possible and he pulled back, drawing back on the bow, prepared to fire.

As he stared, he locked eyes with an orange eye.

His hand trembled.

What was that?

There came another flurry of movement and Jason continued to slide, trying to maintain his balance, but the snow slipped beneath him, leaving him tumbling down the slope. As he struggled, he tried to rotate around to see what it was, but he could barely control his descent.

He continued staring, trying to figure out where the men had gone, but he was picking up speed and he couldn't stop. Even if he were to try, one of the attackers would reach him.

What was he thinking?

The farther he went down the slope, the more likely it was that he wasn't going to be able to get back up. He didn't want to get trapped down here.

Driving his heels in the snow, trying to slow himself, he felt something else flutter past him. Another explosion of snow near him caught his attention, and Jason released his pressure on the snow and tumbled down the slope.

It was better to get farther downslope than to be attacked.

He picked up speed, sliding faster and faster and holding his bow out from him, much faster than before, and tried not to think about what would happen when he needed to stop.

If he *could* stop.

And then he hit something.

Whether it was a bank of snow, a chunk of ice, or something else, he slipped up into the air, and when he landed, he did so with a hard thud.

His breath burst from his lungs and he rested in place, afraid to do so much as breathe. He needed to get moving, but he was afraid to go anywhere until he knew if he was injured.

Taking a deep breath, he checked his arms and his legs. Thankfully, it didn't seem as if he were hurt.

He got to his knees, swinging the bow around, prepared to aim, but there was no movement. There was no color at the edge of his vision, nothing that indicated anything was close.

It was possible he wouldn't even be able to tell. The man in the dragonskin had been obscured, so if they were to approach, he might not even know.

Jason needed to get moving.

Getting to his feet, he started back up the slope. He would be careful, watching for their presence. If he came across them, he would bury himself deeper this time. Either way, he had to return to the village.

The only problem was that he didn't know how far he had slid.

It was possible that he had slid even farther than he'd gone with Therin. If so, how long would it take to return? As he traipsed up the side of the mountain, keeping low and moving carefully, he caught a glimpse of movement.

Jason dropped to the ground, burrowing beneath the snow, and glanced out.

Had they already managed to find him? He thought he'd slid far enough that he would have moved away from them, but what if they had slid along with him, keeping pace?

The idea of that terrified him.

Nothing approached.

He lay there, ignoring the cold creeping through his jacket and pants, ignoring the pain burning through him. He waited, afraid to so much as move anywhere.

When nothing else came, he poked his head up, looking around.

As he did, he could swear that there was movement.

He hesitated, staring outward.

And then it was gone.

Crawling to his feet, he started forward, winding around the mountain, and crashed into Therin.

8

Therin took a step back, watching Jason for a moment. His furs were crusted with snow and a deep frown creased his face. It took a moment for Jason to realize Therin held a long dagger in his hand, but he quickly slipped it beneath his jacket.

"What are you doing here?"

Jason glanced behind him, relieved it was Therin and not anyone else.

"I'm glad to see you." Something cold in his pocket caught his attention and he reached for it, realizing the rock he'd found had stayed with him. He pulled it out and held it in his gloved hand a moment. It was colder than holding on to an icicle.

"What are you doing here?" the other man said again, studying Jason—and what he held in his hand.

Jason slipped it back into his pocket. "I was heading back to my village, and I came across three men. There was something else..."

He hesitated to say more. That had to be imagined, didn't it?

"What else?"

"Probably nothing. Some strange creature." Therin's eyes twitched a moment. "But the men grabbed me. They were going to..." Jason wasn't sure what they would have done to him.

Therin locked eyes with him for a moment before turning his attention upslope. "What three men?"

"I don't know. They wore dragonskin clothing. They were clean-shaven. Dark hair."

Therin's brow furrowed. "Where were you when you saw them?"

Jason waved a hand behind him. "Somewhere up the slope. I was still quite a ways from the village, I think, but to be honest, I don't really know how long I had to go. It could have been another few hours."

"How did they find you?"

"They came across me."

"How?"

Jason shook his head. "I don't know. I'd just caught a hare"—that he'd had to leave behind. Considering how hard hunting could be, leaving anything pained him —"and I burrowed into the snow, but they still found me."

Therin turned his attention upslope, and a sense of heat emanated from him that reminded Jason of what he had experienced before from the strange man. He stood with his arms stuffed into his pockets, completely motionless.

It was strange how relieved he felt at finding this man. He was thankful he had, but now he wondered whether Therin was even safe. He had the same silver eyes as the other men did. He had the same sense of sorcery about him. If nothing else, it was incredibly likely Therin was *with* the other men.

And yet, Therin had done nothing to threaten him. He had wanted him to go back to the village. He hadn't tried to capture him.

"Who were they?"

"Dangerous men."

"Dangerous like you?"

Therin looked over his shoulder at Jason, darkness lingering in his gaze. "More dangerous than me."

Dangerous men close to the village.

His mother and sister were there.

The village didn't have any real defenses. The main protection it had was its isolation. Other than that, the men were hunters, most skilled with the bow, but not soldiers. Certainly not magic users. They wouldn't be able to withstand something like that.

He had to get back to warn them.

"Why are they here?"

"They're after something. There should be no other reason for them to be here. We're too far away from the city."

"What city? Varmin?" Even Varmin didn't feel right.

They were far from it, but not so far that it would be unusual to have visitors from there, especially with the festival taking place. Then there was the strangeness about the men. The sense of magic he felt from them.

Not Varmin.

Therin looked back at him, pushing back the hood of his cloak. The silver in his eyes practically shone in the fading daylight. "Is Varmin close?"

"Not really. The back side of the mountain. It takes several days with the right gear. Longer"—much longer, he didn't feel the need to add—"without it."

"What sort of gear?"

"Snowshoes. Climbing supplies. Harnesses, rope, that sort of thing." The men had none of that.

"They're not from Varmin," Therin said. He watched him, looking as if he might say something before shaking his head, almost in frustration. He waved. "Come on."

Therin continued down the mountainside and Jason followed him. He remained silent for a while, but as he hurried along, he shook away the quiet. "Where are we going?"

"The three men you encountered are what's known as Dragon Souls. They're incredibly dangerous, deadly skillful, and powerful."

"Sorcerers?"

Therin paused and looked at him. "I've already told you it's not sorcery."

"I know what I saw." Therin started down the slope, moving away. "How do you know so much about them?"

"Because I was once one of them."

Jason hurried after the man, once again noting how no tracks seemed to remain behind him, unlike where Jason walked. He left deep footprints in the snow, and though the wind was picking up, shifting the snow around his footprints, he didn't pass nearly as quietly as Therin did. It was almost as if the other man could disappear.

"What's a Dragon Soul? They have the same silver-colored eyes as me."

Therin glanced back at him, locking onto his silver eye for a moment. "They do." He continued onward. "Dragon Souls are men gifted with a connection to the living dragons. They can use their power."

"That's how you lit the fire? With that sorcery?"

Therin grunted. "A sorcerer implies I have magic of my own. I merely use what I can from what the dragons have given me."

Inherent magic and borrowed. Both are dangerous.

A different realization came to Jason then. Therin had seen a dragon.

"What are they like?"

"You've seen what they're like. It's lucky you managed to get away. I suspect they believed you a slave."

The man's comment came back to him. "They did. Why?"

"Dragon Souls keep slaves, and they often breed with them. They need someone who has a connection to the dragons to train them. The slaves are able to work with the dragons, but they don't have enough power to use them against the Dragon Souls. They need the slaves because they're not threatening."

Therin looked over at him then. There was a dangerous glint in his eyes.

"You already knew you had dragon sight. I could see it when we first met. I can see it now in the way that you look at things, favoring your silver eye. That as much as anything is a giveaway. There is no shame in it, Jason."

"A dragon killed my father," he said.

Therin stopped, crossing his arms over his chest. "What do you think Dragon Souls do with the dragons?"

"You told me they use their power."

"They use power from dragons they control. You can blame the dragons for what happened to your family, but if anything happened, it was not the fault of the dragon."

Jason ran to catch up to him but stumbled, scrambling back to his feet to hurry after him again. "You can't take the blame off the dragons. I know what they did."

"You know what your people claim the dragons did, not what they were responsible for." Therin continued down the slope. "The dragons are trained. They are controlled, but they are also trained. The trainers are the ones responsible for the way they behave." He paused, glancing over at Jason. "Do you have any animals in your town?"

"We keep dogs."

"Do you blame the dogs if they bite someone?"

Jason understood what he was getting at. "The dog

might have to be put down if it's too violent. Do you do the same with dragons?"

"Not often," Therin said.

They continued down the slope a bit longer. "Why are the Dragon Souls here? We don't have any dragons. There haven't been any seen in decades."

"Yet you blame a dragon for what happened to your father."

"My father wasn't killed in the village. He'd descended for trade in Varmin." It wasn't even *in* Varmin where his father had been lost, but outside of it. "He was the cannon master. He was responsible for making it farther down the mountain to find the necessary supplies."

"And what supplies are those?"

"You were there. You saw what my people do."

"You draw attention to yourselves."

"It's not about drawing attention. It's about celebrating."

"What do you celebrate?"

"We celebrate that there hasn't been a dragon attack on the village in many years."

Therin glanced back, and he looked as if he wanted to say something, but he didn't. Instead, he continued onward.

"Where are you going?"

"To stay ahead of the Dragon Souls."

"You don't even want to know why they were here?"

"I know why they were here."

"You said that, but I've told you there hasn't been a

dragon attack in decades. There are no dragons in these mountains."

"I have experienced the Dragon Souls enough to know the reason they would come hunting these mountains. And I understand the kind of things they think they'll find. You're lucky you got away, but I don't know if you'll be able to return to your village very easily. They will not stop their search."

"But I've told you—"

"I'm aware of what you told me. And I am aware of what Dragon Souls search for."

Therin continued to make his way down the mountainside, and Jason struggled to keep up. The other man moved quickly, gliding atop the snow, reminding Jason of what he'd seen when he had been captured, however briefly.

"That's why you were there, isn't it?"

"I was there because it was where I was needed."

"Did you find anything?"

Therin glanced up the slope again, frowning. As before, a sense of heat built from him, radiating away from the man. "Nothing useful."

"Where are you going now?"

"Continuing my search."

Jason kept up with Therin as they walked. He plunged deeper into the snow with each step, his boots sinking, and wished he shared Therin's way of gliding across the top of the snow. The other man didn't appear to struggle at all, mand with each step he took, Jason was forced to take double that.

"Why did you think there was a dragon?"

"Rumors, mostly. I've been following rumors, and in that, I thought I was going to find…" He shook his head, looking down the slope of the mountain before turning his attention back to Jason. "It doesn't matter what I thought I was going to find. It wasn't there. Perhaps I'll go to this Varmin and see what I can find."

"If the dragons are trained, why look for them?"

"There are some that are free. And there's the…"

Jason frowned. "What? Who else has dragons?"

Therin's eyes narrowed a moment. "The rebellion."

He continued to glide along the surface of the snow, making no mark in it. Jason couldn't help but feel amazed by that, nor could he help but feel astonished by everything that he had found around Therin. There was something about the man that impressed him, and yet it seemed almost as if Therin were reluctant to use those talents.

"The rebellion fights the Dragon Souls?"

Anger seemed to cross his face. "Yes."

Jason frowned at the answer. There was something Therin wasn't sharing with him, though he didn't know why or what that might be. "Why are you out here hiding?" When Therin didn't answer, Jason waved a gloved hand at Therin's furs. "You're dressed in furs, but you have the same magic as the Dragon Souls. You're hiding."

"Because of who I'm dealing with. I understand how dangerous they are, and I know that if I make a mistake, I won't survive it." He met Jason's eyes. Therin's silver eyes were unreadable, and yet, there was something about them, some sort of power Jason was able to feel. The longer he looked at the other man, the more certain he was that Therin was using more power than what he was letting on.

Therin paused. Even when he stopped, he didn't sink very far into the snow. He made a little more of a mark in it when he was standing still than when moving, but not nearly as much as Jason did. When he stopped, he sank deep into the snow, the bearskin boots doing nothing to give him the same lift that Therin had.

"I've had others with me, and I lost them. I understand the dangers of having someone else accompanying me."

"How long have you been doing this?"

"Long enough."

Therin looked as if he fit in the village, though Jason suspected that was part of the point. Because of the beard, he could have been from anywhere.

Not at all like the Dragon Souls. They didn't fit in. Their clean-shaven faces would end up freezing out here. Then again, the Dragon Souls had dragonskin clothing. With something like that, they were protected in ways that others were not.

"Why aren't you a Dragon Soul any longer?"

"I can't serve what I don't believe," he said softly.

He continued onward, and Jason tried thinking of

something he could say, but he couldn't come up with anything. He had no idea what the other man had been through, and no idea of the kind of things he had experienced. All he knew was that he was here now.

After they had walked for a while, continuing downward the entire time, Jason glanced back, looking over his shoulder. Every so often, he had a sense there was movement near him, though he didn't know why that should be. He had noticed something before, and yet, there hadn't been anything there. Perhaps it was nothing more than his imagination, but he couldn't shake the sense that something was out there.

"What is it?" Therin asked.

"I keep thinking I see something. It might be nothing."

"What do you think you see?"

He shrugged. "Normally I can see movement pretty well, and every so often, I catch a glimpse of something out of the corner of my eye."

"How certain are you of this?"

"Not at all. That's why I keep looking." Jason stumbled, catching himself, but not before he ended up with a face full of snow. When he got up, he shook his head. "It's probably nothing more than my mind working me over after what I experienced."

The other man grunted. "Possibly."

He paused again, and when he did, he reached into his pocket, pulling something out. He held it out, turning slowly in place, looking.

"What are you looking for?" Jason asked. "I can feel…"

What was it that he could feel? He wasn't sure what it was, or whether or not it was even real. "Power, I suppose."

The other man studied him. There was something unsettling about those silver eyes. How bad must it be for others to have him look at them with one silver eye?

"You have the gift, Jason. The dragon touch. You have it."

"I don't have anything like that." He turned away, closing his eyes. He didn't want to have anything to do with the dragons. It was bad enough that he had dragon sight, and if Therin believed he were dragon touched as well...

That was a power he would rather not possess. It would be easier—better—not to have anything else like that.

"You don't have to fear it. It won't hurt you."

Two kinds of magic...

"The dragon—"

"Was controlled."

If that were the case, it meant Dragon Souls had been in Varmin. *They* had been the reason his father had died. Why, though?

Tessa hadn't spoken about it very often, and he was careful not to push her about it. Then again, he didn't really want to know what Tessa had experienced, the way she had seen his father suffer. She was the last one to have been with him alive. Because of his father, Tessa had managed to escape. She still lived. His father did not.

Therin turned away and continued onward,

descending rapidly. Every so often, Jason would drop to his buttocks and slide down to catch up to the man. It was almost as if Therin were sliding while standing, gliding along the surface of the snow, and yet even if that were what he was doing, he didn't leave any marks; he left no sign of his passing. There was no evidence that he'd been here at all. It amazed Jason.

"How do you travel the way that you do?"

"Walking?"

Jason pointed to his tracks, and then to Therin's. "Not just walking. You're moving in a way that you aren't leaving any evidence of yourself."

"It is safest not to."

He held out the dragon pearl that Jason had seen before, and this time, there was a sense of heat radiating from it, the same sort of heat he'd detected when the other man had been using his sorcery. Was it the dragon pearl, or was it something about him that made it seem that way? Jason didn't know, but perhaps it was just some quality of Therin's.

"I use the power stored within the pearl. It connects to something within me."

"Sorcery," Jason said.

"Sorcery assumes *I* have the power. The stone, this pearl, connects to something within me. The power is not mine. The power is the pearl's. There is no sorcery. There is no magic. I am merely using the power stored within this."

"How are you able to do that?"

"I'm able to do it because I have trained my mind to control it."

Jason stared at the pearl. It seemed to glow softly, though he wondered how much of that was his imagination. It was possible he only thought it was glowing.

"There are a few who possess power, Jason. Those who do are able to use it without any sort of artifacts such as this. They don't need a pearl. They have power within them."

"And you don't have that power?"

"I do not. This is power of the dragons. Much like the dragonskin you long for, though different. Different than even the dragon bone swords so many carried. I have simply used the pearl to help ensure I don't get trapped by the snow." Therin glanced over to him. "You could do it."

Jason shook his head. "I'm not sure I could." Or that he wanted to.

Jason couldn't deny that he could feel the pull from the dragon pearl. There was energy within it, and he didn't understand why he should be able to detect that, only that it was definitely there.

"We will go a little farther and then we will stop for the night," Therin said.

"Can they find us?"

"It's possible." Therin shook his head. "But I need to stay ahead of them. Were they to discover I was still active, I imagine they would change the nature of their focus."

They trudged along through the snow. Rather, Jason

trudged along through the snow while Therin floated. With each step, he could feel the snow seeping into his boots, and his feet were cold. He tried to ignore it, trying not to focus on the way the snow bit at his feet, the ice squeezing his toes, making him miserable.

It was easy enough to drop onto his bottom and slide down the slope. He was able to keep up with Therin when he moved that way, but he didn't have much control, and he was forced to jam his heels into the snow to stop himself. Therin seemed to notice this, and he smiled at Jason.

Jason dropped down onto his bottom again, sliding to catch up to the man. When he did, his heels got caught in the snow and he went twisting, sliding onto his stomach and falling forward. Snow got into his face, his mouth, and worked its way inside of his coat, freezing him. Then his bow smacked him on the forehead.

Jason shook his head as he got to his feet.

Therin held out the dragon pearl. There was something warm about it, almost unpleasantly so. Jason held on to it, squeezing, but he hesitated, afraid of squeezing too tightly. He didn't want to end up drawing some sort of power into himself. He preferred to avoid the power of the dragon as much as he could, but he also didn't want to suffer.

"Hold it. Feel the energy within it."

Jason squeezed the dragon pearl. It fit in the palm of his hand with a comfortable warmth. "It seems slippery."

"Good. Now focus on that. The warmth. Let that fill you."

Jason homed in on that warmth, and gradually, it began to get even warmer. He almost dropped it. There was something about it that reminded him of dragonskin.

"I feel it," he said.

"Good. Now see if you can connect to something within it."

He glanced up. "What am I supposed to connect to?"

"To the power within you."

He did drop the stone then, and he turned to Therin. "I'm not like that."

Therin reached into his pocket, grabbing for something else. When he pulled his hand out, holding it out to Jason, there was another dragon pearl within it. He let it rest in his palm and locked eyes with Jason.

"The power needs to come from within you. What you need to find is your way of reaching it."

Therin reached for the stone that Jason had dropped, digging through the snow. If it was warm, Jason expected it to melt through the snow, dropping all the way to the hard rock that existed beneath layers and layers of snowfall. Somehow, it hadn't fallen that far and Therin stood back up, holding on to the other stone, and slipped it into his pocket.

"When you're ready, I'll let you try again."

Therin started back down the slope, gliding along the surface of the snow once again, leaving Jason to watch him.

He trudged ahead, each step taking him deeper into the snow, and tried to keep up with the other man, but it was a struggle. As much as he wanted to keep pace, with the way he sunk into the snow, he found he couldn't.

After a while, Therin began to pull ahead.

Jason was forced once again to drop to his backside and slide along the snow to catch up to the other man, and when he did, Therin only glanced in his direction, saying nothing.

9

F lames danced in front of Jason, casting a pleasant warmth. After the cold he'd experienced throughout the day, a cold that bit through him, he welcomed anything warmer. He held his gloved hands out, keeping them right in front of the fire, letting it warm him.

"Here," Therin said, thrusting something into his hand.

Jason looked over, half expecting that Therin was going to give him the dragon pearl to work with again, but it was a strip of dried meat.

His stomach rumbled. A pot resting on the fire was filled with melted snow, and a comforting sense came from within it of whatever spiced tea he made. Jason took a bite of the jerky, tearing it free. He chewed slowly, savoring it, and when he swallowed, his throat burned.

He tried to think about when he'd last eaten anything, and couldn't recall it. Had it been the broth several days before?

The sweet bread. He was surprised he had managed to stay satiated for as long as he had, but then, part of that might have been his fear more than any real satiation.

"We're going to try again." Therin pushed the dragon pearl into his palm.

The stone pressed into the surface of his glove. Through the glove, he could feel the warmth. He continued to chew at the meat and when it was gone, he pulled off one of his gloves, holding the pearl in his palm.

"Focus on how it feels to you," Therin said.

Jason took a deep breath. The pearl was incredibly smooth. And the warmth coming from it was pleasant, though he tried to pretend it was not. He didn't want to acknowledge that anything about a dragon would be pleasant.

"As you feel that warmth, focus on what you detect. Focus on how that echoes within you."

Jason squeezed the pearl. There was no echo within him. There was the slight warmth of the pearl itself, but other than that, he sensed nothing more.

He looked over at Therin. "What if you're wrong and I don't have this ability?"

Therin stared down at the ground, as if studying the snow swirling around them. "When I was found, they brought me to Lorach, a place for Dragon Souls. I was young, probably no more than five or six. And the man who found me believed I had potential. He did what I'm doing to you now, only he forced me to wear the dragon pearl around my neck. He activated it, letting it grow warm and then hot. It stayed with me until I developed enough control to reduce the heat from it. For a long time, I didn't believe I had the ability they claimed, and yet, eventually I did manage to gain control over the dragon pearl. I managed to reduce that heat. I managed to survive." He shook his head and looked at Jason. "Fortunately, there are other ways of learning. There were many aspects to my training I would not force upon someone else, that being but one of them. It was brutal. Effective, though."

Jason held tightly to the dragon pearl, squeezing it. "I don't feel anything."

"Sit. Drink this," he said, pulling a cup from someplace deep within his pocket, pouring the spiced tea into it, and handing it over, "and focus on the pearl. That's all I ask. Only that you focus on it, thinking about the way you can feel it. Nothing more than that."

Jason took a seat much like the other man asked, and held the pearl in his hand. It was warm, but not unpleasantly so. He didn't need a glove, but didn't know if that was because of the pearl or because of the heat from the strange magical fire.

What was he supposed to find from this pearl?

Two kinds of magic...

Jason pushed those thoughts away.

He thought of the things he'd seen from Therin in the time since he'd met the man. Everything seemed impossible. Not only had he healed Morris, but he'd lit several fires without burning anything. And the Dragon Souls had used their power to attack him.

If he could learn to use this magic, maybe he could hunt with it. Not just hunt with it, but it was possible he could use it to light a fire the same way that Therin did.

His family wouldn't have to suffer.

As much as anything, that drove him.

He tried focusing on what he could detect of the stone, but the longer he held it, the less likely he thought it was that he would be able to detect anything at all. There was warmth from it but nothing else, and certainly nothing that reverberated within him the way Therin had suggested there would be. All of it was within his mind, wasn't it?

"I can't detect anything."

Therin smiled sadly. "Perhaps you don't have the necessary connection." Jason handed him the stone, but Therin shook his head. "You hold on to it."

"Why?"

"Maybe you'll develop a connection to it in time. Sometimes it's merely a matter of exposure."

The other man turned back to the fire, tending to it. There wasn't a whole lot to do, as it burned on its own, glowing with an intensity that lit up the night. It crackled like a normal fire would, and it radiated warmth the same way, but there was something else about it that struck him as atypical.

It was almost more tolerable than it should be. He found it pleasant, though he didn't know why that should be. Every time he'd been around flames like this before, there had been a limit to how close he was able to get, and yet with this fire, he was able to sit almost alongside it. Perhaps that was the nature of the magical flame, and because of that, he was able to come closer than he normally would be able to do.

"Won't the Dragon Souls be able to see the flame?"

"I've done a few things to make it more difficult for them by attempting to mitigate the extent of the flame." Therin met his eyes. There was a flash of something within those silver eyes that made Jason wonder if there was something he could determine from the other man, but he wasn't able to find anything. "There is control. If you don't want to understand the nature of the connection, then I won't share anything more with you."

"I'm open to understanding it." He didn't really know much about Lorach, and other than hearing the stories of how dangerous the dragon riders were, he knew nothing. His people had remained isolated, hidden and protected, long enough that stories of dragons had become just that: stories.

"Tell me about Lorach. I don't know that much," he said.

"It's unfortunate."

Therin turned toward him, looking across the fire. As he did, the flames seemed to dance in his eyes, almost as if he were summoning the power within them, using that in some strange way. Was that what it looked like when the Dragon Souls used their power?

"Lorach is an impressive city. I first went there when I was young—much younger than you are now. You quickly learn the Dragon Souls have a position of authority there, but that doesn't mean others don't. The king rules, and he has incredible power."

"Because of the Dragon Souls."

Therin tipped his head in a nod. "Because of the Dragon Souls. But it's more than that. He has power of his own." He fell silent, staring at the flames. As he did, the fire seemed to dance within his eyes even more wildly. Jason heard nothing more than the steady crackling of the flames. There wasn't even a hissing from the snow, almost as if the fire didn't affect it at all.

While waiting for Therin to say something more, he stared at the snow, trying to better understand why it wasn't melting under the heat of the flame, but there wasn't anything he could determine. The dragon pearl rested there, the flames crackling around it, almost as if radiating from the dragon pearl itself.

A soft rumbling came from behind him and Jason swiveled, looking up the slope.

"Is that an avalanche?" he asked.

"I suspect that is the Dragon Souls searching." Therin sat up, and as he did, the flames began to lower, though the heat persisted from them, still keeping Jason warm. He was thankful for that, appreciating that the fire offered him as much comfort as it did. "I left the Dragon Souls when I began to question their methods. And now I pursue free dragons."

Therin placed his hands in his lap, and flames began to leap from the surface of his palms. It started small and then began to build, shapes twisting within it. As Jason watched, he realized one of the shapes was familiar. It was a dragon, made completely out of flames.

"The Dragon Souls control many dragons. There have been dragons for as long as our people have existed, and the connection to the dragons has existed for nearly as long. The Dragon Souls recall a time when they hunted free dragons, searching for them, but these days, the dragons are all bred, the eggs harvested, ensuring Dragon Souls have control over the lines of dragons. Occasionally, rumors emerge of something else."

"What sort of rumors?"

Therin smiled slightly. The flames shifted, becoming smaller, and the shape in his palms diminished. "Those of dragons."

"With the rebellion you mentioned?"

Therin nodded slowly. "Those who would sacrifice the dragons in their fight with Lachen." He looked up at Jason. "I don't always agree with the Dragon Souls, but the dragons are protected there. Safe. Now I search for free dragons." He watched Jason, an unreadable expression in his eyes. Dark. "I don't suppose you've seen any."

Jason shook his head. "I don't know that I'd even recognize a dragon."

"You would know," Therin said. "They're dangerous. Which is why I look."

Jason sat back, resting his hands in the snow. They

weren't nearly as cold as they had been. He looked at the other man across the fire, meeting his silver eyes. "Why do you care about the free dragons?"

"Because I need to know if they're what the stories say." When Jason didn't say anything, he grinned. "Powerful in a way we would never understand."

Jason shook his head. "The dragons are powerful. I wasn't there the day my father died, but the stories that came back suggest the dragon he interacted with was incredibly strong."

"I'm not saying our dragons aren't powerful. All I'm saying is that there are others I suspect exist."

"And that's why you came to my village?"

"I follow rumors."

"Why did the rumors bring you to the village?"

"Probably because of the display you used to celebrate your freedom. It would draw dragons to it. Fire to fire."

"We weren't trying to draw dragons."

"You might not have been trying to, but displays like that have a way of succeeding. Unfortunately, none came."

Jason stared at the man. "You were hoping we would draw a dragon?"

"I was hoping there might be something. And then when you shared with me that the ballistae were fired, I had to wonder whether or not there was a sighting, but more likely than not, your people didn't encounter anything."

"There was a group of kids my age who were talking about firing one of the ballistae," he said.

Such a foolish thing, but at the same time, it was the kind of thing he could imagine Reltash having done, even though it would weaken the village. More than that, it would be unlikely that anyone would even know it was him. They could have fired it off in the night and disappeared into the darkness. No one would have been the wiser.

"Perhaps that's all it was."

"Why out here?" Jason looked around, scanning the darkness. It seemed such an odd place to come looking for a dragon. This place was cold and bleak, not the kind of spot he would've expected to attract a creature like the dragon—a creature that enjoyed heat and fire and other sorts of things that simply weren't around the mountaintop.

"Perhaps it's nothing," Therin said.

"Why?"

"It's possible there's another type of dragon."

Jason held his gaze, waiting for the other man to say something more, to reveal he was joking, but he didn't. He looked serious. For his part, Jason started chuckling.

"You're kidding, right? You think there's some sort of ice dragon out here?"

"I didn't say that it was an ice dragon. All I said was that it might be a different kind."

He laughed again, and Therin turned away.

"Rest. In the morning, you continue onward."

"Where to?"

"We can continue to circle down the base of the mountain. I can get you to a smaller village and you can gather enough supplies to make it back up."

Jason lay down, resting his head on his arms, staying close to the fire. At least he was warm. It seemed a surprising comfort out in the open like this, surrounded by snow, and in a place where he should be cold, and yet he was not.

It took only a few moments before his eyes drifted closed, and strangely, in his dreams, he thought that he saw visions of dragons crawling around him.

10

J ason sat up. Wind howled around him, tearing at his clothing. The fire was gone, and there was no sign of Therin.

Had the other man left him?

How had he managed to sleep for as long as he had? In a place like this, without any sign of warmth, he would have easily succumbed to the cold. The fire was the only reason he was able to survive, and if Therin had taken the dragon pearl and disappeared, Jason wasn't sure he would be able to withstand the temperatures.

He got to his feet. Everything about him was cold and stiff, and he stretched, trying to work the pain out of his joints, but it was difficult to do. He'd been motionless for so long. Daylight had long ago come, and though he couldn't see the sun as it hid behind the clouds, he could feel the shifting temperature. The wind made it cold, but if it weren't for the wind, it would be comfortable.

He turned in place, looking all around. There was no sign of Therin. Looking for his footprints was an exercise in futility. The other man didn't leave any marks. Even now, Jason was unable to identify any sign of the other man.

He was alone.

He glanced at the slope of the mountain. He wasn't going to be able to make it back to the village on his own, and he couldn't do so without the necessary supplies, and so Therin's plan to continue working his way down the side of the mountain until he reached one of the smaller villages was the safest bet.

Jason had never traveled that far. The farthest he'd gone was to some of the villages on the backside of the mountain, but never down to the base. It was too dangerous.

He took a deep breath. He had no other choice.

Jason started through the snow. At least he had his bow and arrows, and he had the dragon pearl, for all the good it would do him. He checked for what else he had, realizing the strange rock he'd found must have slipped out of his pocket while he'd slept.

A rumbling sounded behind him and he glanced back up. He couldn't shake the feeling the rumbling represented an avalanche, but the more he listened, the less it seemed that it was. If it was an avalanche, there should have been some sign of snow pressing down, and yet nothing about the upper slopes changed.

That troubled him. Maybe it was nothing more than the beginning of an avalanche, or perhaps the snow shifting in a section of the mountain he wasn't able to see, but he couldn't help but feel as if there was something more to it. If somehow he was in danger, he didn't want to get caught out here in the snow alone. There was nothing with which he could protect himself. He needed shelter of some sort.

Worse, he couldn't help but fear that Dragon Souls might be out here as well.

If there were Dragon Souls, he needed to stay ahead of them.

Jason picked up his pace, hurrying through the snow. Every so often, he would drop to his backside and try to slide, but the snow had shifted overnight, making it more difficult. He found he got caught on sharp edges, and it was painful. What he needed was to keep moving.

He turned when he heard another rumbling.

He stared, looking out at the blank expanse of white, watching as wisps of snow lifted off the surface of the mountain. Every so often, he thought he caught a glimmer of movement, but it turned out to be nothing more than the snow.

As he started to turn away, something else caught his attention.

A dark figure.

At first, Jason thought it might be Therin, and he considered waving his hand, drawing attention to himself, but as he stared, he wasn't sure if it was Therin.

The man wouldn't have been coming from that direction, would he?

As he stared, he realized that it wasn't just one figure. There were three.

The Dragon Souls.

Jason moved more quickly. He had to run, wanting to stay ahead of the Dragon Souls, wanting to do anything but get caught by them, and as he staggered through the snow, trying to take step after step, trying to keep ahead, he couldn't help but feel as if they were catching him.

He hazarded a glance behind him, but the wind was picking up fast and strong enough that he wasn't able to see anything other than the gusting of snow as it lifted off the surface. It whipped around him, concealing everything in a white haze.

At least he hoped that it would conceal him, too. With his bearskin clothing, he would blend into the blizzard, but for how long?

He had no idea what the Dragon Souls might be able to find. It was possible they had an enhanced version of his eyesight, a way of seeing through the cold and seeing movement as heat signatures. If so, he wasn't going to be hidden nearly as well as he hoped.

Which meant that he had to move quickly. If he could get down to the village, he could blend in.

He didn't know anything or anyone in the village, and heading there without money meant he was going to go in depending on kindness. That wasn't something he thought he should be risking.

There was no other choice, though.

Standing frozen for a moment, he got another glimpse of the figures. They were moving quickly—as easily as Therin had moved across the snow, gliding along the surface of it.

Therin had been trying to help him understand, trying to show him he could use the dragon pearl and the power within it, but he hadn't been able to connect to it.

He reached into his pocket, squeezing the stone. It was warm, and with the cold being what it was, Jason was thankful for that, but he needed more than just warmth. He needed the power the stone promised, and he wasn't even sure if there was a way for him to reach it.

Connect to it. That was what Therin had said.

He had no idea what it was going to take to connect to that power. Even if he could, he wasn't sure that he would know what to do once he did.

Maybe that was not necessary. Maybe he didn't need to know how to use the connection, but only needed to hold on to that power, to draw it out of the pearl and through himself.

As he hurried along the snow, he tried to think about what he wanted from it. He tried to think about how that stone would feel, the warmth that it had, and tried to draw it through him.

Nothing happened.

Of course nothing would happen, as Jason didn't have any of that magic within him. He wasn't a sorcerer, and he certainly didn't have the necessary power to control a dragon pearl the same way these others did. All he could do was try to keep moving, to stay ahead of them, and live.

That was it, wasn't it? They already thought him a slave. That was what Therin had said. What would happen if he were captured?

He had to push those thoughts out of his head.

He needed to survive. His sister and mother needed him to survive and return to the village.

Dropping to his bottom, he tried to slide along the surface of the snow. If he couldn't walk above it the same way as a Dragon Soul, maybe he could slide in a way they couldn't.

Come on, dragon pearl.

The stupid thing didn't work for him, and it was foolish to even think that it might. He thought about throwing it, but he enjoyed the warmth. He enjoyed the way it seeped into his glove, working along his arm, up into his chest, rolling down through his belly and into his legs. That warmth flowed into him.

It felt almost like he were sitting in front of the fire.

He continued to pull on that power, letting it flow, and realized he was sliding down the mountainside much faster than he had been able to do before.

Two kinds of magic...

It didn't matter. Not if it worked.

Jason was thankful he managed to hit a section of the mountain that no longer provided resistance. He ignored the snow working up his coat, getting onto his back, freezing him, and he ignored the way it occasionally crawled down his boots, seeping into his stockings and his feet. He ignored the way it sprayed up along his face. All of that was painful, unpleasant, and he tried not to think of it.

The longer he slid, the faster he went. He was tempted to dig in his heels and slow himself the way he'd done when he'd been traveling with Therin, but if he were to do that, he ran the risk of the Dragon Souls catching him. At least this way, he had to think he was staying ahead of them. He was moving quickly, and much more rapidly than he was able to do when walking.

Suddenly, he hit a lump in the snow and went flying.

When he landed, his bow next to him, his breath was knocked free of him and he bit back a cry. Jason hurriedly grabbed his bow as the wind whistled around him, spinning him… and he went headfirst down the mountainside.

Jason tried to grab for the snow, to spin himself around, but he had no control. Now he was facing the wrong direction, and he did drag his heels, trying to grip the snow, but as his boot started to come free, he resisted the urge to even do that. He didn't want to lose one of his boots. Men had lost feet because they had lost their boots, and Jason was not about to freeze his foot off because of this slide.

How had he ended up like this?

He tried to spin around while he was sliding, and he managed to get up, with the wind whistling around him. An occasional tree cropped up, and it was the first time that he'd even seen a tree growing like this. It had long needles, and as he passed beneath one, it whipped his face, poking at his cheeks, and he jerked his head back. He almost slammed into the snow but managed to lift his head at the last minute.

He got back up and kicked his legs around.

He was still sliding, moving quickly, with no control over it. It was almost as if the snow had caught him in an avalanche, dragging him with it. As he looked around, he realized that was exactly what had happened. He was tumbling down, pushed down by the snow behind him, forced with increasing speed. If he were to stop, he would run the risk of getting caught in the avalanche, covered by it, and would have to find some way of digging his way out. He had heard of people caught in avalanches who had not survived. It was better to let it carry him down as far as it would and stay ahead of it.

More trees began to crop up and Jason had to kick himself off to the side, trying to steer himself. It was increasingly difficult to avoid striking them, and yet, he didn't dare try to slow himself. He was sliding with increasing speed, the avalanche pushing him down. He found it strangely exhilarating.

Were it not for the terror rolling through him at the idea of one of the Dragon Souls catching him, he might be excited by the ride. As it was, he was afraid he would not be able to stay ahead of the Dragon Souls and survive the avalanche.

Snow continued to push him, faster and faster as it

went, and Jason looked around for some way to slow himself if it were necessary.

Maybe he could grab one of the branches and pull himself up.

Doing so would be painful. It would jerk on his arms, and it might be too much to withstand. He would have to slow himself first. Yet slowing himself ran the risk of the avalanche consuming him.

What he needed to find was a particularly tall tree he could climb—and do so quickly. He had considerable experience climbing mountains and working his way up icy slopes, but none climbing a tree.

As he surveyed the nearby trees, the choice was made for him.

His arms caught a low-hanging branch.

Jason dug his heels, trying to slow himself, and wrapped around the branch. Snow pushed on his back, its weight heavy against his coat, and he pulled, trying to climb, working his way up the side of the tree. Finally, he made it onto the branch.

The snow continued to push down on him, and he scrambled up the tree, squeezing through branches, avoiding the needles as they tore at him.

The snow pushed on him and he slammed into the trunk.

At least he had something that he could hold on to.

The snow piled up against him, heavy and forceful. It was painful, but it no longer forced him down the slope. Now he was pinned against the trunk, trapped in place.

All he could do was wait.

It seemed that the snow continued to push for a long time. He lost track of how long he was there, clinging to the trunk, his arms wrapped around it, ignoring the pain as it slammed into him over and over again. The weight was enormous, far more than he'd ever experienced before.

And then the rumbling ceased.

Jason moved an arm.

He freed some of the snow, holding his breath. He freed more and started to climb, digging his way upward. As he went, slowly climbing, he finally found a space near the top of the tree.

How much snow had collapsed?

It was a wonder the tree hadn't fallen over under the weight of it.

Getting his hand free, he looked up, and sucked in a breath of air. He checked his bow, thankful it was still with him—and somehow undamaged.

Strangely, from atop the tree, the sky seemed blue. Clouds rolled in the sky and the sun shone. It had been days since he had seen the sun. Most of the time at the top of the mountain, the sky was a hazy, cloudy mess. There was always the threat of snow, always the threat of another storm, and yet, that haziness protected them.

Jason didn't know the last time he'd seen a blue sky like this. It certainly had not been for quite a while.

He took a deep breath of the crisp air and shifted up the trunk of the tree a little bit higher, trying to get a better vantage. When he did, he turned his attention up the slope, worried he might find movement, anything that might signify the Dragon Souls were there, but there was nothing.

Letting out a relieved sigh, he started to turn, looking down the slope. There were other trees, and it was strange to see a forest of trees all around him. He'd never experienced anything like that. Finding branches was rare enough, and they were prized. It was part of the reason he valued his bow and arrows as much as he did. If he were to lose even one of the arrows, replacing it would be difficult. It had taken considerable effort on his father's part in order to have the equipment he needed. Few in the village ever burned wood, preferring dung. The only time wood was burned was during the festival, a way of taunting the dragonriders. Or those who had too much money, those who ran the mines and were willing to pay.

Jason breathed in and turned his attention downslope.

As he did, his breath caught.

There was a town.

11

T herin had mentioned a village at the base of the mountain, but this wasn't a village at all. This was an actual town, and it sprawled outward, filling the entirety of the base. Jason had no idea how long it would take to climb back up the side of the mountain, but it certainly was going to take long enough that it wouldn't be easy. Without any money, he had no way to secure the necessary supplies. Therin was supposed to have helped him, and without him, how was Jason going to gather what he needed?

Perhaps he could barter with some of the people in the village.

Then again, what did he have to barter with?

The answer was in his hand. He still gripped the dragon pearl, and had managed to hang on to it during the descent. Even better, he held on to it while the snow was crashing into him. Maybe it had kept him warm during the fall. It had to have some value. Especially if it was valuable to the Dragon Souls.

He didn't have any idea who he could go to for trade with the pearl, but he would have to find somebody. That was going to be his first order of business, and from there, he could look for other supplies. He might need additional clothing, and he certainly would need something to light a fire along the slope. Perhaps some food, though he might be able to hunt on his way up. Given that he was so far down the side of the mountain, it was more likely he would encounter other creatures. If that were the case, he wouldn't have to worry about meat quite as much.

The first thing to do was to get down there and find out what he could about the village, and whether there was anyone there who might be able to help him.

Jason continued his descent and dropped down to his bottom, sliding once again. He didn't move at nearly the same speed as he had before, but once he was free of this tree, he managed to steer away from the other trees, and then into an opening.

The snow was harder packed here, easier to navigate. He got to his feet, shaking some of the snow out of his coat, taking off his gloves and dumping them out, and looked around.

There was evidence of movement past here. Footsteps —dozens of them—indicated others had traveled in this direction. Could it be that they didn't have nearly as much snowfall as they did up the side of the mountain?

The wind wasn't quite as bad, either. No longer did it

howl as it had, almost as if they were in a protected section.

He made his way toward the town. Jason paused every so often, looking for any sign of movement, searching to see whether there was anyone else around him. The Dragon Souls weren't here, but that didn't mean anyone else might not be. It was possible others were here, and if they were, he wanted to be careful about approaching them. He was certain he would be dressed differently— possibly even strangely, compared to them.

When he reached the outer edge of the village, he paused. The homes were small, cozy, and not snow-covered the same way his village was. The snow was hard packed around the town and, in some sections, even cleared completely, revealing dirt.

Jason stared at that, shocked by it.

They didn't dare have the earth exposed in the village. If it were, it would be easier for the dragons to see them. The whole point of having the snowpack was to conceal them from the dragons, to avoid another attack. In this part of the mountain, dragon attacks must not have been nearly as frequent.

Unless they didn't fear dragons at all.

What if these people were servants of the Dragon Souls and of the king Therin had mentioned?

They were still quite a ways from Lorach, far enough away that Jason had to think it would be unusual to encounter anyone from that kingdom.

As he looked around, he realized they were in a small

valley, and the valley itself might protect them from the dragons. They would have more notice of their coming. Maybe they had weapons set up the same way his village did, anchored around the entirety of the village, the same as his people did.

Jason started into the village.

He remained close to one of the nearby houses. The roof was made of bundles of branches similar to the tree that he'd climbed. The needles had dried and they were stacked together, giving protection. Piles of those needles littered the ground, and he couldn't help but wonder what it might be like to burn them. Would they burn well?

As he glanced behind him, looking at the trees, he couldn't help but think that these people didn't have to worry about finding firewood. They would have plenty to burn. They would be able to stay warm.

The smoke drifting up from chimneys within each of the homes told him that much.

More than that, it was the fact that he was warm. It wasn't nearly as cold as it had been farther up the mountain. It was almost as if the sun warmed things, melting the snow, and he unbuttoned his coat. He continued to creep into the village, looking around. He had no idea where he was going, and when he encountered his first local, he froze.

He'd been worried about looking like an outsider, and yet, he needn't have been concerned. The first man he encountered was dressed in a thick brown fur. It was different than the white bearskin Jason wore, but only in the color. It was patched together, the stitching keeping it intact, and the man tromped past him, turning up one of the streets.

Jason decided to follow. If nothing else, he would at least look as if he were with that man rather than on his own.

As he trailed the man, he encountered others wandering through the streets. Many of the men were dressed in jackets that were far lighter than what he'd ever worn before, but many others were dressed in furs like the man in front of him. The man meandered through the street before turning a corner. Jason had looked to see where he'd gone when someone grabbed his arm.

He spun around and came face-to-face with the dark-furred man.

"Are you following me?"

Jason shook his head. The man's breath stunk, and there was a dark gleam in his brown eyes. Maybe it was more than his breath that stunk. His furs, too. "I'm not following you."

"You look like you have been. Why?"

Jason tried to pull away but the man was strong, holding on to his arm in a tight grip. Every time he tried to jerk his arm free, he found that the man was there, keeping him from moving it away.

"I don't know where I'm going."

"What?"

Jason shook his head. "I don't really know where I'm going. I'm trying to—"

The man shoved him free and Jason staggered back, tripping over his feet and landing on his backside as he looked up at the man. He was tall, though not as tall as most from Jason's village. Other than the furs, there was nothing else unusual about him, and thankfully there was no silver in his eyes as there had been with the Dragon Souls.

Jason started to get up and the man spun, heading away.

Getting to his feet, Jason dusted himself off.

"Don't mind him," a voice said from nearby.

Jason jerked his head around.

"What was that?"

"I said don't mind him. He comes in here about once a month, and he's usually angry about something." A figure stepped out of the darkness, and Jason realized it was a boy about his age. He was slightly shorter, stick thin, and had spiky black hair. His eyes were crystal blue and seemed to match the sky overhead.

"You aren't from here, are you?" the boy asked.

"No."

"Are you from Atriul?"

Jason hadn't heard of that place, and he shook his head.

"Hovarth?"

Jason shook his head again.

"Where are you from?"

He pointed up the side of the mountain.

The boy's eyes widened. "Where?"

"All the way up."

His breath caught. "There's nothing up there. We've tried to climb, but..."

Jason let out a sigh. What was he doing here?

The answer was easy. It might have taken him only two days to get down, but heading up was going to be harder. He'd seen that in the times when he'd gone with his father to Varmin. The return climb required more effort than it took getting down.

"I'm looking for someplace I can trade. I need supplies."

"What sort of supplies?"

"Supplies to get back."

"You came down to get supplies to get back?"

"I got caught out in the storm. I was sort of forced down."

The boy watched him, and then he nodded. "Come with me."

He started heading through the streets, waving Jason to follow.

He hesitated at first but then decided, what better way to find what he needed than to go along with someone who was local? The boy seemed friendly enough, and certainly not at all like the dark-coated man who'd almost attacked him.

Maybe he should be asking about Therin. If he could find out what happened to him, he might be able to figure out how he could get back.

"What sort of things are you looking for?" the boy asked.

"Food. Maybe some rope," Jason said, thinking about what would be beneficial. A length of rope would be helpful, and even more than that, he would need some snowshoes. Considering the way he'd sunk into the snow while walking with Therin, he'd need something to let him stay above it and move more quickly. He thought that he could make them with the branches he had seen, but if he could buy them, then it would be easy enough to just start back. Making snowshoes would take time, and he had no idea how much time he wanted to risk.

Then again, he'd already been gone for a few days, long enough that his mother and sister probably thought he was gone for good. No one survived very long outside of the village. It was possible they'd sent search parties for him, but they could only search so far and so long, and eventually they would have to turn back. If the storms had been as bad as it had seemed, they wouldn't have been able to spend much time outside looking for him.

And a part of Jason had this nagging suspicion there was something else that was taking place. With the ballistae fired, as he thought they had been, the possibility existed that there had been a dragon sighting.

That had to be why the Dragon Souls were there, wasn't it?

Therin hadn't believed that, though Jason was no longer sure what to make of Therin. The other man had abandoned him, leaving him on the side of the mountain. What kind of person did that?

"A shelter. Even some snowshoes."

"You didn't wear snowshoes?" The boy glanced down at Jason's feet before looking back up to his face. "How did you make it down the side of the mountain? I hear the snow is a hundred feet deep."

"Not quite that," Jason said.

"It sounds like it is impossibly deep. The hunters outside the village talk about snowstorms that leave impossible amounts of snow."

"There is a lot of snow, and it's cold, but it's not quite that bad."

"I still can't believe you're from there."

An idea came to him. "Have you seen another man? Thick beard. Dressed in furs."

"Other than Old Henry?"

"Who's Old Henry?"

"He's the man you met when you first came to town."

Jason nodded. "That's not him. He's dressed similar, though." It was strange. He hadn't made the connection before, but it did seem that Old Henry had been dressed similarly to Therin. Maybe they knew each other. And if they knew each other, then Jason might need to follow Old Henry to see if there was anything the other man might reveal to him.

"I haven't seen anything like that. Then again, most traders head to the south side of the town."

"Why the south side?"

"Because it's better connected. Well, at least better connected than any place other than to the north." The boy grinned. "I'm William, by the way."

The boy stuffed out his hand and Jason took it, shaking it. "I'm Jason."

"It's good to meet you, Jason. Maybe when we find the supplies you need, you can tell me about your town."

Jason shrugged. "It's not that exciting."

"Maybe not to you, but it is to me. I still can't imagine what it must be like living up there. Anywhere but here," he said wistfully.

Jason looked up the side of the mountain. From here, it was impossibly steep and impossibly high. Had he not come down it, he would have wondered how he was going to survive making it back up.

They continued to weave through the town, and as they went, Jason looked at the buildings. Most of them were homes, similar to what he'd seen on the outside of the town, but as they started to cross through the center, they encountered other buildings. Some of them were structured a bit differently, and many of them looked to have signs hanging out front.

They were no different than the kind of shops they had in his village. Then again, the entire town was similar, though different than what he encountered in his home. It was strange, and he couldn't shake that strangeness, but there was also something relaxing about being here, away from the whipping wind, the fear of cold, and the simple challenge of trying to keep warm.

"Don't you have to worry about dragons?"

"About what?" William asked.

"Dragons. Don't you have to worry about them?"

William cocked a brow at him. "What are you talking about?"

Jason frowned. "Creatures that fly and shoot fire from their mouths?"

William started to laugh. "You can't tell me your people believe in such stories."

"We believe in them because they're true."

William paused, turning and facing Jason. He crossed his arms over his chest and locked eyes with Jason. "I can't tell if you are trying to make fun of me or not."

"Not. Definitely not. My entire village is defended against dragon attacks. We haven't had one in several decades, but they're real enough."

William stared at him for a moment. "We don't have anything like that. And as far as I know, we've *never* had anything like that. The worst we have to deal with are wolves. Occasionally garols."

"What's a garol?"

William grinned again. "You come here asking about dragons, and you don't know anything about a garol?"

Jason shrugged this time. "I guess so."

"They're cats, and almost as large as wolves. They hunt in packs, and we have to keep on the lookout for them. They haven't bothered us in a while, but when they do, it's usually because they are hungry. Then again, when that happens, hunters typically are aware of it because the deer populations around us start to change." The other man shook his head, laughing softly. "I still can't believe you believe in dragons."

Jason fell silent and followed William. They stopped in front of a shop with a sign hanging out front.

"This is a general store. You should be able to find anything you need inside."

Jason nodded. "Thanks for your help, William."

"Oh, you're not getting off that easy. I still want to know more about your home."

"When I finish," he said.

He stared at the door, debating, and then a realization struck him.

If they didn't believe in dragons here, there was no value to the dragon pearl.

Jason didn't have anything worth trading.

J ason stood frozen, staring at the sign, and William watched him.

"What is it?"

He glanced at the other boy, taking in his fine features, his narrow jawline, his spiky black hair. This was a person who didn't believe in dragons, who didn't know they existed.

Then again, Jason had never seen a dragon, himself.

He had seen dragonskin. He had seen dragon bone weapons. And he had seen the dragon pearls along with the magic that was used by those who possessed those items.

All of that told him that dragons were real.

More than that, his father had died because of a dragon.

He didn't know how, though.

He'd assumed that his father had come down the side

of the mountain, arriving at a village like this, and had been attacked by a dragon, but if that weren't the case, then what had happened to his father?

"Aren't you going to go in?"

"I don't have any money," he said.

"How did you expect to trade for anything?"

Jason sighed and then reached into his pocket, pulling out the dragon pearl. He held it out to William.

The other boy took it, holding it in his hand. "It's warm. Is it some sort of special rock from your homeland?"

"It's a dragon pearl."

"Is it?" William grinned again. "Did you take this off of a dragon?"

"A Dragon Soul gave it to me."

"What's a Dragon Soul?"

"It's a…" Jason no longer knew what to say. He had come down here, thinking he would find help, but more than that, he'd come thinking everything he knew would be known by the people in this village. And yet, if they weren't aware of any of that, then there was no point in trying to argue what he had known.

What he needed was to find Therin. The other man would have money, Jason was certain of it, and more than that, he would have experienced trading.

It still surprised him that Therin would have abandoned him, and yet, maybe he hadn't. Maybe Therin had gone off hunting and Jason had been the one to have left him. When the avalanche came, he had no other choice but to hurry down the side of the mountain. It was lucky he had survived.

Maybe Therin was still coming. If that were the case, he needed to wait, preferably on the outside of the village, watching to see if the other man was going to approach.

"This is a mistake," he said.

"It's not a mistake. I can help you."

"I don't have any money," he said again.

"Like I said, I can help you," William said.

"Do you have money?"

"No… but there's something else I can do." William motioned for him to follow, and Jason sighed before doing so.

They wandered along the side of the street and took a few smaller turns, and the buildings began to press closer together.

William glanced over at him. "Have you ever played caral?"

Jason shook his head.

"That's what I figured. Anyway, when we get in there, I want you to tell them the same things you told me."

"About the dragon?"

William grinned. "Exactly. Tell them about the dragon. And then pull your special stone out at the last minute."

"Why?"

"You'll see."

They paused in front of a small building. It looked a little more dilapidated than some of the others. While many of the others had been painted, this one appeared to be faded and less well cared for.

The door hung askew, and William nodded to himself before pushing it open. Jason followed him inside.

It was dim, and it took a moment for his eyes to adjust. Even while they were adjusting, his silver eye allowed him to make out the forms inside. There were about a dozen people, and they all sat around tables. Many of them had drinks resting on the tables in front of them, and some of them had food.

Jason's stomach rumbled. It had been a while since he'd eaten. The meat Therin had given him had satiated him some, but he was still hungry.

William cocked his eye at him. "You can't go doing that now."

"What?"

He jabbed Jason in the belly. "That. Keep that to yourself. Here." William reached into his pocket and pulled out a hunk of bread and passed it over to him. "If this is going to work for you, you're going to need all of your money. You can't have the Stag's Horn getting any of it for their food. Besides, I can tell you that you don't really want their food."

William weaved through the tables before taking a seat near the back.

"Gary. This is my new friend Jason. He's from the mountain."

Gary looked up. He was probably ten years older than Jason and had a neatly trimmed beard. He had a dangerous gleam in his eyes that reminded Jason of men like Reltash. There was something about him that Jason didn't like right away.

"Is that right?" Gary drawled.

"It is. And he's in the mood for a little gaming. I thought you might be interested."

"I've told you that you aren't allowed here anymore."

"You don't get to tell me where I get to go, Gary. Besides, I thought you'd be interested in learning about what my new friend Jason knows. As I said, he comes from a village high in the mountains."

"A lot of people claim that."

William took a chair and pulled it out, throwing himself down into it. "A lot of people claim they know about dragons?"

Gary frowned, and there was movement in the shadows that stepped forward.

Jason looked around, worried that this was a mistake. There was something about this place that left him unsettled, making him think it was not exactly safe. Why would William bring him here?

"Go on," William urged. "Tell him."

"Tell him what?" Jason asked.

"Tell him what you told me."

"What do you want me to tell him?" Jason asked.

William glanced over his shoulder. His eyes seemed to urge Jason to speak, giving him a wild expression. His hair sticking straight up did nothing to change that. "About the dragons."

Jason licked his lips, his mouth suddenly dry. He felt uncomfortable here, but perhaps that was the point. Maybe that was what William wanted. If that were the case, then it was working.

"I think this is a mistake," he said.

"It's not a mistake," Gary said.

Two men appeared on either side of him, and they had their arms crossed over their chests. Jason noticed the long swords strapped at their waists.

He had a belt knife he'd used to escape the Dragon Souls, but he didn't have any sort of training with hand-to-hand combat. The only thing he had was a bow, and in this place, a bow was not likely to help him all that much.

"Sit." Gary leaned forward, looking at Jason. "Are you playing some sort of game with me?" Gary glared at William.

Jason suddenly decided that he wanted to be anywhere but here. This *was* a mistake. He had been around men like Gary before and recognized the anger in his voice. The other two alongside him reminded Jason of the people that Reltash liked to surround himself with. Usually they were those who had some strength, and more than that, they were dangerous.

"It's no game, Gary. Then again, if you want to play caral, I'm happy to do so."

"Tell me about these dragons," Gary said, looking up at Jason.

Jason took a deep breath, running his hands along the tabletop. It was worn, with what looked to be places where knives had been stabbed into it. "What do you want me to tell you?"

"Tell him what you told me," William urged.

"What?"

William sighed and turned back to Gary. "He doesn't want to say it, but he comes from a village that knows about dragons. They hunt them. He told me that they have great weapons designed to destroy them."

Gary looked over at Jason. "Is that true?"

Something in William's eyes suggested to him that the other man needed him to say it was true.

"My people have experience with dragons. We've been attacked by them. We've gotten to the point where we can protect ourselves against them."

"Do you hunt them?"

"Not anymore."

"Because they hunted them out," William said.

Jason shook his head slightly.

William ignored him, turning back to Gary. "He even has a memento of the dragons."

Gary looked up at Jason. "Do you?"

Jason sighed and pulled out the dragon pearl. If that was what this was about, then he failed to see what William was hoping to accomplish. If he was trying to convince Gary to let them into some sort of game, Jason didn't know why.

"What is this?" Gary glanced from Jason to William.

"This is from a dragon," William said knowingly.

Gary studied it, rolling it in his hand. "Feels as if he just pulled it out of his pocket."

"It's called a dragon pearl," Jason said.

"Yeah? And how did you take this from a dragon?"

Jason's mind began to race, trying to think through what Therin had said about the dragon pearl. They were valuable, he knew that, but where had he gotten it?

He didn't even know. All he knew was that Therin had claimed the dragon gave the pearls up willingly, and because of that, he was able to use it in order to access great power.

Was there anything he could use to help convince Gary?

If William wanted to get Gary to let them play, this was going to have to be his bet. More than that, he needed to sell this dragon pearl as valuable. If he could do that, then he might procure enough money to buy the items he needed to return to the village. That had to be what William was after, though if that were the case, then why not just tell him?

Jason debated what to do but pulled out a seat, looking over at William before turning his attention to Gary. "The dragon has to give it to you," Jason said. "And when it does, you can use it for incredible power."

Gary rolled the stone in his hand, looking up at Jason. "What sort of power?"

"You can use it to control fire," he said.

Gary grinned at him, and the two men on either side of him laughed.

Perhaps this was a mistake. He didn't know enough about this man, and certainly didn't know whether he was dangerous, though he suspected someone like him would be.

"Show me."

"Show you what?" Jason asked.

"Show me how you control fire."

"I…" He glanced over at William, who now had a sheen of sweat across his forehead.

This was a mistake.

Worse, it looked to Jason as if William now knew it.

Not only was this a mistake, but there was nothing he would be able to do with the dragon pearl that would convince Gary he could control fire.

What would happen when he was unable to do that?

"I can't do it without the stone," Jason said.

Gary handed it back, rolling it across the table. "Show me." He set his hands on the table, leaning forward. There was an intensity in his eyes and his brow was furrowed.

The other two men took a step toward Jason. He picked up the dragon pearl, rolling it in his hand. He could feel the warmth, the slick surface of it, and tried to think of what Therin had said about reaching for that power. It was somewhere within him.

Even if it was, how was he going to be able to use it?

He didn't know anything about how to summon the magic. All he knew was there was power within it. He'd seen that much from Therin, seen the way the other man had accessed it, and though he might want to summon that power, he didn't have enough control or knowledge to do the same.

He stared at the dragon pearl, trying to will it to work.

One of the men standing on the other side of Gary started to laugh, and Gary shot him a silencing look.

Jason tried not to look up, not wanting to see anything about either of the men, not wanting to do anything. All he could think of was trying to figure out some way to make the dragon pearl glow with heat. He'd seen the way Therin had made the fires dance, and how he'd made the flames work without anything to burn.

What he needed was some way to do the same thing.

"He can't do it," one of the men rumbled.

His voice was deep, angry sounding, and it reminded Jason of Reltash.

He thought of all the times Reltash had picked on him since his father had been lost, and he tried to ignore that, but it filled him with irritation. He had to know better than to allow Reltash to harass him like that. Gary was much the same.

Jason could tell that about him without knowing anything else about Gary. He was a bully, and it seemed to Jason that William had been bullied by Gary. That had to be why he'd come here. He wanted to prove something to the other man.

Jason held the pearl in his hand, cupping it, holding it outward, trying to coax the flames from it, but there was nothing.

All he felt was the warmth within the dragon pearl.

It was not at all like what he'd sensed when he'd been with Therin.

Maybe Therin had been helping him more than he'd realized. It was possible the other man had made it seem as if Jason had control, that he was somehow able to reach for the power within the dragon pearl, and yet, now that he was without the other man, there was no one to get help from.

Gary turned his attention to William. "You tried to scam me again?"

"I'm not trying to do anything. I just thought that you would want to—"

Gary leaned forward, getting to his feet and looming over William. "I think it's time for you and me to take a walk."

"Gary. You know I wouldn't—"

"I know what you would do. You've been here often enough, trying to convince us to let you participate, and yet, we also know what you have done."

William started to shake and Jason got to his feet, shoving the dragon pearl out between the two. "This really is a dragon pearl. I've seen the power from it. I can't as easily bring forth the power myself, but—"

Gary turned to him and nodded to one of the men near him.

He started toward Jason, who took a step back, but as he did, he held the dragon pearl out.

Heat began to burst from the dragon pearl and flames danced in his hand.

The other men stopped, and even Jason stood frozen, staring at the dragon pearl.

He had never held one it when it was burning like this, and surprisingly, it wasn't burning his hand.

The other two men took a step away and Jason recovered, forcing his hand forward, making Gary look at him.

"Look. *This* is a dragon pearl."

The other man turned his attention to the pearl, ignoring William for now. "How are you doing that?"

"I told you. It's the power of the dragons."

William let out a relieved sigh. "Now do you believe me?"

"I believe him. *You* are a different matter."

Jason continued to hold the dragon pearl out, not sure what else to do with it. The fire danced in his hand, spinning around, almost as if it were something alive. It didn't burn him, but it was a strange sensation as it floated in his hand like that, the flame somehow hovering right above the surface of his palm but not causing him any pain.

"I'll trade you for it," Jason said. If he had the ability to use it to create flames, he *shouldn't* trade it, but what good would something like that be to him if he couldn't return to his village? It was the only thing he had of value.

"You'll do what?" Gary asked, turning to him.

Jason nodded, motioning to the pearl. "I'll trade you. I'm happy to let you have it. All I need is—"

Gary slammed his hand underneath Jason's and the pearl flipped out of his hand. The flames whipped out and the pearl landed on the table. The man stared at it for a moment before reaching for it.

When he did, he smiled. "It looks like I don't need to trade for anything."

He took it and stuffed it in his pocket.

"You don't know how to use it," William said.

"That's fine. It seems like he does. So I don't need you."

He nodded to the two men. They grabbed William, dragging him out of the building. William shouted something, but Jason wasn't able to make it out.

"Now comes the question of what I need to do with you."

"That pearl is mine."

Gary glanced down at his pocket for a moment before looking back up at Jason. "It seems like it's mine now."

"And if I start you on fire?"

Gary stared at him for a moment. "Seeing as how you seem to have a difficult time getting your flames to work in the first place, I very much doubt you have enough control over this stone to set me on fire."

"Are you willing to risk it?" Jason asked, trying to sound as dangerous as he could. A man like Gary needed him to push back. "I need enough coin to buy supplies. That's my price."

"Your price for what?"

"My price to prevent me from incinerating you."

The other two men suddenly appeared, and Gary glanced at them.

"My friends here might have something to say about

that."

"Maybe. But if they do, what's to prevent me from acting before they have a chance to stop me?" Jason cocked an eye at Gary. "You want take that risk? I know you don't believe I have the capability of lighting a fire quickly enough to cause any danger, but what if I do?"

He forced a dark smile.

Gary watched him for a long moment before grinning. "Nice try."

He nodded to the other two men.

They grabbed Jason, lifting him.

Jason held his hand out and focused on the dragon pearl. He didn't know what happened before, or whether he was even capable of making the same thing happen again, but at least he could try. He thought about what it had felt like when the pearl had been in his hand, the slick surface, the way the flames had danced above his palm, but he couldn't come up with anything that would work.

Gary watched him and continued to grin.

"See? You don't pose any threat to me."

Jason breathed out a sigh.

They started dragging him away, and all of a sudden Gary screamed.

"Okay."

Jason turned back and Gary slapped at his pocket.

Had he done that?

Maybe Therin *had* activated it somehow.

"My price."

Gary glared at him. "What exactly is your price?"

Jason jerked his arms free of the two men. "It just went up." He took a seat at the table, leaning forward toward Gary. "You can keep the dragon pearl, but now that you decided to try to steal it, its price doubled."

"You never named a price."

"Why don't you give me what you think is appropriate, and then double it."

Gary glared at him.

Jason shrugged. "Fine. Then I start you on fire." He raised his hand and, having no idea whether or not it would work, he held it out.

Gary hurriedly reached into his pocket, grabbing for something.

Jason suppressed a smile as the other man lifted a faded brown leather pouch of coins and threw them across the table.

"That should be enough," Gary said.

Jason lifted the pouch and shook it. The coins jingled inside. He had no idea how much was in there. He was tempted to pour it out and count it, but at least it was better than nothing.

More than that, he had to think it would be enough to get him some supplies.

Jason tipped his head to the side. "Don't make me come back here. If you've cheated me, I can start that pearl on fire from anywhere."

He got to his feet, stuffing the pouch into his pocket.

He started away and Gary called after him.

"Is it really what you say?"

Jason glanced over his shoulder. "It really is."

Gary grinned.

Jason hurried out of the room and back out to the street.

He took a deep breath, looking around, and had just started one way when he heard a voice hiss from the other direction.

"Over here," William said.

Jason hurried in his direction and joined the other man. They were ducked behind a building and William was looking along the street, toward the tavern.

"You were lucky to get out of there alive," William said.

"No thanks to you."

The man paled. "I'm sorry about that. I thought… Well, I suppose it doesn't matter what I thought. Anyway, it's good you got out of there."

"It doesn't seem as if he cares very much for you."

"Gary? Nah. We're great friends. He doesn't know it."

Jason chuckled. "What happened?"

"He claims I cheated when playing caral the last time, but he's just mad that he's terrible at it."

"Do they hurt you?"

William shook his head. "They wouldn't do anything to me. At least, not inside town. If they caught me outside of town, it would be a different story. Anyway, did you really make it burn like that?"

Jason could only shrug. He had no idea what happened, and had no idea how that was even possible, but it certainly *seemed* as if he had some control over it.

"I guess so," he said.

"And you were willing to sell it to him?"

"I need to get back to my village."

"I wouldn't have sold it. I didn't really think you could do what you said, and..." William grabbed him, pulling him back behind the building. He raised a finger to his lips, and pointed.

Jason poked his head around the corner just enough to see Gary and his two other men starting along the street.

Another man followed, and it took a moment for Jason to realize that it was Old Henry. The dark-furred man crashed into Gary, grunting at him, before continuing on down the street.

Gary glared at his back, and the two men with swords motioned to their weapons before Gary shook his head.

William pulled Jason back.

"I thought they were going to stab Old Henry. He might be annoying, but he don't deserve that."

Jason leaned back, resting on the wall.

"I think I have enough coin to get the supplies I need," he said.

"Good. When we're done, then we can stop someplace to eat."

Jason nodded toward the tavern they had just come out of.

William wrinkled his nose. "Gods, no. I wouldn't take you there. Now that you got money, we're going to eat something good."

13

J ason gripped the package close. He had food—far more food than he'd had in a long time—and a spool of rope. There were other supplies, items he thought he might need on the climb back to the village, and yet he still hadn't managed to get snowshoes which would help make the journey quicker. He could head upslope without them, but it would probably take him twice as long.

He'd have to find the rest of the supplies in another place. William wanted to eat, and with Jason's stomach grumbling as it was, he couldn't help but feel as if that were a good idea.

"Where are you going to have us go?" Jason asked.

"There are a few options."

"I just need food," Jason said.

"And I told you, I'm going to take you someplace where you can get what you need. I just think you have to decide what you're in the mood for. Harkens has some of the best smoked meats, but"—he glanced down at Jason's pocket, where the coin pouch was hidden—"he's expensive. I don't how much you have left, but..."

Jason had been careful about revealing to William how much coin he had remaining. He didn't want the other man to try to snatch it.

"I have enough to feed me," he said.

"Hey! Haven't I been helpful?"

"A little bit. You almost got me killed, too."

William shook his head. "Gary never would've killed you. At least, not in the village."

"You said he wouldn't kill you in town."

"Fine. Gary would never kill me in town, but I doubt he'd do anything to you, either. He's all talk."

As soon as he had enough supplies, it would be time to start back. Strangely, the idea of heading back up the side of the mountain left him with a little bit of dread.

He needed to know how his mother and sister were doing, and he really did want to get back, but life here seemed so much easier than what life was like up in his village.

"What are the other options?" Jason asked.

"Well, now that you asked, there are a few places that have great cooking, and to be honest, the drink is just as good." When Jason didn't answer fast enough, William let out an exasperated sigh. "Don't tell me that you don't enjoy a mug of ale every now and again?"

Ale was rare in the village. Every so often they would manage to port up a cask of wine, but that was typically reserved for the village elders and rarely allowed to anybody else within the village.

William grabbed his arm and dragged him to the street. "If that's the case, then I know *exactly* where I need to take you."

They weaved around a few streets and then stopped in front of a building with a sign hanging out front. Jason couldn't make out the images depicted on the sign, but the sound of music drifted from within, along with laughter.

"What is this place?"

William grinned at him.

"Is it any place like the last one?"

"It's *nothing* like the last one."

He pushed open the door and headed inside. Jason hesitated a moment before following the other man. Once inside, the sounds engulfed him. They were louder here, but there wasn't the same darkness. Lanterns had been hung, casting a bright light. There was a hearth in one corner, crackling with heat and flame, and a faint haze hung throughout the inside of the tavern. The floor was all made of wood and his feet thudded across it.

He followed William as he made his way through the tavern, and the other man took a seat along the far wall, a space where there was barely enough room for the two of them.

William grinned over at him. "This has always been my favorite place, but I don't usually have money for it."

"Why not?"

William shrugged. "I don't usually have money."

168 | D.K. HOLMBERG

"That's why you gamble?"

"It's not gambling when you know you're going to win."

"It's still gambling."

William sighed. "Anyway, when I do have a few extra coins, I like to come here. The food is really good, and the ale... well, the ale is probably the best you'll get in town."

He raised his hand and after a few moments, a young woman came sauntering over. She wore a brightly colored dress of striped orange and yellow, and her golden hair was braided around her round face, hanging over each shoulder. She flashed William a smile, shaking her head. "What are you doing here? You can't have enough money to eat."

"I don't. My friend does."

The woman straightened up, appraising Jason for a moment. "He doesn't look like he has much money, either."

"He has plenty." William nodded to him. "Show her." Jason hesitated and William pushed on his shoulder. "She's not going to serve us until you prove that you can pay." William looked up at her. "Rochelle, I promise this is unlike the last time."

"That's what you said the last time you were here."

"This really isn't like the last time."

Jason glanced from Rochelle to William. She was attractive, and there was a playful gleam in her eye and a hint of a smile on her face. He could see by the way

William looked at her that he came here for more than just the food and drink.

Letting out a heavy sigh, Jason reached into his pocket, pulling out the pouch of coins. He shook them and Rochelle leaned forward, glancing at it.

"That's Gary's."

"Traded with him," Jason said.

Rochelle stared at him for a moment. "I hope so. Otherwise you're going to have trouble when Gary comes in here looking for it. You know what we do when people come in here fighting," she said.

"I know, Rochelle."

"Good." She grinned at Jason. "What can I get you?"

"What are my options?"

"Most of the time, this one comes in here looking for a pitcher of ale, but I don't know if that's what you want."

Jason glanced over at William and shrugged. "I'd try the ale. I need something to eat, too."

"Sure. What do you feel like?"

"What are my options?"

She started to laugh before realizing that Jason was serious. "Oh. Well, we have quite a few things." She pointed to a board along one wall. Written on it were a list of different types of foods and Jason stared, mouth agape.

Could all of those foods be found here?

There was venison, but there was also beef, and a few different animals he didn't even recognize. In addition, there were potatoes and carrots and other vegetables written on there.

She grinned at him again. "I can tell I'm going to need to give you a few minutes."

She spun, disappearing into the crowd, and William pushed on his shoulder. "See? I told you you'd like this place."

"I can see why *you* like this place."

William leaned back, raising his hand. "That's not it at all."

"No? I thought you said there were other places that had just as good food and drink."

"Well…"

Jason smiled. "I can see why you like her."

"She's never really given me the time of day."

"Why not?"

"I'm not like Gary."

Jason stared through the crowd, and though he couldn't see where Rochelle had gone, he could see the crowd moving around her. "I didn't get the sense that she cared all that much for Gary."

"Everybody cares for Gary. He has enough influence in the town."

"If he has such influence, why was he out at that last place?"

"Quite a few reasons, but mostly because he has an easier time with some of his other ventures."

"What sort of ventures are those?"

"The sort that avoid the attention of the constables."

Jason only nodded, but he had a hard time understanding what sort of thing that might be. It seemed there was quite a bit about this town that he didn't really understand.

Within a few moments, Rochelle returned, setting a copper pitcher onto the table. She set two mugs down and filled them from the pitcher.

She tipped her head toward William. "Can I have a word?"

William frowned. "Why?"

"Just come with me."

William clamped Jason on the shoulder, getting to his feet. "I'll be back."

Jason lifted the mug, sniffing it. It had a strange aroma, and as he brought it to his lips, taking a sip, it wasn't unpleasant, but it wasn't anything like he'd ever tasted before.

He watched Rochelle and William, and every so often, she glanced in his direction.

She was worried about him.

Not that he could blame her. If the situation was reversed, he suspected he would be worried about him, too. Here he came dressed in strange bearskins, an outsider, and he had managed to acquire Gary's coins. From what he could tell about Gary, everybody in the town had a certain fear of the man.

Rochelle turned away, and William glanced toward Jason before spinning and chasing after her. Jason sat there, sipping at the ale.

After a moment, someone sat down across from him. He looked up. "My friend is going to be—"

He cut off. It was Old Henry.

His dark furs seemed out of place in the tavern. As did the angry gleam in his eyes.

"What was that about a friend?"

"I just said he was coming back."

Henry stared at him. "You stopped following me."

"I wasn't trying to follow you." Jason tried to ignore the flush working through him but the heat washed up his face, and he suspected the other man knew.

"You aren't from town."

"Neither are you."

Old Henry grunted. "What gave that away?"

"Your furs."

"You wear furs. But then, yours aren't meant to blend into the forest like mine are." He watched Jason for a moment, his mouth pressing into a tight line. "And then there's your eye."

He said eye and not eyes. He recognized Jason, which meant he knew about dragon sight. Did that mean he knew about Dragon Souls as well?

"Who are you?" Jason asked.

"The folk around here call me Old Henry."

Jason steadied his breathing, setting the mug of ale down. He didn't like the way it made his head start to spin, almost as if he were getting dizzy. "That's not an answer."

"I seem to think it is."

"Who are you really?"

He stared at the man. There was much about Old

Henry that struck him as similar to Therin. It couldn't be a coincidence. Henry didn't have Therin's thick beard, and yet there was something else about him that seemed off.

"There are certain things you shouldn't trade for," Henry said.

The man reached into his pocket and pulled something out, setting it on the table in front of Jason. His gaze flicked down to it and his breath caught.

The dragon pearl.

He had little doubt it was the same one he'd sold to Gary. He'd only seen two before, and the other one had more color streaked throughout it. The one Therin had given him had no color. It was completely black. It seemed to catch the light, reflecting outward, almost seeming to glow, though Jason suspected that was merely an illusion.

"Where did you get that?" Old Henry asked. There was a dangerous tilt to his head as he leaned forward, watching Jason.

"It was given to me," Jason said carefully.

"There aren't too many outside of Lorach who carry items like that. Seeing as how you're dressed, I have a hard time imagining you've ever been to Lorach. Where did you get it?"

Jason stared at the dragon pearl, unable to take his gaze off it. He couldn't help but feel there was power coming from the pearl, and yet, that had to be his imagination.

"I told you. It was given to me."

"That wouldn't be simply given. It's too valuable."

"I don't know anything about that."

"Obviously. Otherwise you wouldn't have made the foolish mistake of trying to sell it."

"I needed supplies."

Henry held his gaze for a moment and then laughed darkly. "Supplies? You trade something like that for supplies?"

Jason started to reach for it, but Henry snatched it back.

"Someone like you who doesn't appreciate what it is shouldn't be carrying it."

"I appreciate what it is."

"It seems to me that you don't, otherwise you wouldn't have sold it, like I said."

"And like I said to you, I needed—"

"Supplies. I heard you." Henry reached across the table, taking William's mug of ale and glancing at it for a moment. He brought it to his nose, sniffing it before setting it back down. He cupped his hand over the top of the mug, and it might have been Jason's imagination, but it seemed almost as if his hand started to glow. Heat radiated from it, and he lifted it away before tipping the mug back and taking a long sip.

"You can use the power," Jason said.

"What was that?"

"The power from the dragon pearl. You can use it." His mind started to race. It hadn't been him who'd accessed the pearl's power with Gary at all, had it? "You were there."

"I find a fool coming out of the mountains, and then I find the same fool carrying around something worth more gold than most in this village would ever see. And you trade it for scraps."

"Not scraps. Supplies."

Henry grunted. "A waste, that's what it is."

"Who are you?"

Henry stared at him for a moment, and he said nothing. He continued to sip at the mug of ale as Jason watched him. There something off about Henry, more than just his understanding of the dragon pearl and what it meant.

Why was he here?

The timing was strange, and it seemed to him that Henry had to know something about Therin. It didn't seem to Jason that he should have suddenly appeared in the village at the same time Jason had.

"Aren't you going to say anything?"

"What do you need me to say? You have items you shouldn't have, and you're using things you don't fully understand."

"You took it off Gary."

Henry rested his forearms on the table, looking at him. "I wasn't about to allow someone like that to keep it."

"What if he—"

Jason didn't have a chance to finish. William took a seat next to him, sliding onto the bench. "I'm sorry. I just had to... Old Henry. What are you doing here?"

Henry glanced at William. "Leave."

"What?"

"Get moving."

William licked his lips, glancing over at Jason, his eyes going wide. "What's going on?"

This was his opportunity to try to get a better sense of what Henry was doing. More than that, this was his opportunity to see if there would be any way to avoid getting caught up in whatever Old Henry wanted from him.

"It seems as if Henry here is familiar with the dragon pearls."

Henry shot him a hard look, and Jason looked away rather than deal with the heat of the man's gaze.

"Are you really sure you should be talking about that here?" William asked.

"The boy is right," Old Henry said.

"Boy? I'm seventeen."

"And still a boy."

"Listen. I don't know what's going on between the two of you, but I just came over here to warn Jason that Gary is upset about what happened."

"I made a trade with him fair and square," he said. Then again, he wasn't sure he had made such a trade. It was all dependent upon him having what he claimed, and if Henry had taken the dragon pearl from Gary, it was likely the other man would have been upset.

"I don't know what you did or didn't do, but I heard from Rochelle that he's—"

William grabbed him, pulling him around.

"What is it?"

"Gary. He's upset about the fact you cheated him."

"I didn't cheat him."

"According to Rochelle, that's not the way that he sees it. And knowing Gary—and the people he works with—that's all that matters to him."

Jason glanced over his shoulder, and as he did, he realized what William was saying was right. Gary was working his way through the tavern, and he seemed to be heading in his direction.

14

H enry grabbed the dragon pearl off the table and got to his feet. He started toward the back wall of the tavern, moving quickly and with a hint of a limp.

Jason glared at him. "I need to go after him," he said.

"After Old Henry? Let him go. We can slip out through the front door, but we're going to have to go quickly. Rochelle promised she would try to slow Gary."

From where he sat, Jason could make out the broad back of Old Henry as he started to head out of the tavern. Once the man was gone, so was any chance of answers, and there was also the risk of losing the dragon pearl and whatever it meant for finding Therin again.

Maybe finding Therin wasn't something he needed to do. Answers might come from another source. He slipped out of the chair and started after Old Henry.

"Jason—"

He ignored William and hurried after Henry. Commotion behind him caught his attention and he hazarded a glance over his shoulder, noticing Gary shoving his way toward him. He kept himself low, hurrying forward, and reached a door along the back wall of the tavern. Once there, he looked for any sign of Henry, but the man was gone.

William slammed into him. "What are you doing? What is it about Old Henry?"

"He knows something."

"He's crazy. We've seen him around here for years. There's nothing he knows that will help you."

Jason wasn't convinced that was true. It seemed to him that Old Henry knew plenty, but the challenge was finding out what that was and how to reach the other man.

"How would he have left?"

"Probably through the kitchen, but we can't—"

Jason ignored him and pushed through the door. As William had suggested, the kitchen greeted him. It was warm, cozy, and the heat and sense of various foods baking caught his attention. There were four different cooks working at different stations throughout the kitchen, but there was no sign of Old Henry here.

He saw a door on the far side and raced toward it.

He wasn't going to stay here and get caught by Gary.

One of the cooks got in his way and Jason spun, moving around him, and reached the door as a shout came from behind him. It was Gary.

Jason refused to slow.

Stepping through the door, he reached the street.

It was starting to get late, the sun having fallen and darkness greeting him. He didn't know his way around the city at all and worried if he wandered through here, he'd end up getting lost, but William pushed up against him, joining him.

"Where would Old Henry have gone?"

"I don't know. I don't really pay attention to him."

"You have to have some idea where he would've ended up."

"Not really. Like I said, Old Henry is—"

"He is what?"

The voice came from the darkness on the far side of the street, and Jason raced toward him.

"Henry. Who are you really?"

"I'm no one of any concern."

"That's not true, and you and I both know it."

Henry regarded him for a long moment, his gaze lingering on Jason, heavy and almost painful. "You and I both know nothing. You shouldn't even have been here."

He glanced over Jason's shoulder and his brow furrowed. As it did, a sense of heat began to build, rising up from behind them, and Jason spun to see flames streaking along the street.

He'd created a wall of fire. Gary stood at the door to the tavern, almost as if afraid to emerge.

William sputtered. "What was that?"

Henry grabbed Jason and William and jerked them forward. They went staggering along the street and

Jason was pushed from behind, urged with increasing speed.

"Now you have that fool after us," Henry said.

"If you took the dragon pearl off him, it would be *you* who has him after us," Jason said.

"I wouldn't have had to take it had you not attempted to sell it."

"What was I supposed to do? I can't get back to my village."

"Not sell the pearl."

Jason tried looking over his shoulder, but the man shoved him forward. They reached the street and he pushed them along it. It was wider here, and lanterns had been lit, the light pushing back the growing darkness. Jason was able to see along the street fairly well, his eyesight enhanced by his dragon sight. He noticed the streaks of color, movement that came from the side streets, but as he looked around, he wasn't sure whether or not he was seeing what he thought he was.

Henry didn't give him the opportunity to relax and look around, and without that, he didn't have the ability to take full advantage of his dragon sight. They were forced along the street, hurried forward, and every so often, the other man would shove them again.

Heat bloomed somewhere in the distance and William froze, looking toward it.

Jason followed the direction of the other man's gaze and thought it was on the far side of the village. Near the mountainside.

Henry leaned forward. He sniffed at the air, and there came a strange sense of heat from him, though Jason didn't see whether the other man had pulled out the dragon pearl. It was possible he kept it in his pocket, and if he had, then he was using power without it.

He shoved them again and they turned, heading along another street.

When they turned the corner, movement behind him caught Jason's attention.

There was no heat signature, nothing that revealed anything to his dragon sight, but he was certain that he saw something.

"Keep moving," Henry grunted.

"Was that—"

Henry nodded. "Keep moving."

Jason resisted the urge to shiver. He was certain it had been someone dressed in dragonskin. Since leaving his village, the only people he'd seen wearing dragonskin were the Dragon Souls.

If they'd found him, did that mean they were hunting him?

"Are they after me?"

"Probably," Henry said.

He shoved them again and Jason went staggering forward, quickly catching himself before streaking away. At the end of another street, he risked pausing, looking behind him. Once again, he could swear he saw movement, though he wasn't entirely certain if that was what it was. There was the outline of something in the darkness, though he could make nothing out with his dragon sight. It was completely concealed, and that troubled him.

He was accustomed to that in his home. There were several who had dragonskin clothing that was opaque to his dragon sight, but since reaching this village, he hadn't encountered anyone that obscured.

Henry shoved him again and Jason shot him a look.

The dark expression on the other man's face made it difficult for Jason to do anything other than hurry forward. When he did, he could feel Henry's breath on his back, forcing him onward.

They wound through the town. Jason had been aware it was a sprawling sort of town, and yet as he made his way through, it felt even larger. They weaved from street to street and seemed to be zigzagging, taking a back-tracking path as they did, heading from one section to another, almost as if Henry didn't know where they were going.

Every so often, the sense of heat would bloom behind him, and Jason would look back. Yet Henry didn't give them an opportunity to spend much time looking over his shoulder, continuing to force him forward.

"Where is he taking us?" he whispered to William.

The other man shook his head. "I have no idea. We've been backtracking, and at this point, I... to be honest, I'm getting a little bit lost."

"This is your town."

"It is, but it's dark, and I don't really know where we're heading."

"Quiet," Henry hissed.

He jabbed Jason in the back, and from the way William winced, he suspected the same thing had just happened to him. Jason fell quiet and focused instead on what he could detect around him. Every so often, there was the heat, but he also noticed movement behind him, and he glanced over his shoulder, thinking that if nothing else, he might be able to uncover whether or not there were other people nearby.

There was the occasional sense of heat from people farther down the street, but it was almost as if Henry was navigating them away from others, guiding them so they wouldn't encounter anyone else. Jason was beginning to feel tired, disappointed he hadn't eaten anything, and wondering whether he'd even grabbed the pouch of coins.

Another burst of heat struck, and this time it seemed to illuminate the night.

Henry paused, giving Jason and William a chance to stop as well. The rest was welcome as the other man looked into the distance, glaring out into the night, his jaw set almost angrily.

The heat began to fade and Henry shoved him again, forcing them forward. William glanced over at him, a question burning in his eyes. Jason didn't have any answer for him. He felt bad that the other man had gotten caught up in this, but then again, William had been the one who had involved Jason with Gary and his machinations. Had he not, Jason likely would've wandered the village on his own and probably would never have attempted to sell the dragon pearl.

No, that wasn't true. He had come to the village thinking he would trade the dragon pearl, thinking it had some value he might be able to capitalize on, but when he'd learned that the people of this village didn't even believe in dragons, he had begun to doubt the value of the pearl.

"Who are we running from?" William asked.

His voice was loud, almost too loud against the night.

"You don't want to know," Henry said.

"If you're running from Gary, I can show you a place he won't be able to find us."

"Gary?" Henry leaned close to him, looming over William. It wasn't that Henry was so much larger than William, though he was taller. It was almost that he had some way of making himself appear more powerful, more intimidating, and William shrank back from the gaze. "Do you think I fear *Gary*?"

"I know the kind of things Gary can do to others in town. I understand wanting to run from them."

"I don't worry about any boy like that."

William looked at Jason and mouthed the word, "Boy?"

When Henry shoved them forward again, he hurried onward, having no choice otherwise. He tried to ignore the sense of heat flaring up, and the longer he focused on it, the more certain he was it came from all directions around the town.

That was what Henry was avoiding. It was almost as if

he were trying to find some way through the sense of heat, but couldn't.

Jason looked over at Henry. The other man's face was contorted in a tight frown, and as much as he wanted to ask about the other man's experience with the Dragon Souls, he was afraid to do so. More than anything, it was clear to Jason that Henry had some experience with them.

They needed to get answers, but Henry was guiding them to safety.

"William doesn't have to come with us," he said to Henry.

Henry looked at William. "They know he's with us."

"They don't. Gary might, but—"

"They know," Henry said. There was a finality in his voice, and Jason resisted the urge to argue.

When they reached a section of the town with smaller buildings, all of them homes, Henry finally started to slow. They reached a particular home that looked dingy and rundown, and the other man stopped them in front of it, pushing open the door and shoving them inside.

"What are you doing with us?" William whispered.

"Quiet," Henry snapped.

Inside the room, Henry shouldered past them, heading toward a table along one wall. When he was there, he quickly lit a lantern. Flames began to crackle softly, giving off a warmth and a brightness.

Henry motioned to a pair of chairs nearby and Jason took one, waiting for William to take the other. The other man looked nervous, almost as if he intended to bolt at any point. If the situations were reversed, Jason thought he might try to do the same. This wasn't his fight. William had gotten caught up in it by accident.

"How many are after you?" Henry asked.

William looked in his direction and Jason shook his head. "I don't know that they're after me."

"The pursuit we just endured would say otherwise. How many?"

"Three, but maybe more."

"Three. Are you sure of that?" Henry asked.

"Not really. As far as I know, there were three. When they captured me—"

"Who captured you?" William asked.

Henry ignored him. "They captured you?"

Jason nodded. "It was up on the mountain. They—"

"They thought you were a slave."

Jason shivered at the idea. It was the same thing Therin had said, and the idea that he was a slave only because of his eye color troubled him. "I guess so."

"You already knew."

"There was another who warned me."

"Another?" Henry asked.

Jason debated how much he should tell Henry. He didn't know whether he could trust this man. He was strange, and though he had the ability to use the dragon pearl, and though he seemed like he was helping, he wasn't even sure if that were true. It was possible that he was guiding them to this place for his benefit.

Then again, he *had* defended them against Gary.

188 | D.K. HOLMBERG

"There was another man. I was with him on the mountain, and he was leading me away from them."

"Away from who?" William asked. He glanced from Jason to Henry. "Will either of you tell me what you're talking about?"

"Who was this man?" Henry asked.

"He said his name was Therin. He claimed he'd been one of them, but had left long ago."

"Did he now?"

"He's the one who gave me the dragon pearl. He said he could help me learn how to use it."

Henry chuckled, grabbing the dragon pearl out of his pocket and resting it on his lap. He pulled another out of his pocket, and set that one on his lap too. When he did, he motioned to them. "What do you see about these?" Henry asked.

"They're both dragon pearls," Jason said.

Henry frowned, his brow wrinkling, making his dark eyes appear even darker. "Yes."

"What am I supposed to notice?"

"You're supposed to notice differences. You have the dragon sight, so I know you can tell."

Jason frowned. He focused on the darker of the two. That was the one he'd carried with him out of the mountains, the same dragon pearl Therin had given him. It was dark, and it carried with it speckles of red and blue, though he wasn't able to determine much more about it. If he held it, he thought he might be able to recognize the heat or the slickness from it, but nothing more than that.

The other one was shaped the same, though it did appear to have more color within it. There were striations of green and seemed almost as if it glowed.

"They're similar, but the colors are different."

"It's not just the colors," Henry said. "One of these is real."

Henry nodded and cupped his hand around a dragon pearl. He held on to it, squeezing it, and as he did, heat glowed from his hands. When he parted them, it appeared there was something other than a dragon pearl in his hand.

Rather than a smooth and dark surface, now it was an irregular shape. A shard of black, completely flat and with jagged edges, rested on his hand.

"This is called a dragon shard," Henry said.

"What's a dragon shard?" William asked, leaning forward. He ignored Henry's warning glance and stared at the strange item on the other man's hand.

"A dragon shard is created by a Dragon Soul. They use it to follow someone they feel has potential."

"What sort of potential?" William asked.

Two kinds of magic...

He had dragon sight. What else was that other than potential? Magic. It was the reason Therin had thought he could use the pearl.

Rather, the shard.

Why would Therin have a shard?

Unless...

Henry leaned forward, watching him.

"He said it was a pearl," Jason said. "I saw him use it."

"You saw what he wanted you to see," Henry said. "Therin is good like that. Makes people see things that aren't there. Feel things they wouldn't otherwise."

"What's it for?" William asked.

"A dragon shard is a dangerous item, and if you were given one, it's because you have perceived value."

Jason leaned back. "I'm just a villager."

"I'm afraid the Dragon Souls think otherwise."

Jason couldn't shake the strange sense the dragon shard left him with. "Therin gave me that," he said softly.

"Who is he?" William asked.

Jason continued to stare at the dragon shard. What purpose did he have in giving them something to track him?

"He's a dangerous man. One of the most dangerous of the Dragon Souls."

"What?" William asked.

Jason tore his gaze away from the dragon shard, meeting Henry's gaze.

"You didn't know," Henry said.

"I didn't know." It made a certain sense. The power he had. The way that he'd helped. Even the dragon pearl. "He didn't tell me."

"What's worse, the man you know as Therin leads them."

15

J ason stared at Henry, uncertain how to react.

Therin led the Dragon Souls?

If that were true, he could have done something to him during their journey. What game was he playing at? Why hide the fact that he was a Dragon Soul—and pretend he wasn't working with the others?

There was something he was after.

Dragons, though Jason didn't see how there could be any dragons in his village.

"What now?" Jason asked Henry. He didn't like relying upon another stranger, but this was one who seemed to know things.

"Now you wait here while I see what I can uncover."

"I could—"

"Do nothing more than get yourself killed."

Henry left William and Jason sitting alone in the small

building. Every so often, Jason would look around, and he couldn't help but feel as if something were off. He wasn't sure who to trust, and certainly didn't know whether he could trust Henry.

The dragon shard Henry had demonstrated rested on the table, and Jason reached for it. He sighed and lifted the dragon shard up. "I'm sorry I carried this to your town."

"You carried it when you thought it was something else," William said. His demeanor seemed to shift after learning that Jason didn't have the same control over dragon items as he had believed, and Jason didn't blame him. For his part, he *had* deceived William somewhat. "It's still amazing, though." He swept his hands around him. "The Dragon Souls. The idea that the dragons are real. All of this."

Jason shook his head. "I'd rather it not be amazing."

"Why not?"

"I need to get back to my village. My family needs me."

William laughed. "What's that like?"

"To be needed?"

"Nah. Family."

Jason stared at him, half expecting him to laugh and admit to joking with him, but it didn't come. "What happened to your family?"

"Oh, besides my mother dying when I was born? My older sister took off a few years ago with a farmer from outside town. She got mauled by a wolf or something and didn't survive..."

"I'm sorry."

William flashed a smile, though for the first time, Jason saw something darker in it. "You couldn't have known."

"Still."

"My father barely sticks around anymore. He's a trader. Gone for long stretches. Longer each year. It's his way of forgetting." William looked down. "Sometimes I think he's trying to forget me, too." He sighed then looked up, the smile returning. "But hey! I've got my luck. That's got to matter for something. Doesn't help with me keeping a job, but eventually that has to change. Eventually I might be able to get out of here like my sister tried."

Jason swallowed. Here he thought that he'd had it rough. William had it far harder than he had—and still managed a sense of humor. "How well do you know him?" Jason looked toward the door Henry had gone through.

"Not well. He's come to town about once a month over the last few years. He usually trades with some of the shops, and then he disappears. He heads out into the wilderness. No one really knows where he goes or what he does."

"Do you have any reason not to believe him?"

"I don't know him."

Jason breathed out a heavy sigh. "I don't need anything to do with the Dragon Souls. I just want to get back home."

"The one in the mountains?"

He looked up, meeting William's eyes. There was

doubt written on William's face. "I *do* come from up on the mountainside."

"You're dressed like you are, but the mountain is impassible beyond a certain point. I might not have traveled that far from here, but I have seen that. What are these Dragon Souls?" William asked, changing the subject.

"I don't really know. I'd never heard of them before. They apparently are powerful and control the dragons."

"So dragons *are* real?"

"That's what I've been saying."

"It's just... We knew it as rumor. Stories we told children."

"Sometimes stories have a way of being real."

"Like the story of you coming from the mountain town."

"I did come from the mountain town," he said.

William sat back, resting his arms behind his head, leaning against the wall. He closed his eyes. "You know, I thought *I* was deceiving *you* when I first met you."

"You did deceive me."

William rolled his head off to the side, cocking one eye. "I did, but it seems like you deceived me just as much."

He fell silent, holding on to the dragon shard, squeezing it in his hand. Why had Therin given it to him? That was the thing he didn't really understand. What purpose would there have been? It seemed as if Therin had tried to help him, and as he thought back to the other man, he hadn't any belief that he had wanted to harm him.

In fact, it seemed to Jason that Therin had helped rescue him from the Dragon Souls.

All of that couldn't have been an act, could it? What if he couldn't trust Henry? What if this man was with the Dragon Souls?

Then again, that didn't seem to fit, either. If he was with them, why would he have been working to help them hide? Why would he have revealed the dragon shard hidden within what Jason had believed was a dragon pearl?

There had to be another explanation, though he had no idea what that would be.

The door opened with a creak and he cocked an eye as Henry crept inside.

"As far as I can tell, they're gone. More likely than not, they will be active again. If they think you're here, and if they think you have something of value to them, they will continue to pursue." Henry took a seat, kicking his legs out in front of him, crossing his arms over his chest, and studied Jason. "There has to be some reason Therin kept you alive. What else can you tell me?"

He shivered at the bluntness of the comment. "I don't know anything. I first encountered him in the village. We had a festival."

"Your Freedom Festival."

Jason nodded quickly. "That's right. You know about it?"

Henry grunted. "Stupid mountain tradition. They think dragons *want* to be in the cold. They can't tolerate it

196 | D.K. HOLMBERG

for long. Why else do you think you haven't seen dragons?"

Jason ignored the comment, and chose not to mention what had happened to his father. "That's where I first met him. We get strangers in the village fairly often during the festival."

Henry leaned forward, resting his elbows on his knees. "How often do you get strangers for your festival?"

Jason shrugged. "There are plenty of small villages that dot the mountaintop, especially along the back slope. Even all the way to Varmin. They come together for the festival."

"How many of those villages have people you don't know?"

"Most have a hundred or more people. There are quite a few of the residents within those villages I don't know. Most of the time they are people I've seen before, but—"

"And you'd never seen Therin before."

"Never."

Henry clenched his jaw, leaning back. He looked up toward the ceiling, scratching at his chin. "Why there?" he whispered.

"What is it?" Jason asked.

"Therin has a particular interest."

"Free dragons," Jason said.

Henry shot him a look, nodding. "Yes. How was it that you know that?"

"He told me."

"He *told* you?"

Jason nodded. "He said that was why he was out. It's why he left the Dragon Souls. He said he was pursuing free dragons."

The other man laughed, almost a bitter sound. "Oh, he's pursuing free dragons all right, but he has not departed the Dragon Souls. Why would he when he can hunt them so much more effectively from within the Dragon Souls?"

"Why would he have told me that?"

"Therin will tell you anything in order to convince you of his purity." The other man took a deep breath. "I know him far better than I would like. And last time I encountered Therin, he was chasing another dragon."

William sat up and leaned forward. "You've seen a dragon?"

"You can't really think they are nothing more than myth," Henry snorted.

"They're stories," William said.

Henry grunted. "You'd be surprised."

"There aren't any free dragons in my village."

"No. It's too cold for them there."

"Besides, if he's after dragons, and if he kept me alive as you say, how are they related?"

Henry watched him a moment before shaking his head. "Maybe you *will* be useful."

"What's that supposed to mean?"

Henry reached into his pocket and pulled out something that he rested on his lap. As he did, he looked up at Jason, watching him. "All it means is that you might be useful. I wasn't sure if you were lucky or smart. Maybe you're smarter than I'm giving you credit for."

"What does he mean?" William asked.

Jason sat stiffly in the wooden chair, trying to think through what Henry might be implying. Not only was Therin after dragons—and free dragons at that—but there was something else he was seeking. There had to be something more.

Why would Therin have been in the village?

The festival.

What had Therin said?

The cannon would attract dragons.

That couldn't be coincidental, could it?

And if the other man was after free dragons, and he believed the festival would somehow draw them, that would explain why he had come.

But Jason didn't think the other man had seen a dragon.

"Why did he want to keep me alive?"

"I suspect he kept you alive because he believed you had access to something he wanted," Henry said.

"The only thing he wanted was dragons," Jason said.

"Exactly."

"But I didn't see a dragon."

"Didn't you?"

He shook his head. He didn't think that he had, and yet, there had been the strangeness he'd experienced on the mountaintop. Not only was there the entire herd of deer—something that shouldn't have existed that high up on the mountaintop—but there were the strange movements he'd seen.

"Dragon Souls can hunt dragons quite effectively, but some locations would be harder for them."

"You're saying he couldn't hunt them in the mountains?"

"I suspect they thought they could, but there's a reason dragons have retreated beyond where the Dragon Souls can reach. I wouldn't have expected they'd flee to the mountains like that, but it's possible they did."

"What do you mean that they retreated?" William asked.

"You really are a fool," Henry said.

"Maybe, but this fool lives in this town, and this fool is curious. Why don't you tell me?"

Henry sighed and grabbed the items on his lap, setting them back in his pocket. "Dragons have been controlled by Dragon Souls for quite a long time."

"Therin made it sound like they were trained."

"It's more than just training, though that's what the Dragon Souls would have others believe. It's a matter of control. Coercion. The dragons are aware of what's been done to them and want nothing to do with it."

"Why would the dragons care?" William asked.

"Would you care if you were forced to do something you didn't want?" Henry asked.

"Yes, but I'm not an animal."

"That's debatable. Regardless, dragons are incredibly

intelligent. They understand what's being done to them. They do everything in their power to avoid it."

"Therin told me some of that, but why would he?"

"It's easier to believe a lie if you sprinkle it with some truth."

"Is that what you're doing?" William asked.

Henry shot him a hard look.

William grinned. "Well, is it? Look, I've seen you around town, and I know you're known to trade here, but I don't know anything about you. I don't think Jason knows anything about you either. What are you doing here? Why do you even care?"

"I care about freeing the dragons," Henry said.

"That's what Therin said," Jason said.

"I'm sure he did. Have you wondered why he's dressed similar to me?"

Jason shared a look with William before nodding. "I did."

"He thinks it makes him more believable. Underneath his furs, you'll find his dragonskin clothing, the same as the Dragon Souls."

"What's dragonskin clothing?"

"It absorbs heat. It allows the wearer to stay incredibly warm even in the coldest of temperatures," Henry said.

William looked over at Jason. "Why don't you wear that?"

"It's also incredibly expensive," Jason said. "My family... well, we don't have much."

"There are other ways of staying warm that don't involve skinning a dragon," Henry said.

"Like my furs?" Jason pointed to his jacket. "Or yours? I've worn a dragonskin jacket before," Jason said. He spoke softly, thinking back to his father and everything that had happened to him. "It wasn't mine or my family's, and it was because of my father's role in the village. But there really is nothing like it."

"No," Henry said. "There really is nothing like it. Not only is it warmer, but it's armored as well."

"Armored?" William asked.

"Don't be so dense," Henry said. He slapped his arm. "It can take a blow. It's why the Dragon Souls are effective as fighters. All of them are equipped with dragonskin clothing."

"How do you peel it off a dragon in the first place, then?"

"It's a difficult process," Henry said, his voice going softer.

He was silent for a moment. "Why are you here?" Jason asked.

"Do I need to have a reason?"

"You need to have more reason than what you've said."

"I'm here to prevent the Dragon Souls from finding dragons in this part of the world. To protect the dragons. To prevent the kingdom from gaining additional strength. And to serve my vows."

"What vows are those?"

Henry shook his head. "It doesn't matter."

"It does."

"No. It doesn't matter."

"Are there others like you?" William asked.

Henry glanced toward the door. Heat began to build from him again, and he jumped to his feet.

"It's time to go. The Dragon Souls started moving again."

"You can tell just like that?" William asked.

"I can tell," Henry said.

Jason shared a look with William, and they crowded behind Henry at the door. He wasn't sure whether he even wanted to go with the other man, but what choice did he have at this point? He no longer knew who to trust, and if Therin was part of these Dragon Souls, it made sense why the other man would have abandoned him on the mountainside, and he might even have been involved in the chase down the mountain.

"Where are they?" he whispered.

"Outside. Be ready," he said.

Henry pulled open the door and reached into his pocket, holding on to something. Probably a dragon pearl.

"How do you know he's not one of them?" William asked.

"I don't," Jason said.

"If he has their magic, and if he has the same knowledge, what's to say that he's not the same?"

Use your instinct when you hunt. Learn to trust it and it will never lead you astray.

He hadn't done that with Therin, though he should.

He'd been intrigued by the fire. The dragon pearl. Everything about the man.

What about with Henry?

His instinct told him to trust him, but what if William were right?

That was the same troubling thought Jason had. If it was all tied together, and if he couldn't rely upon Henry, then they might have to split off. He didn't like the idea, but he also didn't like growing reliant upon Henry keeping them safe.

"Is there any place we could go?" he whispered to William.

"I might have a place," he said.

Henry stepped out into the street and heat built, radiating away from him.

Jason stayed where he was, waiting for a moment.

Henry motioned for them to follow, and he hesitated. If he went with Henry now, he might be able to find out more about what was taking place, but if he stayed with him, then he was depending upon Henry being trustworthy.

Jason simply wasn't sure whether he could.

He glanced over at William, who nodded.

As soon as they were out in the street, William took off running in the opposite direction as Henry.

Jason followed, trailing after the other man as quickly as he could. He glanced over his shoulder, looking back to see whether Henry was watching, and didn't see anything.

Heat built and flames raced along the street.

To his dragon sight, he noticed the flames as streaks of orange and red, far more powerful than anything he'd encountered. They were bright against the night, glowing wildly. He hurried after William, turning away and racing through the streets.

A shout echoed from somewhere behind him and his heart hammered, forcing him to move faster and faster.

They weaved back and forth, heading to the streets, once again running. This time, Jason couldn't help but feel as if his escape was far more dangerous than it had been before. This time, they didn't have anyone with them who had any power over the dragon pearl.

That made Jason more nervous than he'd been.

William guided them to a stop near the center of town. It looked to be another rundown tavern and Jason shook his head, amused at the fact that William had so many options for this type of place. It was quieter than the last; no sounds of music or shouting or singing were coming from inside. He couldn't help but worry that going into an establishment like this would end with them trapped, and he worried about getting stuck in a situation where they wouldn't have any way of escaping. Especially as it involved those who had power over dragon pearls and control over fire, the kind of thing Jason didn't fully understand.

"Are you sure this is safe?"

"It's safe enough," William said.

"Henry thought the last place was safe."

"I don't know that we can trust Old Henry. Besides, he

brought us to some little shack on the edge of town. This spot is filled with people that I know."

"People like Gary?"

"Come on," William said.

"I'm just saying..."

"I know what you're saying, and I'm sorry about Gary. I thought you might be able to help me while I was going to be able to help you. Anyway, I made a mistake. It's not going to happen again."

"If you say so. What is this place?"

"It's another tavern. This one is little different, and it's one I haven't been kicked out of before." He grinned at Jason. "Yet."

"You have a strange way of being proud of getting kicked out of places."

"It's not so strange. I'm lucky."

"You're lucky so you get kicked out of places?"

"I'm lucky, so people get tired of losing."

"I see."

"I'm not a cheat. Not like Gary would have you believe."

"If you say so."

"I'm not," William said. He licked his lips and his eyes flickered toward the door. "I've always been lucky. Not with my family, but otherwise," he added quickly. "I don't know what else to say about it, but in a town like this, luck isn't always lucky, if you know what I mean."

"I guess so, if that means you have to deal with people like Gary."

"Exactly. It's lucky when you win, and lucky when you have more coin to gamble with, but not so lucky when you have to deal with people like Gary chasing after you, thinking you somehow scammed them."

"And you haven't?"

William let out a loud groan. "Like I said, no. Would you just trust me? This place is better than most of them."

"You said that about the last one."

A soft, dreamy expression crossed his face. "That one is better than most of them too."

"How am I to know that Rochelle isn't working here, too?"

"She isn't. Unfortunately."

William cracked open the door, watching Jason, and nodded.

It was brightly lit. Tables scattered throughout had a strange sort of organization. Most had people sitting at them, and food resting on the tables caught Jason's attention. His mouth began to water and his stomach rumbled. Even though he'd been in a place like this where food was plentiful just a few hours earlier, he still hadn't eaten. He needed to change that before he ended up sicker than he already was.

William guided him toward the back, through one door, down a short, dimly lit hall, and then another door.

Jason stood at the doorway, frozen.

Three tables rested inside this room. Men sat around each of the tables, coins piled up in front of them. Different games seemed to be taking place at each of the tables, one of them dice, one with strangely carved figures, and another with wooden cards.

None of that held his attention for long.

Rather, it was Gary who caught his eye, sitting at the table with dice. As soon as they entered the room, he leapt to his feet.

16

"I thought you said this was safe," Jason whispered.

"It should be safe," William said. He turned his attention to the others, raising his hands, flashing a wide smile. "Gentlemen. Are you going to disrupt the game?"

"You stole from me," Gary snapped.

Jason scanned the inside of the room. There were the three tables, probably nearly twenty men crammed into the small space. Most of the tables were filled with food and ale, and stacks of coins rested on their surface. The walls were bare, made of paneled wood, so different from what he had in his village. It was dimly lit, only a few lanterns giving enough light to see by. With his dragon sight, everything seemed to flash with a little bit of brightness, and yet, one of the men didn't fully reflect his dragon sight.

He stared at that man, looking to see if there was anything he could uncover about him, but there was nothing about him that made much sense. It was almost as if he were invisible.

Was he wearing some sort of heat mask and clothing?

Jason nudged William, trying to get his attention, but the other man was focused on Gary.

"He stole from me," Gary said.

"Ah, you know that's not true," William said. "You made a deal."

"I made a deal, but then he had someone steal from me."

"Who stole from you?" William asked, sweeping his gaze around the inside of the room. He kept a wide smile on his face, and Jason found it almost disarming. William was skilled, but he didn't think the other man's luck would extend to a situation like this. If nothing else, it was bound to get both of them hurt.

"Old Henry."

William started to laugh. Jason tried to keep his face neutral and avoid any expression, though it was difficult.

"Look at him. Does he look like the kind of person who would be working with Old Henry?"

Jason looked around at the others in the room. In the shadows, he could see them watching him, though he couldn't tell anything from their expressions.

"Yes," Gary said. "They're dressed the same."

William laughed again. "Old Henry has been coming to town the last few years. In all that time, he hasn't brought anyone else with him. Why would he suddenly do so now?"

"To steal from me."

Gary was becoming more hesitant, and Jason continued to focus on the man he couldn't easily see with his dragon sight.

The only time someone hadn't shown up to his dragon sight was when the other had been wearing dragonskin, and though he wasn't sure this man was wearing dragonskin, the fact that the people in this town didn't believe in dragons made him immediately worried this was someone from elsewhere. A Dragon Soul.

"Listen. We only came here to try our luck," William said.

"You came here to cheat," Gary snapped.

"Cheat?" William swept his gaze around the inside of the room. Everybody was looking at him and not so much at Gary. "When have I ever been known to cheat?"

"All the time," Gary said.

William laughed, though it sounded a bit more forced than it had before. "I don't cheat."

"You just haven't been caught," Gary said.

"I'm lucky. And you're jealous." He grabbed Jason by the arm, dragging him through the room and toward one of the nearby tables.

Jason wanted to resist, wanting to be anywhere but here, but to go now would draw even more attention to himself.

He wasn't sure if allowing that kind of attention was dangerous or not.

"Sit," William whispered.

Jason looked around the table. There was an extra seat, but only one.

"Why don't you sit?" he said.

"Because you're the one with the coin."

William flashed a smile as he looked around. "Are we going to play or not?"

The others turned their attention to Gary, who continued to glare at William and then Jason, but slowly he took a seat.

William let out a slow sigh, turning his attention to the table. "My friend here doesn't have much experience playing shalan. I was hoping you might be able to show him."

"This isn't a beginner's game," one of the men said. He had a heavy beard and deep-set eyes. If he were wearing furs, he might look almost like Henry, and yet he was dressed almost formally.

"And I'm not a beginner," William said.

Jason looked over at the man. What was he doing? They didn't need to be here. All he wanted was to sit down and have something to eat, to escape Henry and the Dragon Souls, but he couldn't shake the feeling there was something more taking place, and he didn't like the idea that he was dependent upon this place for safety. They didn't need the coin.

Was this what William had planned? Did he somehow think to use Jason for whatever it was that he was after?

And if that were the case, he needed to get up and head out of the tavern.

If he did, where would he go?

He didn't know anything about this town, and if the Dragon Souls were still out there, wandering through it, he ran the risk of encountering them.

And then there was Henry. Jason couldn't help but feel as if the old man was dangerous.

Playing a game like this, betting the coins he already had, ran the risk of him not having the necessary money to return to his village. Jason wasn't sure he even wanted to risk that. He'd rather take the coin he had, buy the snowshoes and the rest of the supplies he might need, and head out. He could do that first thing in the morning, start on a full belly, and from there...

William smacked him on the shoulder. "It's your draw."

Jason blinked, staring at the table. A stack of wooden cards rested there, and William motioned to them. As he spun his gaze around the table, he found the man who was invisible to his dragon sight watching him.

Did he know that Jason found him invisible?

It wasn't as if the dragon sight was something he could hide. His different eye made it all too easy for others to identify, and the only hope Jason had was that in the dim light of the back room, the stranger wasn't able to see that one eye was silver and one was blue. From what he'd seen throughout the town, blue eyes weren't uncommon, so in that case, he could cock his head to the side, trying to hide one of his eyes.

Doing so would be odd, but what choice did he have?

"How much should I wager?"

"A copper."

A copper would buy him food for the morning.

Then again, none of this was really his money. Maybe he needed to be freer with it.

If things went well—if William was as lucky as he claimed—he could have enough money to pay Gary back and keep the other man from harassing him.

Jason glanced over the table at Gary. Every so often, Gary looked in his direction. Jason had a sinking suspicion that the other man was not going to let any of this go.

Jason took one of the cards and dragged it across the surface of the table, keeping it facedown. William reached for it and lifted it, bringing it to his face before setting it back down on the table.

When Jason went for it, William tapped him on the hand, shaking his head.

The others around the table continued to take cards, working their way around, and by the time they got back to Jason, he glanced up at William.

"A silver," William said.

A silver would be enough money to buy a shelter to keep out the cold on the way up the mountainside. Snowshoes to avoid sinking with each step. And then some.

He didn't know how much was in the coin purse, but there had to be enough to finish collecting his supplies. This was a mistake.

William tapped him on the arm. "A silver."

"I don't—"

William glared at him.

Jason reached into the coin pouch, pulled out a silver, and set it on the table in front of him. When he was done, he dragged over another card. William reached for it, pulling it up to his face and looking at it before setting it back down on the table.

Once again, Jason tried to reach for it, but William shook his head.

The play went around the table, and this time, several people began to drop out. They did so by pushing their coin toward the center of the table. When it came back around, William tapped him on the shoulder. "A silver."

Someone across from him groaned.

Rather than arguing this time, Jason reached into the pouch, searching for a silver. There were quite a few coppers, but it wasn't until he got to the bottom of the coin purse that he managed to find another silver.

Setting it on the table, he looked up at William, but the other man simply stared at the stack of cards in the center of the table. He said nothing, his expression unreadable.

Jason reached across the table, grabbing for one of the cards, and as before, William took it, glancing at it before setting it back down. Play continued, working around, everyone else dropping out by pushing their coins to the center until it was only the man invisible to his dragon sight and him.

The man studied William before turning his attention to Jason.

"Just the two of us. Why don't you show your cards."

"You haven't paid for the right," William said, flashing a flat smile.

The other man glanced up at William. "That's how you want to play it?"

"That's how it's played," William said.

The other man reached into his pocket, pulling out a gold coin and setting it on the table.

Jason's heart sunk. He had fished through the coin pouch and he didn't remember seeing any gold, and he didn't know how many coppers it would take to equal what he had. He glanced up at William, shaking his head.

"Go all in," he said.

"William."

"Trust me," he said.

Jason breathed out a heavy sigh and looked down into the coin pouch, flipping through there, searching for another gold, perhaps a silver, or something that might be equivalent, but he didn't come up with anything.

Having no idea what cards were out on the table, and having no idea how to even play the game, he wasn't sure that he could even trust William.

Then again, this wasn't his money.

He had enough supplies that he would be able to make it back to the village—at least, he thought he did. The only thing he needed was snowshoes, and perhaps more food, but he still had his bow and arrows, and he figured that the game around the lower part of the mountain would be easier to capture.

Taking a deep breath, he poured the coins on the table

and pushed them into a pile. He took a card, dragging it across, and William took it, looking at it before setting it back down.

The other man grunted and started flipping his cards over. Jason had no idea what any of the cards meant, and though the shapes had meaning, he didn't know what it was.

The man started reaching for the pile of coins.

"Not so fast," William said.

He nodded to Jason. "Turn them."

Jason sighed. He flipped over the first of the cards. Someone gasped. He flipped over another, and then another, and then the fourth. All of them were identical.

Everybody at the table sucked in a breath.

The man across from him froze and held his hands apart, releasing the pile of coins that he'd been pulling toward him.

"What is it?" Jason asked.

"Gather the coins."

"We won?"

"We won. Gather the coins."

Jason stood, pulling the coins toward him, and as he did, he couldn't help but feel the weight of the gazes from everyone around the table staring at him.

Not him. William.

As he gathered the coins, piling them into his pouch, he took a seat, but William tapped him on the back.

"It doesn't seem like we are all that welcome here any longer," William said.

"You're going to leave after one hand?" one of the men said.

"You want to test your luck again?" William asked. He took the cards and slipped them back onto the stack. "I'm more than happy to continue to play."

"You don't get to play. He plays."

"He doesn't know how to play. I'm working with him, but he's not at the point yet where he knows the intricacies of the game."

"Only because you're telling him how to play."

"The only thing I did was look at the cards."

Jason stared at the table. He had no idea how to play the game, but he recognized the four matching cards must have been an incredibly lucky hand. Not only that, but there was no way they could have accused William of cheating. With Jason picking the cards, there was nothing William could have done.

Had William used him again?

If so, he had enriched him.

The coin pouch was quite a bit heavier than before. He didn't know how much gold coins were worth, but certainly it was much more than the pair of silver he almost lost.

"I think I'm with him. I'm going to eat, and then maybe we can play another day," Jason said. He slipped the bag of coins into his pocket and backed away.

"What was that about?" he whispered.

"Not now," William said.

As they reached the door, there came a steady

murmuring from the men around the tables. Jason and William headed back out into the tavern. Jason breathed out heavily and leaned against the door, blocking it.

"I've never had anything quite like that," William said.

"I thought you said you were lucky."

"Yeah? There's luck and then there's luck. Most of the time I'm lucky, but I've never had that many coins to gamble with. I'm lucky, but that doesn't mean I'm smart with my money."

"Where does it go?"

"Can we not do that here?"

Jason swallowed and looked behind him. "What are you worried about?"

"I wasn't expecting him to commit to that much," he said.

"You're the one who challenged him, though."

"I challenged him, but I didn't think he would commit to quite that much. We really should get out of here."

"What would've happened had we lost?"

"Then we would've lost," William said.

He grabbed Jason's arm, sweeping his gaze around the inside of the tavern, shaking his head. "That happened a little faster than I was hoping."

"What were you hoping for?"

"I was hoping for—"

The door to the back room slammed open and Gary emerged with several others behind him. One of them was the man who was invisible to Jason's dragon sight, and they raced through the tavern.

William swore and grabbed for Jason, leading him out, and said, "Well, this is going to be fun."

They raced along the streets, once more running, and yet, this time at least, Jason felt as if they weren't running from people with unthinkable power. It was possible the man invisible to his dragon sight had some sort of power, but more likely he was only wearing dragonskin and didn't know what he had.

They turned a corner and then another, heading toward the outer edge of town.

"This isn't going to be good for you in town, is it?"

William shot him a look. "Probably not, but I've been through worse."

"You have?"

"Well, not a whole lot worse. Besides, eventually you're going to go, and seeing as how you have all the money..."

They turned a corner. Jason was looking at William and crashed into a solid figure.

He bounced off, and William went staggering in the opposite direction. His backside struck the cobblestones and he looked up.

He was greeted by a dark-haired man wearing dragonskin.

A Dragon Soul.

Heat radiated from the man and Jason scooted back, trying to get away from him, but there was only so far he was able to go. He continued to try to get away, and as he did, he could feel the other man's gaze holding him, glaring at him, and heat continued to build.

"Sorry about that," William said, getting to his feet. "My friend and I are—"

The Dragon Soul turned toward William, holding his hand out, and a blast of power burst from him, striking William and sending him across the street.

Jason tried to get to his feet, but he wasn't able to.

It was almost as if the man was using some sort of power to hold him in place. He didn't know enough about the power of the Dragon Souls or of the dragon pearls, but it seemed as if he were being held down.

Jason fought against it, but the Dragon Soul pressed back.

"You have been particularly difficult to find." The Dragon Soul's voice was dark and thick and almost sounded as if it were burned.

"What do you want with me?"

"It's not what I want with you."

He tried to get up, and yet couldn't.

The Dragon Soul took a step toward him and then staggered.

Something had struck him, though Jason didn't see anything—or anyone.

The Dragon Soul dropped to the ground, motionless as soon as he fell.

What had struck him?

It didn't matter. Jason was freed.

William rubbed his chest. He stood where the Dragon Soul had been, motioning toward Jason.

Jason got to his feet, running as he followed William,

and they raced along the street. Behind him, power built from the Dragon Soul, shooting along the street. It struck, connecting with Jason's back, and sent him staggering forward.

William caught him, grabbing his arm, and dragged him forward.

Together, they continued onward, moving as quickly as they could.

"What was that?" William asked.

"That was one of the Dragon Souls."

"The people Old Henry warned you about?"

"Seems like it," he said.

"I wasn't sure if we could believe him."

"The Dragon Souls are real. I was captured by them before, and…"

Heat built from behind him and Jason grabbed William, pulling on his arm, and they turned a corner before either of them could get struck again.

He could feel the heat as it slammed into the space where they'd been.

He should've stayed with Henry, regardless of whether or not he could trust the old man. At least Henry had some way of combating the Dragon Souls.

"Any ideas where we should go?" he asked William.

"Well, the inside of the town doesn't seem to be all that safe. What if we go outside of town?"

"We won't be safe there, either."

"It's possible, but…"

Another burst of heat began to build and Jason

grabbed William, throwing him forward. He was just in time, as a burst of fire streaked along the street where they had been.

"Come on," William said.

They turned a corner, and Jason followed at a run. With each step, the coin purse jingled loudly. Jason clamped a hand over his pocket, trying to quiet it.

They weaved, turning corner after corner, reminding him of when they had run with Henry, but this time there was no sense of intention, nothing like they'd had with Henry guiding them. The other man had far more control, and Jason had been far more confident when Henry had been leading them. With William guiding, he didn't know if the other man knew what he was doing and where they were going.

Every so often, the sense of heat would continue to build behind him. Jason was convinced they needed to continue to hurry forward. If they didn't, he worried they would get struck by the heat, and he had no idea what would happen if he were hit.

In the distance, a dark figure caught his attention. He pointed, and William grabbed him, pulling him down a side street. Jason had lost all track of where he was going and where they were in the town. The buildings blurred together, the shapes all similar and the streets all narrow, making it difficult to tell where he was. William continued to guide him.

They turned another corner, and this time, there was another shape in the distance. Jason grabbed William, pulling them off to the side, and they ran.

"Another?"

Jason nodded. "They all wear dragonskin."

"How can you tell?"

"I just can."

William nodded and they weaved, turning, and suddenly appeared on a wider street. There were several other people out, and a shout behind him called his attention. He spun, realizing that Gary was approaching.

Had they really managed to head back toward Gary and the others?

"This is—"

Jason didn't have a chance to finish, as another blast of heat struck, streaking along the street.

He grabbed William, pulling him back. The heat slammed into Gary and the people with him. Someone cried out, and Jason didn't have it within himself to feel too bad about that. They ducked back along the wall and he looked along the street.

On the opposite end, behind Gary and the others, another dark figure appeared.

They were stuck.

It didn't seem as if there was going to be any way for them to get out of there. Short of going through the buildings, Jason didn't know how they could find a way free from the Dragon Souls.

"You should go," he said to William.

"I'm not going without you."

Jason flicked his gaze from one end of the street to the

other, and as he did, he couldn't help but feel as if they were running out of time. The Dragon Souls were getting closer, marching forward, and heat was building from them. If nothing else, he didn't want William to get pinched between the two of them.

"Thanks for your help, but I don't think you should stay here."

"Listen, I'm lucky. Maybe that will help us somehow."

Jason chuckled. "I don't know that luck is any sort of power."

"You saw how it helped us while playing cards."

"I'm not sure that was helping us."

William grinned. "Yeah, that is kind of the curse of the gift. Every time it seems like it helps, something gets mixed in with it that isn't quite as lucky."

"You could have warned me about that."

Jason glanced at either end of the street. There wasn't a side street here, no place for them to go, and as he stood there, debating what they should do, heat began to build from either end of the street.

Someone near Gary cried out. Jason jerked his head out of the way as heat exploded where he had just been. The Dragon Souls were nearing and would be upon them.

"I think you can still get away. They're only after me."

"I—"

Something rumbled, and then a figure appeared on the street in front of them.

Jason blinked. Henry.

But how?

"Come on," Henry said.

"Henry? How are you here?"

"It doesn't matter how I'm here. All that matters is that we need to—"

Henry didn't have a chance to finish. The Dragon Souls ran forward, heat building from them. Henry held his hands out, pressing away from him in either direction. Flames scorched away from him.

"You shouldn't have run," Henry said.

"I didn't know if I could..." Jason didn't know how to finish, either. He had run from Henry, the one person who had suggested he could help him, but then, Jason had thought Therin was going to help, too. Yet he had betrayed him. Abandoned him.

One of the Dragon Souls neared.

"Henry," the Dragon Soul said, his voice rumbling. "We've been waiting for you to return."

J ason stared at Henry, at the furs, the beard, the dark
eyes, and the heat radiating off him, and he couldn't
help but wonder if Henry was still a Dragon Soul.

Maybe he was no different than Therin.

What had Henry said? It was easier to lie when he
sprinkled in some truth? This was the kind of thing that
fit within that, and he could easily believe that though
Henry was trying to make him believe he was trustworthy
and Therin was not, the reverse was true.

Henry glanced at Jason. "It's time for us to go."

Jason stood frozen in place. He looked at the Dragon
Souls, the two men approaching from either direction
along the darkened street, nothing more than shadows
streaming from the buildings mixing with the sense of
heat coming off the men, and he didn't know what to say.

Suddenly, one of the Dragon Souls fell.

Heat exploded, faster and with more violence than

Jason was able to follow. He was only aware of it after the man had fallen.

Another figure strode down the street, dark furs drawing Jason's eyes, the thick beard calling his attention, and he swallowed.

"Therin?"

Therin flicked his gaze toward Jason. "You shouldn't have left me," the other man said.

"I didn't. You left me."

Henry remained standing in place, one hand pointed toward Therin, the other toward the other Dragon Soul behind him.

"Come on," Henry said.

Jason didn't know what to do, didn't know whether he could move. Instead of following either of them, he stood back, watching.

Henry flicked his gaze toward Therin before diverting his attention briefly to the Dragon Soul behind him. A blast of heat struck the earth and then bounced up, catching the Dragon Soul. The man went flying, his head hitting the ground before bouncing. He didn't get up.

Henry turned fully to Therin then. "It looks like you decided to dress like me."

"I was about to say the same thing." Therin turned toward Jason. "You need to come with me. Quickly."

Henry stepped forward, blocking Jason from being able to go anywhere. "You're not taking the boy."

"I'm the one who found him. Helped him."

"You intend to use him."

"Use him? Strong words from a man like yourself."

"Look at you. Look at what you've become. You model yourself after me. You think you can be like me. You're nothing like me."

"I'm not a traitor," Therin said. He turned his attention to Jason. "We need to go. I can hold him off, but I don't know how long I'll be able to do so."

"Open your coat," Jason said.

"What?"

"Open your coat."

Therin glanced toward him. "We don't have time for this."

"I need to know who I can trust."

Therin grunted. "Fine."

"You too," he said to Henry.

Henry turned his attention to Jason. "You're not going to like what you see."

"Why? Are you intending to betray me?"

"It's not a matter of betrayal."

Jason glanced from Therin to Henry, keeping his gaze fixed on both men. He didn't know who he could trust—if he could trust either of them.

A figure down the end of the street caught his attention and he turned briefly toward it. Another Dragon Soul.

He didn't have much time. He was going to have to make a decision which way he would go, whom he would trust, and it had to be soon. If he didn't, this other Dragon Soul was going to turn the tide.

From what he could tell, Therin had taken out one of the Dragon Souls, but so had Henry.

As he watched, Therin unbuttoned his coat, and something changed. Jason shifted, his dragon sight no longer working. Dragonskin.

Jason held his breath, flicking his gaze toward Henry.

The other man continued to unbutton, and what Jason saw made his breath catch, but for a completely different reason.

Underneath his coat, he was naked.

His skin was raw, burned, and angry looking.

Henry stared at Therin, not taking his gaze off the other man. "Are you satisfied?"

"What happened?" Jason asked.

"Did you get what you needed?"

Jason nodded.

"Come on," Therin said. "I can protect you, but—"

Jason took a step toward Henry, and William followed.

"You're wearing dragonskin," Jason said.

"I told you I was with the Dragon Souls. I've left."

"No. I don't think you have."

Therin stood up, straightening his back, and something about his entire demeanor changed. "You're making a mistake."

"Maybe," Jason said.

At the same time, he wasn't sure what else he was supposed to do. He didn't necessarily want to go with Henry, but he also didn't want to go with Therin. He just wanted to be safe.

Henry tossed something toward Therin.

The sudden movement made the other man wince. Flames burst, an explosion shooting upward. Henry grabbed them and they went running.

Jason was tired, winded, and his entire body ached, but fear made him stronger than he would've otherwise been. He continued to run, feeling William behind him, chasing him, and the two of them raced through the streets after Henry. They reached the edge of town but Henry didn't slow, hurrying out beyond the edge of town, racing toward a cluster of trees.

"Where are you taking us?"

"To safety."

Behind him, the sense of heat and flame continued to build. Jason tried to ignore it, to focus on staying with Henry, but he risked looking behind him.

What if he'd made a mistake?

He still didn't know if he should have trusted Therin. The other man had said he was once with the Dragon Souls, which meant he would likely have had the dragonskin, but there was something about him that made Jason hesitate. He was forced to trust Henry instead, even though he didn't know if the other man was fully trustworthy.

When they reached the edge of the trees, heat exploded behind them. Henry forced them behind the trunk of a tree and paused. He looked behind him and tossed something back toward the town. As before, it exploded, fire bursting into the night.

"What are you throwing?"

"It doesn't matter."

"Are those dragon pearls?"

Henry frowned, shaking his head. "I wouldn't throw a dragon pearl. It's a waste of power."

"Then what is it?"

"I call them dragon seeds. They're little more than a fragment of bone. An explosive."

"Bone?" William asked, glancing from Henry to Jason. "What kind of bone?"

"Dragon bone," Henry said.

He grabbed them, forcing them deeper into the forest.

They ran through the forest, and it seemed as if Henry knew exactly where he was going. He guided them quickly, dragging them off, weaving through the trees. Every so often, Jason was aware of heat behind him, but he tried to ignore it. He recognized the way that Henry guided them, taking them not just away from the town, but heading toward the mountain slope.

"We aren't going to be able to lose them that way," he said.

"I don't intend to lose him that way," Henry said.

"Then how?"

"You'll see," he said.

William was slowing, and Jason glanced over at him.

"I don't know how much longer I'll be able to keep up."

"Then don't. You could return to town."

"He stays with us," Henry said.

"He's not part of this."

"He is now. They saw him with you. If he returns, the Dragon Souls will take him, torment him, and try to use him against you."

"Why am I suddenly so important?"

"You shouldn't be, but it seems as if you are."

Henry continued forward and Jason scrambled after him, trying to keep up. As he did, he stared at the other man's back, looking for answers he knew he wouldn't find.

All he wanted to do was rest. That wasn't quite true. He wanted to eat and then rest. Then he wanted to get back to his village, back atop the mountain, find a way to relax, and when he did, he would avoid coming back down the mountainside. He wouldn't complain about his lot in life. He would continue to serve, maybe try to train with Mason, eventually learn to fire the cannon the same way the other man did. His father had trained him for that, hadn't he?

Jason breathed out, trying to catch his breath, and as he did, heat slammed into him.

It was overwhelming, powerful, and he couldn't shake the feeling that he was not moving quickly enough to stay ahead of the Dragon Souls.

Henry glanced back, seemingly unfazed by all of this. He was moving quickly, and it reminded Jason of how Therin had managed to walk above the surface of the snow. It was almost as if Henry glided through the forest.

"What happened to you? You were a Dragon Soul. You had to be."

"I left."

"Like Therin claimed?"

"Therin never left."

"I suppose he'd say the same thing about you."

Henry grunted and ducked behind a tree trunk, pausing for a moment to look back at the forest. He pulled a flask from his pocket, tipping it back, drinking, and handed it over to Jason. Jason took a sip, enjoying the water, though it was warm and tasted too heavily of copper and minerals. He passed it over to William, who wrinkled his nose as he took a sip.

"Therin is using me to try to convince others of his change of heart."

"Why would he do that?"

"He's doing it because he thinks it will give him access he wouldn't be able to have otherwise."

"What kind of access is there that he can't get otherwise?"

Henry didn't answer, turning away and continuing deeper into the forest.

Jason and William shared a look, and the other man shook his head, shrugging. "I don't know. He's been around here for a long time, so I think you made the right choice, but... I don't know."

Jason swallowed. His throat burned from the effort of hurrying through here, and he felt as if he weren't sure whether or not he had made a mistake, but he couldn't help but think that this was the right thing.

What was Henry doing with them? What did he intend?

Every so often, a sense of heat built. At first, Jason thought it came from the Dragon Souls chasing them, but the more he focused on it, the more certain he was that it came from Henry.

"That's you, isn't it?"

"Those are my dragon seeds."

"What are you doing?"

"I'm trying to delay anyone who might be following us."

"And you're dropping the dragon seeds behind us?"

"Dropping them, throwing them, trying to keep them from catching us. If they don't know where I'm attacking in the dark, they have to be careful."

"Or you're creating a trail for them to follow."

Henry glanced over his shoulder. "What makes you think I don't have some way of tossing them so they can't find them?"

Jason focused on the explosions, and realized they came from all over behind him. It wasn't just one spot, and it seemed as if they *did* create a pattern arranged outward.

Perhaps Henry was right.

They weaved through the forest, no longer going at such a breakneck pace, and he was optimistic that they would be able to get ahead of the Dragon Souls.

He didn't know what Therin was after, other than that the man believed Jason must have some way of finding a dragon. Why, though? Nothing about Jason would suggest he would know where to find a dragon, or even how.

He said nothing, and the longer they went, even William remained silent, trailing along with him, walking as quickly as he could.

"How much longer do we have to go?" Jason asked Henry.

"Do you want them to catch you?"

"No, but we're getting tired."

"Tired is better than dead."

"If he wants me for something, then he wouldn't kill me."

Henry glared at him. "There are some fates that are worse than death."

It reminded him of something his father had said once.

Jason followed Henry.

William grabbed his arm, turning toward him. "I don't know too many fates worse than death."

Henry paused and pulled open his jacket, revealing the burns again. "I can assure you there are many worse things to experience than dying."

"You're still alive."

"Now I am."

The other man spun, jogging onward, into a forest that continued to get thicker, the darkness deeper. Jason was thankful for his dragon sight as he wound between the trees, darting from one place to another as he followed Henry. Without his dragon sight, he would probably lose sight of the man quickly. He made a point of checking on

William, ensuring the other man was with him and didn't get lost.

It seemed as if they walked for hours before Henry paused again. When he did, he pulled out his flask, taking a sip before handing it to the others. This time, Jason noticed it had a strange metallic taste to it. There was something familiar about it.

"I know this stream," he whispered.

"What's that?" William asked.

"The stream he got the water from. I know it."

"How do you know a stream?"

"In the mountains, there aren't too many places where water flows freely. When it does, it usually has something within it that keeps it from freezing. Whatever that something is gives it a specific taste."

It was the stream from the cave near the village. Where he'd *almost* gotten to safety.

Jason looked at Henry, meeting the other man's eyes. "You've been to our village."

"I haven't been to your village, but I have been to some of the northern villages. Do you think that stream only flows through your lands? No. It flows down the mountainside, and I gather the water there."

It was a strange thing to even remember that stream. It was one his father had liked to go to, telling him there was something about the stream itself that was special. Thinking of his father like that made him smile to himself, however sadly. Over the last year, he hadn't had all that many happy memories of his father. He'd been so focused on what he'd lost, and had neglected the things his father had given him over that time. Perhaps that had been a mistake.

"We need to keep moving," Henry said.

They meandered, and they didn't go much farther before another burst of heat struck. Jason glanced back, thinking it was only a dragon seed, but Henry stiffened.

"That wasn't a dragon seed, was it?" Jason asked.

"No. The Dragon Souls are getting closer."

"I haven't noticed one of your seeds exploding recently."

"I haven't either. It seems as if they found a way around them."

"They can do that?"

"They know as much as I do. More. And Therin is clever."

As they raced through the forest, Jason looked behind him every so often, detecting the sense of heat exploding. William watched, his brow furrowing, a question written on his face.

What was going to be the end result of all of this? Once they escaped with Henry, what were they going to do?

That was the part he didn't fully understand, and the part he wasn't sure could be answered. Once they managed to get free of these Dragon Souls, he still didn't know whether they'd be safe.

Every so often, he would glance over at William. William had withdrawn, remaining quiet. Jason didn't know if there was anything he could say that would draw his attention. At least, there was nothing he could say that would draw his attention and not alert Henry of the fact he was trying to do so.

The trees began to space out more widely, and the farther they went, the harder it was going to be to conceal themselves as they had when going through the forest. Henry began to pick up his pace. Jason raced after him, following, but he did so with reservations.

"How much further do we have to go?" William asked.

"Quiet," Henry snapped.

Jason shared a look with William.

"Tell us where you're taking us," he said, reaching Henry.

Henry didn't even slow, giving a dark-eyed stare in his direction.

Jason debated turning away, but for now, his fate was tied to Henry.

The other man continued to run, tracking almost directly through the forest, making his way in a straight line. At least, as straight as he could with the trees in the way. Snow drifted down on them, and his boots crunched through it. He watched Henry, looking to see if the other man glided above the surface of the snow, and found he did.

William was having a harder time in the forest. He wasn't dressed nearly as warmly as Jason or Henry. He would freeze if they eventually stopped. Even though Henry had some control over the dragon pearls, Jason didn't know if he had enough control to keep William warm.

Another explosion came from behind them, and he jumped.

This one was close, and it sounded almost as if it were close enough for him to feel.

The Dragon Souls could glide across the surface of the snow the same way Henry was able to do. They didn't need to trudge through it, not like Jason and William did. Every footstep they made ended up with them buried deeper in the snow, which meant they were traveling far more slowly than the Dragon Souls.

Jason grabbed for William, pulling him along.

Henry suddenly spun, putting himself behind them. "Head straight north. You do know which direction north is?" he asked Jason.

Jason glanced at the sky before nodding.

"What are you going to do?"

"I'm going to see if I can't delay them a little bit. With the way you're sinking into the snow, we've gotten slowed down."

Henry veered off and Jason pulled William with him, heading north, following the stars. If nothing else, his time in the mountains had taught him how to navigate.

Then again, in the mountains, everything was either up or down. There wasn't much in the way of navigation. Still, the stars were brighter there and easier to see. His father had taken the time to work with him, wanting him to know how to follow the stars.

"Are you sure we should be listening to him?" William asked.

"I'm not sure about anything anymore." Jason hurried forward. The snow continued to thicken, making it even more difficult for them to race along. With each step, he felt himself sinking deeper and deeper. They would have to get wherever they were going soon or they would be caught by the Dragon Souls, unless Henry had some way of helping them navigate the same way he could. It would be easier if the other man could guide them above the surface of the snow like he did. If that were possible, then they wouldn't have to struggle quite as much.

Wind started to pick up, whistling around them and gusting between the trees. It was cold and biting and reminded him of all the wind out of the north in the village.

The falling snowflakes were wet and heavy. It was a precursor—at least, it would be in his village. Eventually that wet, heavy snow would transition over to the dry and sharp flakes, the painful kind that would bite at exposed skin.

Jason shifted the hood of his coat, pulling it up over his ears. He glanced over at William, realizing the other man didn't even have a hood.

This was going to go poorly.

As they plunged through the snow, explosions of heat continued behind them. Jason shook with each one. It seemed like thunder, a steady rumbling, one after another, and the ongoing drumbeat practically guided them onward.

He trembled under it. If something were to slow them, they would be caught up by that thundering. The wind whistled. It pushed against them, almost as if it wanted to keep him in the forest. Jason leaned into the wind, trying to power forward.

The trees were continuing to thin, providing less and less cover. It had been easier deeper in the forest, where the ground was hard packed, the snow less plentiful, and the wind not quite as violent.

And then they were in the open.

From here, there was nothing but the vast expanse of the mountain stretching in front of them.

This couldn't be what Henry wanted them to do. If he intended for them to head up the mountain, they were ill equipped for it. He wasn't going to be able to make good time and William wasn't dressed for the weather.

"Where to now?" William asked.

"He said to go north."

Another explosion came from behind them, and Jason staggered before heading up the mountainside. At least he had his bow and arrows.

North.

As he went, it felt as if the air were shifting. It was less cold than it had been, and the star guided him around the side of the mountain.

That was strange. He'd always thought that the mountaintop was due north, but perhaps from where they were, it wasn't exactly north.

He paused, glancing over at William before looking back toward the forest. It was difficult to see anything in the darkness, even with his dragon sight. There had to be something in the forest, but he wasn't able to see anything, and certainly no striations of color that would suggest that Henry—or any of the Dragon Souls—were coming toward them.

"What is it?" William asked.

"He told us to go north, but…"

"But what?"

"But north isn't up the mountainside."

"I don't think I can climb the mountain," William said.

"I don't know where else he wanted us to go."

Jason looked into the darkness, trying to see if there was anything he could make out. The darkness stretched in front of him, almost all-encompassing. With the cold, there was no movement.

As he looked for anything that might guide them, he turned his attention back to the stars, but that still veered them away from the mountain peak.

Shaking his head, he headed north. That was what Henry had wanted them to do.

As they wound along the side of the mountain, he found they were climbing somewhat, but slowly. It wasn't nearly as steep as Jason would've expected had they been trying to climb up the mountain the way he had come down. The chill began to fade and the wind let up. He was thankful for that, and it seemed almost as if it were growing warmer.

"What is that?" William asked. "Why does it seem almost as if we are—"

Heat exploded in front of them.

Jason froze.

If heat was in front of them, it meant the Dragon Souls got around them somehow. Yet it didn't seem possible the Dragon Souls would've been able to navigate around them while they were working their way up the side of the mountain.

Unless there were other Dragon Souls.

He shivered and stopped, looking around.

Their only option was to head up the side of the mountain. While that might have been different than what Henry wanted them to do, it seemed as if it would take them away from the heat and the threat of the Dragon Souls.

"I think we need to climb," he said.

"Jason, I don't have the necessary clothing."

"The other option is for us to head back to your town."

William turned and looked behind him, but shook his head. "I can't do that, either."

"Then we need to climb."

They veered off, turning away from the North Star and heading up the slope of the mountain. It was hard. As they climbed, the cold began to whip around them, biting at them, ripping at Jason's clothing. Jason pulled his jacket tighter around him, and knew that if he was cold, William would be freezing.

He looked over at the other man and saw him shivering, his teeth chattering and his ears already starting to turn blue. He wasn't going to be able to withstand the cold for very long.

This was a mistake. There was no way to keep the other man warm.

Heat exploded in front of them.

Dragon Souls.

"I think—"

He didn't get a chance to finish. A thunderous roar exploded, different than the sound and feeling of the explosions he'd been running from through the forest.

"What was that?" William asked through his chattering teeth.

"I don't know."

Before he had a chance to think much of it, flames burst from nearby, illuminating the night.

A figure emerged and Jason stared, unable to do anything else.

"Come on," a voice said.

"Henry?"

"Of course it's me. What did you think?"

"I..." He looked past the other man, trying to peer into the darkness, but was unable to see anything. The heat was there, and he could feel it, but he couldn't see anything. "I thought that was the Dragon Souls."

"No. Not the Dragon Souls. It's a dragon."

18

Henry scrambled down the slope and grabbed William, wrapping his arms around the other boy. William shivered, and the color of his face left Jason worried.

"We need to get him warmed up," he said.

"Then help," Henry said.

Jason slipped an arm around William and helped guide him, following Henry. Every so often, the sense of heat ballooned behind him, reminding him of the Dragon Souls they'd evaded. The heat he detected in front of him was different. It was similar to what he had noticed when he had been following the North Star, when he'd thought it came from the Dragon Souls in front of them.

Could it have been Henry and his dragon all along?

They climbed a little ways. As they went, a faint tracing of light began to glow against the darkness. It didn't take long for that light to resolve into something of a flame. And then...

Jason stopped short, unable to go any farther.

An enormous creature rested on the slope. It had long wings that were unfurled, and it rested on massive forelegs. Its spiked body ran the length of the mountain, curling alongside it, and its powerful tail followed the lines of the mountain. A giant head—larger than any creature Jason had ever seen—swiveled toward him, two glowing orange eyes turning in his direction. Heat radiated off the entirety of the creature, illuminating a scaled side with dangerously sharp spikes protruding from its body.

"That's a dragon," William said.

"I told you we were heading toward the dragon."

Jason stared at it. Anger built within him.

We're safe from the dragons in the north.

They *had* been safe.

Then his father had died.

How could the dragon survive the cold?

"You said it couldn't tolerate the cold."

"Not for long. That's why we're going."

"What are we going to do?" William asked through chattering teeth.

"We're going to ride the dragon," Henry said.

"I can't ride a dragon," Jason said.

"Normally, you would not. Our need is great, and the dragon understands that."

"The dragon understands?"

Henry pushed him, and Jason went staggering up the slope and barely caught himself in time. He stopped in front of the dragon, and the creature looked at him.

Jason had a sense of the dragon staring at him, almost as if it knew something.

This was no dumb animal. That much was clear. He could see that from the way the dragon looked at him, the intensity—and intelligence—shining in its eyes. It flicked its gaze from Jason to William and then to Henry.

"Put your hand out," Henry said.

"So that it can eat it?"

"So that he can get to know you."

Jason shivered, and it had nothing to do with the cold. He stretched his hand out as Henry said, not knowing what else he could do. The dragon lowered its massive head and brought its nostrils up toward his hand and breathed in.

It created a powerful suction of air, and Jason felt drawn toward it.

He resisted, digging his heels into the snow, holding himself steady. He locked eyes with the dragon, and realized almost too late that if this was like any other predator, meeting its gaze like this was a threatening gesture.

He wasn't sure what he was supposed to do with the dragon, but he wasn't about to look away at this point.

The dragon snorted. There was no other way to describe what happened. A burst of hot air pressed Jason back, knocking him to the ground.

"He approves," Henry said.

"Approves?" Jason couldn't tear his gaze off the dragon, but he noticed movement near him and finally managed to peel his gaze away. Henry was helping William up the side of the dragon, and the other man was saying nothing as he followed.

"Come on," Henry said.

He reached his hand out and Jason got to his feet, but did so slowly.

"What are we going to do?"

"We are going to climb on the dragon, and if you stop talking, we might be able to get away from here before—"

Henry jerked his head downslope, and he squinted.

"We need to go," he said. "Now!"

Henry shifted on the dragon's back and came to sit near the base of its neck, resting close to the head.

Jason hesitated for a moment before getting to his feet and starting up the side of the dragon. Even before he had found a place to rest, the dragon had jumped, lifting into the air, beating at the sky with enormous wings. It was a strange, undulating sort of movement and the wind whipped around him, tearing at him. Heat radiated off the dragon, warming him. He hadn't even realized how cold he was until he pressed himself up against the dragon's back and rested near William.

As he did, he breathed out, looking down toward the ground, though he was unable to see anything. The dragon circled, spiraling higher and higher into the air, and the wind whistling around him should have been cold, but it was almost pleasant.

"Where is it taking us?"

"He's a he, and he's taking us where we need to go."

Jason clung to the dragon's back, unable to move anywhere else. As he did, he tried to ignore the sinking feeling in his stomach, the fear rising through him, and he tried to ignore the fact he was sitting on top of the dragon —a creature his people had been trained to fight, to kill, and a creature his people had weapons surrounding the village to defend against.

The longer that they were going, the more that they flew, the more uncertain Jason felt. The dragon continued to circle, going higher and higher into the air, and finally, it twisted.

Jason was almost tossed off. He was forced to grab on to the spikes on the dragon's back, clinging to the creature, trying to avoid getting thrown off. The fall from here would be fatal, he had no doubt, and yet, Henry seemed thrilled with the movement, laughing wildly as the dragon banked off to one side and then streaked away.

North.

That couldn't be a coincidence, and Jason tried to watch where they were going. It wasn't up the slope of the mountain. Riding on top of the dragon would have been an easy way to return to the village, but it didn't seem that was where they were headed.

"You could take me home."

Henry twisted, glancing back at him. "What sort of weapons does your village have?"

Jason shook his head. "They wouldn't—"

Henry glared at him. "They would. I've been around far too many places where they fire on dragons."

Jason licked his lips. Nausea rolled through him, and he wondered how much of it was from sitting on top of the dragon and how much was from the strange movements.

He couldn't even hold Henry's gaze.

He turned his attention to William and found the other man breathing more easily, though he was lying on the back of the dragon. His color had improved, the heat from the creature's back warming him, and he no longer shivered quite as violently as he had.

He should have been better dressed for the weather.

How would he have known, though? William wasn't expecting to run from Dragon Souls, to escape from his town, and to need to run out into the night and come up the mountainside and risk exposure to the elements. William wasn't expecting any of this.

And yet, he had not argued a bit.

Jason sat up and shifted, moving along the dragon's back, trying to position himself so that he could see better. He tried to ignore the nausea rolling through him, the strange sensation he had sitting on top of the dragon, the awkward way the wings fluttered, carrying them higher into the sky. He tried to ignore all that, and knew he failed. Despite that, he was determined to know where they were heading.

They weaved between mountain peaks.

He had never seen anything quite like it. He'd seen the

mountain range stretching away from his home village, but this was different. Not all of the peaks had snow capping them. In sections, there were stretches that were darker, as if covered by trees. And yet his people struggled to have anything to burn.

"It's enormous," he whispered.

"The dragon or the world?" Henry asked.

"Both," he said.

Henry chuckled. "Bigger than your mountain world, that's for sure."

They continued to fly, and Jason lost track of how long they traveled. The only thing he could think of was that they had avoided the Dragon Souls, but for how long?

"Were they chasing your dragon?"

"No," Henry said.

"Then why were they there?"

"Just wait," Henry said.

The dragon turned, and it seemed to Jason that they began to descend, dropping toward the ground. He was forced to squeeze onto the dragon, grabbing a set of enormous spikes raised out of the dragon's back. They streaked toward the ground, heading faster and faster, wind whistling around them, and he mimicked Henry as he leaned close to the dragon's back. Doing so shielded them from the wind somewhat, but it didn't protect them altogether. The dragon's wings were pulled into its body, and it shot like an arrow toward the ground.

Not like an arrow. It was faster than any arrow, and more powerful. The cold wind began to whip around him.

As the dragon plunged toward the earth, Jason worried the dragon intended to kill them.

He kept his focus on Henry, who seemed not troubled at all by the way the dragon dropped to the ground, but then again, Henry was the one who had brought them to the dragon.

Jason could only hold on, and feared releasing his grip, feared that he might end up falling from the back of the dragon.

And then the dragon stretched out its wings. It caught the wind and they slowed almost immediately. Light stretched out in the mountain valley in front of them.

Jason stared, trying to understand what he saw.

A city.

"What is this?" he asked.

"This is Dragon Haven."

"What is it?"

"This is a city of dragons."

"What kind of city?"

Henry sat up, looking back at him. "You'll see."

The dragon quickly dropped, pulling its wings out on either side, and they settled down to the ground.

When they did, Henry scrambled off but Jason hesitated before following. William looked around with a confused expression on his face before climbing down.

When he was on the ground, he looked over at Jason. "We were on a dragon."

"I know."

"We flew on a *dragon*." His spiked hair stood even taller after the wind had gusted through it.

"I know."

Jason looked all around. The trees were different than they were even in William's village. They had massive leaves, and the air hung with a different fragrance. Squirrels darted around within the trees, birds chirping as well, but more than anything, there was a complete absence of snow.

He'd never been anywhere where there was no snow.

The air was warm—hot, even.

Within his furs, he found himself uncomfortable, and for the first time in as long as he could remember, he unbuttoned his jacket, pulling it open, and was tempted to take it off altogether.

Henry motioned for them to follow, and Jason did, but as he went, he glanced back at the dragon. The dragon had already jumped, taking to the air again, and Jason didn't know if there was any way to follow it.

"Where now?" he asked.

"Now we go and find out what to do with you," Henry said.

"What do you mean?"

"You have the attention of the Dragon Souls. We need to know what to do with you."

"You could have left me."

Henry stopped, turning toward him, crossing his arms over his chest. "I couldn't have left you with the Dragon Souls. They would have used you."

Did he really want to be here, either?

He swept his gaze around and saw the dragon in the sky, circling over the city.

As he looked up, he realized it wasn't the only dragon. There were others, and they all circled, looking like birds flying in the sky. They were enormous, and still terrifying.

Henry shook his head. "You don't get it, do you?"

"I don't get what?"

"You're caught in the middle."

"In the middle?"

"You'll see, and unfortunately, there isn't much for you to do but choose a side."

Henry turned and headed down a hard-packed road.

William trailed after but glanced back at Jason, practically beseeching him to follow.

Jason looked all around the city. It was larger than his village, and larger than what he could remember of William's town. The buildings all blended into the forest, and were constructed differently than any from his village. Whereas in his village, most of the buildings were made of stone pulled from deep beneath the snow, sealed together with snow and ice, giving everything a cold feeling, the buildings here were constructed of wood, with roofs covered with branches and leaves. They were different even than the buildings he'd seen in William's hometown. There the buildings had been made of wood, but the roofs were thatched or slate, and narrow streets were paved with cobbles. The streets here were narrower, and meandered.

No snow clung to the rooftops. In a few of them, chimneys puffed out warm smoke, and Jason could imagine a pleasant fire in each of the hearths. Not dung, but wood. It gave off a soothing aroma.

As he followed Henry, he noticed dragon sculptures situated along the street, almost as if they were observing the newcomers, deciding whether or not they were welcome here within Dragon Haven. All of the dragon sculptures were made of a dark stone, and Jason reached toward one of them, running his hand along the surface of it, finding it smooth—and surprisingly warm.

Henry arched a brow at him, and Jason pulled his hand back.

The streets were smooth stones, massive and made of the same dark stone as the sculptures. They seemed to radiate warmth as well, giving off a pleasant sensation, one that was matched by the heat of the sun overhead.

Henry guided them to an enormous building near the center of the town. When they paused in front of it, Jason could only stare. Two enormous dragon sculptures sat on either side of the entrance. As he craned his neck, looking around, he discovered another dragon sculpture on the opposite end of the building. It was several stories high— easily the tallest building he'd ever seen.

"You will wait here," Henry said.

"And then what?"

"And then we will decide what to do with you," he said.

Jason could only shake his head. He didn't want them to have to decide what to do with him, and he had no idea why they had brought him here, and worse, he wasn't sure that he wanted to remain.

And yet, he didn't have a sense that he had much of a choice. If he wanted to get back home, there wasn't going to be any way other than traveling by dragon. He didn't even know how far they'd gone, though they had flown for quite a while. He could imagine it would take days— weeks—to return to his village by climbing the mountains.

That was if he was even able to make the journey. He wasn't sure he was equipped to do so, and he didn't know whether there was anything dangerous in the mountains that he would have to fear.

"I still can't believe Old Henry has a dragon," William said.

It wasn't long before Henry returned, and this time, he wasn't alone.

A woman wearing a long, flowing black gown followed him. Her hair was twisted into an elegant spiral atop her head. It was almost as if she wore a crown in it. She had a leaf tucked behind one ear, and her eyes were a deep blue.

"This is them?" she asked. Her voice was soft, almost musical, and when she neared, Jason had a strange sense of power from her.

"This is them. I came across this one in the town. Dragon Souls were chasing him."

"And the other one?"

"The other one tagged along."

"Interesting." She turned her attention to Jason, standing in front of him with her hands clasped at her waist. She watched him, regarding him with a strange expression, sweeping her gaze over the entirety of his body. There was an intensity to her eyes, and there was something else about her, a power that seemed to radiate from her. He had felt it before, but that had been with the Dragon Souls.

"Where is his home?" she asked, reaching out and touching his bearskin jacket.

"He's from a village atop the mountains."

"And the Dragon Souls came for him there?"

"Not there, but somewhere along the mountainside."

"Therin was there?"

"He was."

"That is troubling."

"Would either of you care to tell me what's going on?"

The woman studied him again, cocking her head to the side, and a hint of a smile curled her lips. "He has a bit of heat to him."

"He does. He can be a bit dense, but I think it's because he hasn't seen much."

"I'm standing right here," Jason said.

"Again, he can be a bit dense," Henry said.

Jason glared at the other man, but he ignored it.

"Bring them inside," the woman said.

"Inside where?" he asked.

Henry shot him a withering look.

He ignored it. There was no point in paying any attention to it, not at this point.

Henry followed the woman up the stairs between the dragon sculptures and into the building. William followed, and when he reached the door, he cast a glance back at Jason, almost as if trying to encourage him to follow.

Jason hesitated, his gaze sweeping along the street. He still couldn't believe the smooth stone he walked upon, the way that it radiated warmth. Despite the smoothness to the stones, they weren't slick. His boots had a good grip to them, and he didn't worry about falling, tripping over the stones.

The city seemed larger than befit the number of people he had seen so far. It was a strange realization. In the brief time they had been here, Jason would've expected to have encountered more people than he had, but it seemed sparsely populated.

The rebellion.

Therin had mentioned the rebellion, and even when he had hidden his true motivation, he hadn't concealed his feelings toward the rebellion.

What sort of rebellion was this?

Why were they here?

The dragons, most likely.

Was this where he wanted to be? Was this the kind of place he wanted to spend his time? All he wanted was to return to his village. To help his mother and sister, and from there...

Could he even fall back into the life he'd been leading?

Knowing what he now did, he wasn't sure that he could. Every day had been spent searching for food, for survival, and in the brief time he'd been away from the village, he'd seen far more. It was enough to believe there was a different way to exist.

But where?

He could imagine bringing his mother and sister down to the town, and from there, they could find a place, perhaps have William help them, but that involved him returning. More than that, that involved him finding his way down to that town again. The trek down the mountainside would be difficult, and he wasn't sure his mother would be in any shape for a journey like that.

Taking a deep breath, Jason hurried up the steps and entered the building.

The doors closed behind him, and he looked around.

Flames were lit all around him, situated in points all around the inside of the building. It gave off an almost unpleasant heat, something he never would have imagined before.

The woman had taken a seat on a tall chair near one end of the room. Not just a chair—a throne.

Henry stood in front of her, William a few paces behind him.

There were others in the room, but Jason wasn't able to see them very well.

Were they wearing dragonskin? He cast his gaze around, looking through his dragon sight, trying to see if he could make out anything about the others in the room, but nothing came to him.

If they were wearing dragonskin, that seemed surprising, given Henry's view of it.

Then again, if they had dragons, why wouldn't they be able to use their skins? Not all creatures lived that long, and he had to believe even the dragons had an end to their life. When they were gone, their skin would be valuable.

Jason approached carefully, slowly, and as he did, he glanced at Henry, but the other man ignored him. He took a place next to William.

"Welcome to Dragon Haven," the woman said. "You are granted our protection while you're here, but know that we have little tolerance for violence toward the dragons."

"Where am I?"

Henry shot him another look, and within it, Jason could practically hear the other man saying he was dense. And he felt it. He had no idea where he was or why he was here, nothing other than the fact he was in a place that revered the dragons.

"You are with the resistance. You are with those who would see the Dragon Souls defeated. You are with those who serve the dragons."

"Serve the dragons?"

The woman nodded and turned.

As she did, a shape appeared out of the darkness.

The heat within the room made much more sense, and Jason's breath caught.

There was a dragon in the room with them.

19

He and William sat in a small room off to the side of the main chamber. The dragon had curled up on the floor near the back of the room, a smaller creature than what he'd seen outside. Dark scales glowed softly, visible even from where he stood. Heat radiated in a way that made him realize he would never be cold in a place like Dragon Haven—not the way he had always been in the village.

The room was warm, but everything in this place had been warm. He'd taken his jacket off, setting it to the side, leaving his gloves alongside it. It was unusual for him to do that. Even in his village, he didn't often take his jacket and gloves off. The home he shared with his mother and sister wasn't warm enough to remove them very often, and when he did, he often felt as if he were naked and placed in a sort of danger. Partly that came from the fact that the home was not all that well heated, and without his jacket and gloves, he could easily succumb to the elements. Part of that was simply a matter of familiarity.

William had been silent ever since they came here and Jason glanced over at him, worried for him. It was more than just his silence. It was the apprehensive way he looked at everything, the discomfort he obviously had.

"I'm sure they can get you back to your village," Jason said.

"I'm not sure I want to go back," William answered. He turned to Jason and held his gaze. He ran his hands through his hair, making it stand even taller. "There's nothing for me there. Not really. And besides, after everything I've seen, I don't know how I could. I mean, dragons are real!"

"I told you they were."

"You told me they were, and you told me there was power in dragons, but this… this is something else."

Jason could only nod. This was something else, and it was something worse, if he were to be honest with himself. Here he was in a place that revered the dragons, that celebrated them, and seemed to serve them. And he had ridden on a dragon to get here.

He kept thinking back to what he'd experienced, what he'd always believed, and the preparations his people had taken to protect from the dragons. They had been prepared to destroy them. He knew what had happened to his father. He knew what his people had gone through. There were people who had lived in the village long enough to remember the last attack. That couldn't be wrong.

The door opened and Henry and the woman came in. There were two others with her. One was a girl about his age. She had the same blue eyes, high cheekbones, and golden hair as the woman he'd met. Even the way her hair was twisted onto the top of her head was the same. Her daughter, most likely. An older man followed. He was of a similar age as Henry. His jaw was clean-shaven and he was muscular, large enough that he would've fit in within Jason's village. William had gotten to his feet, but Jason remained sitting.

"You may sit," the woman said.

William took a seat and Jason shifted. He didn't know the right behavior. In a place like this, with his sort of ignorance, he worried that his lack of knowledge might be dangerous.

The woman took a seat across from him. "I imagine you have questions."

The others took seats, with only Henry still standing. He paced behind the table and Jason watched him, looking for answers or guidance or something, but Henry didn't pay any attention to him.

"Henry tells us that you were pursued by Dragon Souls."

"That's right," Jason said.

"And that Therin was among them."

He nodded again. "Therin told me that he was not one of the Dragon Souls any longer."

The woman smiled sadly. "Perhaps that is the case."

Jason shot Henry a look. "What?"

There was a moment of silence, and the woman took a deep breath. "Introductions are in order, I believe. I am Cherise L'aral. This is my husband, Olar. And my daughter, Sarah."

"You're the rulers here?"

Cherise smiled, shaking her head. "We don't have rulers the same way you would see them." She glanced toward the dragon curled along the wall, and said it in such a matter-of-fact way that it took Jason off guard. "Dragons were never meant to be subjugated the way the Dragon Souls believe. We recognize that, and we listen to their guidance."

"How do you know what they want?"

"They tell us," Cherise said.

"They tell you?"

"That's not why we're here," Henry said.

The others turned toward him, and Cherise held his gaze for a moment before nodding. "We aren't here for that. You're right," she said. She swiveled her seat, turning her attention back to Jason. "We need to know why the Dragon Souls are after you."

"I've told Henry all I know."

"You have, but I think there is more than what you have told him."

"I haven't been keeping anything from him."

There had been no point in doing so. Jason had no idea who Henry was when they first met, but there wasn't anything he really knew. The Dragon Souls had chased him down the mountainside, and he'd assumed it was because he'd avoided their capture, but maybe there was another reason to it. If there was, then he had yet to uncover it.

"Perhaps there is and you don't know it." Cherise locked eyes with him. "The Dragon Souls have not ventured that far away from Lorach before. We need to know what drew them."

"I thought they searched for dragons."

"Perhaps that's all it is, but there should not be dragons in your lands."

Jason grunted. "There shouldn't be, but my people would argue otherwise."

He bit back saying anything more. It was a mistake, and he knew better than to share. Given the way these people viewed the dragons, telling them his people hunted them, that they had ballistae set up around the village in order to protect themselves against the dragons, probably wasn't wise.

At the same time, he thought they already knew. He'd shared plenty with Henry during their journey, and the other man likely knew enough.

"There's a difference between dragons passing by and dragons living. Thriving," Cherise said.

Jason turned away from her gaze, only to find Sarah watching him.

"I'm sorry. It's just that my experience with dragons has been different than yours."

"I understand. You aren't the first person we brought here who has suffered much."

"No?"

Cherise glanced toward Henry. "Some have suffered even more."

Jason looked at Henry and found the other man ignoring him.

"My father was killed by the dragons," he said.

"That's what Henry tells us. And yet, our experience is that such a thing is not unique. The way the Dragon Souls demand the dragons serve forces them to behave in such violent ways."

"Therin said the dragons were trained."

"Trained in a sense," Cherise said. "The training is different than what you and I might view as training. They are forced to serve, and they are controlled."

"If the dragons are so powerful that you serve them, how are they forced to serve?"

"What has your experience with dragons been?" Sarah asked.

Cherise glanced in her direction, but the younger woman ignored her.

"I don't have much in the way of experience."

His only experience really was with riding the dragon here. Other than that, his knowledge came from the stories his people told, the celebrations they had. The more he learned about the dragons, the more he wondered how much his people really knew.

"We should show him," Sarah said.

"I don't think he's ready," Cherise said.

"For him to understand, we need to show him."

"Show him," Henry grunted.

Cherise regarded Jason for a long moment, and then she smiled. "It seems as if I have been outvoted."

She got to her feet and nodded to them. Jason stood, as did William, and they followed her out of the room. They headed into a narrow hallway and then out another door. Once they did, they were outside.

It was the first time Jason ever had been outside without a jacket and gloves and hat and felt comfortable. He stood in his shirt and pants, but still with his boots on, and found himself warm. A breeze gusted through the trees, pleasant and fragrant. It carried with it the scents of the forest, of flowers, and of other spices that he had never smelled before. All of it was overwhelming.

It was so different than what he experienced in the village: the cold, the absence of odors, the fear of stepping outside without warm clothing.

"Come with me," Sarah said, looking at him.

Cherise watched her daughter, and Jason followed Sarah, wandering with her. They wound through the trees until they reached a clearing. Once there, he stopped.

A low wall surrounded a central grassy plain. Everything was so *green*.

That wasn't what caught his attention.

It was filled with dragons.

Not just dragons, but *young* dragons. They were still large—much larger than any deer or wolf he'd ever seen—

but they weren't nearly as enormous as what he'd experienced flying to this place.

"Go up to them," Sarah said.

"Are they safe?"

She laughed, and Jason watched her. It was an almost
carefree sort of sound, the kind he'd never experienced.

"Safe? They're dragons."

William didn't need any prodding and he hurried
forward, reaching the nearest of the dragons, holding his
hands out. One of the small dragons—with strangely dark
scales, almost as if they shifted with the reflected light—
approached him. The dragon leaned toward him,
breathing in, and William started to laugh. The dragon
spread its wings, trying to flap them, but didn't take to
the air.

It couldn't fly.

"Why can't they fly?"

"They are dragonlings. In another year or two, they
will be able to fly, but right now they're not. They're
dependent upon their caretakers."

"You?" Jason asked, looking from Sarah to Cherise and
then to her husband.

Cherise nodded. "Us. We ensure the safety of the
dragons as they continue to develop, and we help them in
the time that they are growing. That's our price of
service."

Jason frowned to himself. "You're their servants."

"It's not like that," Cherise said.

"No? Then what is it like? You serve the dragons. You take care of their young. And you—"

"And we defend the dragons against the Dragon Souls. Much like they defend us," Henry said.

"How do they defend you?"

"You're still alive, aren't you?"

Jason glanced over at William. The other man was still crouching in front of one of the dragons. He was touching the dragon on the head, and he was smiling. It was almost as if he were enthralled by the creature.

"Why show me this?"

"You fear the dragons," Cherise said. "Like so many have over the years, but you fear them for the wrong reasons. It's not the dragons who are at fault for what happened to your father. It's the Dragon Souls." She crouched down as one of the small dragons approached, and it crawled up into her arms. "What you see as powerful and dangerous, we view as intelligent. They are different than us, but not violent."

Jason studied the small dragons, and yet he couldn't shake what he knew of the dragons, the understanding he had of what they had done over the years, and he couldn't shake the sense that their experience was different. Wrong.

Then again, what did he really know? His experience was tied to the village, and nothing beyond that.

"Why would the Dragon Souls have come to my village?" He looked at Henry, staying at the edge of the forest, almost as if unwilling to get any closer. "Why would Therin have come?"

Cherise took a deep breath, looking around. "They shouldn't have. The mountains have long served as a line of demarcation. The dragons struggle to cross the snow and the cold, and the Dragon Souls have feared pushing, believing there is nothing beyond the mountains. They have no reason to travel through there. Not only is there not much life to be found, but there are no further dragons to subjugate."

Jason turned his head toward the small dragons in the clearing. "This would suggest otherwise."

"We came here because they would be unlikely to travel this far. They don't know that we're here."

"Are you sure?"

"We often worry about them finding us, but Dragon Haven has been protected for many years."

Jason looked at the three of them. "How many of you are here?"

"We aren't as many as we would like. This land is safe, but we haven't been able to flourish as we should have. Now there are only a few thousand of us here," Sarah said.

A few thousand was still quite a few, and yet, given the size of the town, it wasn't nearly as many as he would have expected.

"And how many dragons?"

"Counting these?"

Jason looked over at the small dragons. There were five of them, and they seemed completely uninterested in him. He was thankful for that. He wasn't sure how he would react if one of the dragons came running at him.

"Sure. Counting these."

"Barely two dozen," Cherise said.

"That's it?"

"Freeing dragons from the Dragon Souls is difficult," Olar said.

"How many dragons do they have?"

"Hundreds," Sarah said.

As Jason continued to look at the dragons, he couldn't help but wonder about them. "Why would Therin have come into the mountains without a dragon, then?"

"Dragons don't care for the snow and ice," Sarah said.

He looked over at Henry. "You brought a dragon there."

"Out of necessity," Henry said.

"How?"

"How did I bring a dragon?"

Jason nodded.

"It's not as difficult as you'd think. I called to it."

"How did you call to it? You were in the village as long as we were."

Henry held his gaze for a long moment. "I called to it."

There was more here than what Henry was admitting to, but Jason wasn't sure that he even cared. All he knew was he was in a place where he didn't belong, and he wasn't sure how he was going to get home.

"None of this explains the Dragon Souls and what they were doing there."

"Perhaps he will."

A dark shape appeared overhead, and Jason looked up.

An enormous dragon circled, dropping to the ground. At first, Jason thought it was the same dragon that had brought him here, but this one seemed even larger, and there was a purplish hue to its scales. He didn't remember seeing any purplish hue on the dragon he'd ridden on. This dragon landed and breathed out a streamer of fire that rolled over the small dragons in the center of the clearing.

When the fire calmed, the dragon turned his attention toward them. Yellow eyes locked onto Jason. There came a stirring within his mind, and then it faded.

"What have you brought me?"

It was a deep and rumbling voice, and at first, Jason thought it was Henry or Olar before realizing he heard the dragon.

He stared. "You talk?"

"Don't mind him," Henry said. "We're working on him."

"Who is it?"

"This is the one we told you about."

"He's the one the Dragon Souls chased." There came another strange stirring in the back of his mind, and the dragon stared at him. "He's seen it."

"We think so," Henry said.

"He has," the dragon said.

"I have what?"

Henry stepped away from the trees, the first time since

they had arrived there that he did. He glanced at the massive dragon before turning his attention to Jason. "The Dragon Souls have long been trying to breed dragons that can live within the mountains. They want to extend their range, and until they're able to survive in the cold, they can't do so. They can fly overhead and they can land briefly, but the cold is too much for them."

Jason looked up at the enormous dragon. "You've said that, but it still seems strange to me. I've been around people who wear dragonskin—"

The dragon roared.

"I'd be careful talking about that," Henry warned.

"I'm sorry," he said. He felt foolish talking to the dragon like that, but at the same time, he thought they needed to know what he had experienced.

"Dragonskin coats absorb heat."

"Your experience has been different," Henry said. "The skins are different, and the needs of those who wear them are different, but that doesn't mean dragons themselves can withstand the same temperatures. They can tolerate them, but they are limited to how long they can do so."

Could that be why they had rarely encountered dragons in the mountains?

His people were protected, set up so that they could defend themselves against the dragons, and yet, in the last two decades, there'd been no dragon.

They'd believed the dragons defeated, and yet, if the truth was something else as Henry claimed, then the dragons simply had no interest in being within the mountains. If that were the case, then his people weren't in any danger.

"The Dragon Souls were there," he said.

"They were," Henry said.

Jason looked up at the enormous dragon, staring at its eyes. Something about them was familiar.

Why was it? It was different than the orange-eyed dragon that had brought him here. Something about the way the dragon looked at him, the stirring in the back of his mind, seemed familiar in a certain way, though he didn't quite know why that should be. He pieced together what they were telling him. The Dragon Souls had come to his village, but they also were seeking a way to expand their reach, to find dragons that could handle the cold.

"Do you think there's another dragon out there?" he asked.

Henry stepped forward. "One of the things Therin has long chased is—"

"Free dragons."

Henry nodded. "There's something about dragons born free that makes them stronger. Larger. Though the Dragon Souls have many dragons, most of them are born in captivity. They're not nearly as impressive as those born free." He turned his gaze toward the enormous dragon. "Those dragons are able to reach a much larger size."

"Your dragons are larger than theirs?"

"Considerably larger."

"What does that have to do with me?"

"As I said, Therin is after free dragons. He's using his knowledge to try to encourage dragons to be born free. But not just born free. Born into places where others wouldn't survive."

"Like the mountains," he said, remembering what Therin had said.

"Exactly," Henry said.

"You think he was trying to breed some sort of dragon?" Not just any dragon, but an ice dragon. That was what Therin had said. Jason remembered it well.

Henry shook his head. "We don't think that he was trying to breed them. We think he already succeeded."

20

J ason sat with his legs crossed in front of him and his back pressed against a tree. He breathed in the sense of the forest, the earthy odors, the mixture of dying leaves, the scent of flowers somewhere distant, and felt uncomfortable. None of this was home to him.

Footsteps near him caught his attention and he looked up to see Sarah approaching. She was dressed in a green robe, and she held her hands behind her back, watching him.

"You don't have to be so nervous," he said.

"I'm not nervous," she said, touching her hair.

"You don't have to hesitate coming toward me," he said.

She flashed a smile. "What makes you think I am?"

"You're watching me."

"That much is true."

"Why?"

"Because you make me uncertain."

Jason laughed, almost bitterly. "I make you uncertain? Everything about this place makes me nervous." He looked up. "The trees. The smells. The sounds. Even the warmth."

"The warmth?"

"Where I'm from, it's bitterly cold. You have to wear furs like… Well, like I have back in your building. Without them, you can't survive very long outside."

"That sounds awful."

"We haven't had a dragon attack in decades. We're safe."

"It doesn't sound like living."

Jason looked around him. There were a few thousand people here—more than he'd ever known his entire life. Several dozen dragons. Still, they were isolated. Like his village, in a way. "Is this living for you?"

She frowned at him. "Henry thinks you saw the dragon."

"I know what Henry thinks, but I didn't."

"The dragon thinks you saw the dragon. That's why Therin wanted you."

Jason shook his head, staring at the ground. A trail of insects led away, heading toward one of the nearby trees. Even in his village, there were no insects. It was a strange thing to see so much life all around him.

"How can it know?"

"Dragons know many things."

"You think the dragon can read my thoughts?"

"Yes," she said.

Jason looked up at her, and he started to smile, but he realized that she wasn't joking. She actually believed the dragon could read his mind.

And who was he to think otherwise? As far as he knew, the dragons *could* read his thoughts. There had been the strange stirring in the back of his mind when he'd encountered the dragon, and it was possible that it was able to dip into his mind. If so, should he be scared? If the dragon was able to read his mind, it would know how he felt about dragons in general, and how he felt about what he believed they were responsible for doing to his father.

"If the Dragon Souls acquire a dragon that can survive in the mountains, your village won't be safe."

"My village hasn't been completely safe anyway," he said.

"You just said—"

Jason breathed out, shaking his head. "I know what I just said. And I know that it makes no sense. You're right. If the Dragon Souls come for my village, the people won't be safe."

"We just need you to help us find it."

"I'm not sure I can."

They had made it clear that was what they wanted from him. And yet, part of that was dependent upon him having seen what they thought he had. The longer he was here, the less certain Jason was that he'd actually seen what they believed. The dragon seemed to believe that, and yet, how could it know?

Probably the same way Therin had known.

"Why would they have been there?" he asked.

"Dragon eggs have a very distinctive signature to them," she said.

"What does that mean?"

"Well," she said, taking a few steps closer to him and taking a seat on the ground. She situated her hands on her lap, looking over at him. "Once a dragon egg hatches, there's a certain distinct sense to it. It's the same reason Henry has been searching."

"You've known about the eggs?"

"We've known the Dragon Souls—Therin, really— placed them in certain locations, and yet, we haven't known where, or whether they were even successful."

"I thought you said dragon eggs had a certain signature."

"They do, but when the Dragon Souls were placing eggs, not all of them were going to survive. Some of them were placed into pretty extreme locations."

"Why?"

"It's something about the developmental process," she said.

"What do you mean?"

"What I mean is that the egg takes on some of the characteristics of the location where it's developing. In this place, the eggs will take on some of the traits of the forest. The eggs the Dragon Souls keep and hatch in Lorach will take on those characteristics."

"Which is why Therin thinks that having eggs develop

in the snowy mountains will help them develop a tolerance to it."

She shrugged. "Most likely."

"But why?" Jason looked around at the trees. Somewhere the sound of a bird chirping caught his attention. Insects buzzed nearby. There was so much sound. Activity. Life.

It was nothing like the north.

"Again, I don't really know why. And yet, both Henry and the dragon think that you have seen it."

"I don't know that I have." He looked away, staring into the forest. "In my village, there isn't much to see. I try to hunt, and don't often succeed."

"Why not?"

"Because there isn't much there to catch."

"What do you do?"

"If I don't catch something, then I go hungry."

"That sounds… awful."

"It's not ideal," he said. He breathed out. "Before I left the last time, I managed to catch a deer."

"Is that good?"

He nodded. "Very good. An animal like that should feed my family for a month." And longer, since he'd been gone.

"The dragons make sure we never go hungry," she said.

"The dragons hunt for you?"

"They hunt things like that. Otherwise, we grow corn and beets and carrots and—"

Jason stared at her. "I get the point."

"You don't have those?"

"We don't have much in the way of vegetables. We trade for them and grain, but even that's difficult."

"What do you have to trade with?"

"Tellum," he said.

"What does that mean?"

"It's a particular type of metal that blends into the mountain. It absorbs the heat, which is why we haven't frozen in my homeland. It's still rare—which means not all have it."

And with his father being gone, Jason was destined to end up in the mines, though he had no interest in doing so. It was, however, the only time anyone was ever really warm.

There were some who advocated moving into the mines, though with the metal they pulled out, they were able to stay relatively warm outside.

"Do you think the dragon egg could have been placed there?"

"I don't think so," he said.

"Why not?"

"There would've been people coming through. They would've known."

"There must be some place that you could have found it."

He shook his head. "There isn't…"

Only, he wasn't sure if that was true. What if there was a place where the dragon egg could have been, and it would've been a place no one else would've known about?

Not only concealed, but there would need to be a supply of fresh water.

Jason's breath caught.

There was a place where animals often went, a location that he often went to hunt. And it was a spot his father had visited frequently. It was a place where he'd felt something when he'd been by there. Where he'd seen *something* when the Dragon Souls had chased him...

The flash of golden eyes he'd seen came back to him.

He got to his feet. "I might know where the dragon was."

"You might?"

"I don't know if it is or not, but..."

He looked around. It was near that stream where he'd seen the deer running.

It was far enough down the mountainside that it would have been difficult for others to have reached it, and it would've been relatively untouched.

Could Therin have been looking there to see if anything had happened to it?

It would make a certain sort of sense, but why would he have come all the way to the village? The cannon. That was what he had said. The cannon attracted dragons. And he had hoped to attract a dragon.

"What would your people have done if they saw the dragon?"

"Try to destroy it," he said.

"They would destroy something like that?"

"Dragons are dangerous."

"They are not," Sarah said.

Jason took a deep breath, meeting her eyes. She stared up at him defiantly. "Your experience is different than ours. I can tell you what my people would have done had they seen a dragon." Then again, if this dragon was different, they might not even have recognized it as one.

"Come on," she said. She grabbed his hand, dragging him through the forest, and he didn't resist. She pulled him as they went, and they reached the edge of the town quickly, and she hurried him toward the building, and again inside.

"What is it?" Cherise asked when they approached her.

"He thinks he knows where he saw it."

"Then he needs to go. If the Dragon Souls find it, it's dangerous for the dragon."

"What would you have me do?"

"I would have you save it, Jason Dreshen."

Save it?

The dragons haven't attacked the village in decades, but they remain dangerous. A threat. Our people must remember what it once was like when the dragons flew free. We must remember, as others will not.

"Why should I do that?"

"Because the dragons need our help."

He turned away, and though he didn't know whether or not dragons did need his help, he also didn't know whether there was anything he would be able to do to help.

Henry appeared, looking at him. "What is it?"

Cherise held his gaze. "He believes he knows where the dragon can be found."

"Then we go."

Henry grabbed his arm, pulling him toward the small room and his jacket, which he forced into Jason's hands. He tossed his gloves and pants, and nodded.

"Get ready."

"I'm not sure this is the right thing," he said.

"We don't have much time. We managed to escape the Dragon Souls, but if they're truly after a dragon, they won't stop their search."

Sarah was watching him, and there was a look in her eyes that practically begged him to help. He didn't know any of these people. He didn't know Henry that well. He didn't even know William all that well.

The only thing he knew was his village.

If the Dragon Souls headed toward his village, he knew there would be danger.

His brief experience with the Dragon Souls told him they didn't really care about others. If nothing else, it was possible the Dragon Souls would destroy his village. That, as much as anything, was reason enough for him to go with Henry.

He pulled on his jacket and his pants, slipping on his gloves. "Let's go."

"You're willing to serve the dragon?" Sarah asked.

"I'm willing to help my people."

And he would do it despite the fact that some of the people in the village didn't care all that much about him.

He would do it because his mother and his sister were there. He would do it because it was the right thing to do. It was what his father would have wanted.

"Where are we going?"

William popped his head through another door, glancing from Jason to Henry.

"Back to my village," he said.

"Then I'm coming," he said.

"You aren't dressed for it," he said.

"I'm sure they have something I can wear."

Jason looked over to Henry, who shrugged.

"See? Besides, didn't we already establish that I'm lucky?"

Jason frowned. "I thought your luck was dangerous."

"Well, my luck is not always lucky, but…"

Maybe they could use it. They hurried through, gathering supplies, and when they headed back outside, Henry marched them into a clearing. He looked up at the sky, saying nothing, and Jason followed the direction of his gaze. It took a moment, but a dark shape began to circle, descending.

"How did you call it?"

"I just call it," Henry said.

"That isn't an answer."

"That's the answer you're going to get."

The dragon dropped to the ground, and Jason recognized the orange eyes. This was the same dragon they'd ridden here on. It was almost as if Henry and the dragon had some sort of connection, a bond of sorts, and when Henry climbed on its back, he looked down at them.

"Are you coming?"

Jason scrambled onto the dragon's back, and William followed. He'd somehow acquired thick furs, and though they were of a dark color, they would at least be warm.

"I'm coming too," a voice said.

Jason glanced over. It was Sarah. She was wearing what looked like bearskin, almost as if it matched his own.

She flashed a smile. "If there's a dragon, you need someone who understands them."

"It's going to be dangerous," Henry said.

"Then you will protect me. Besides, if there's a dragon there, I will ensure it's safe."

"How do you know this dragon will be safe in the snow?" he asked Henry.

"The dragon isn't going to stay."

"How do you intend to get back?"

"I'll call it."

They all got settled on the dragon's back, and Henry must've given some sort of alert because the dragon took flight. They spiraled steadily into the sky, the air growing cooler as they went. Despite that, warmth radiated off the dragon, giving enough heat that he wasn't cold. He was almost hot in his clothing, and then they got higher still. The air shifted, now the wind gusting, biting, and familiar. Sarah huddled against the dragon and William stayed low as well.

"You need to avoid the mountaintop," he said.

"We will," Henry said.

"If they see the dragon, they're going to fire the ballistae."

"I understand."

"There's a stream along the mountain. You might need to be up close to see it."

Henry twisted, meeting his gaze. "We will find it."

They streaked through the air and everything began to shift, the ground going from streaks of dark green to brown and finally to the familiar snow. A chill settled through him, and Jason couldn't help but wonder if he was doing the right thing. If nothing else, he was serving his people. He was doing what his father would have wanted for him.

What would he do if there *was* a dragon in the mountains, as they suspected?

Probably nothing.

He would let Sarah and Henry take care of it. That was their responsibility.

Besides, he didn't even know if there would be one. All he knew was that the Dragon Souls believed there could be.

He'd seen their violence. He'd seen the way they had destroyed, and if it meant they were going to head into his village, attacking people he knew, Jason had to do something.

The dragon began to descend. It swept down, angling for the ground, sweeping with a furious speed. Jason held on, clinging tightly to the dragon's back, and within moments, they crashed onto the ground.

"Go," Henry urged.

Jason scrambled down, following Sarah and William, with Henry taking the rear.

When they were down, Henry tapped on the dragon's back, looking in the creature's eyes, and nodded.

Within a moment, the dragon took off, circling back into the sky and disappearing.

Jason breathed in. All around him was familiar cold and snow and nothing but white. It was unpleasant, the cold trying to crawl through his coat, dig into his skin. After having been warm, this was almost unbearable. He tried to ignore it, to think of nothing but warm thoughts, but now that he'd experienced the warmth of the dragon, and the warmth of Dragon Haven, he thought maybe he wished he was back there.

"Where are we?" William whispered.

Jason looked around. "The top of the mountain. We're near my home."

Wind swept out of the north, whipping across the snow, cold and biting. It was frigid, and it swept the loose snow free, creating a blizzard of white in front of him. Sharp snowflakes drifted down from the sky, joining with the wind. This was going to be a terrible storm. He had experienced storms like this before, often enough that he recognized the cold threatening him. This was the kind of storm he would fear staying out in.

"Where to?" Henry asked.

"We need to find the stream," he said.

"We need to find someplace to stay warm," William said.

"There is no place to stay warm," Jason said. He started off, heading up the side of the mountain. It would be easier with snowshoes, and he still had the pouch full of Gary's coins, enough money that he would be able to purchase snowshoes, though there was no place to do so.

"How did you survive here?" William asked.

"We just do."

Jason shielded his eyes from the snow that was pelting down and tried to look through the blinding white. It was getting late, and soon the storm would become overwhelming. If he didn't find the stream—and the dragon, if it was here—before darkness, they would very possibly freeze.

Then again, it was possible Henry had a way of calling to the dragon and summoning it, but would the dragon be able to find them in the midst of a blizzard? He looked over at Henry, and he noticed worry on the other man's face. He had the same thought.

Jason continued trudging up the side of the mountain, and he wound slightly toward the west. He wasn't entirely sure where they had landed, and though the slope of the mountain was familiar, and the snow was familiar, nothing else about the landscape was.

That was the danger of this place. Everything looked the same, everything blended together, and with the snow falling, it was easy to lose their place. He didn't want the others to know that he wasn't entirely sure where he was going. Instead of admitting that, he continued to climb.

Behind him, someone was shivering, and he glanced back to see William with his arms wrapped around himself. Surprisingly, Sarah was doing better than William. She was having an easier time climbing the mountain as well, and it looked almost as if she were gliding along it, the same as Henry.

Jason chuckled, shaking his head.

"What is it?" William asked.

"I just understood why Sarah decided to come with us."

She looked at him, frowning.

"You can control the dragon pearls, too."

"What makes you say that?" William said.

"Well, notice how you and I sink into the snow. Look at her and Henry."

William turned his attention to the two of them, and he sucked in a sharp breath before starting to cough. "How are they able to do that?"

"Because Henry was a Dragon Soul, and I suspect Sarah has had some training."

She locked eyes with him and said nothing.

"Are you going to find this place?" Henry asked.

"I'm looking for the stream, but in whiteout conditions like this, it's difficult to find."

"You don't recognize anything around here?"

Jason shook his head. "It doesn't work like that here. There aren't landmarks. Everything gets covered in snow. We get snowfalls pretty much every day, and the wind picks up, whipping away any other traces that might give us anything to follow."

"Don't you have any trees?"

"None," Jason said. "It's why the stream has been so valuable. It serves as a landmark." Considering they had precious few of them, the stream gave them an idea of where they were going and where they needed to go, and it helped guide them.

All he needed to do was find it.

In the fading light, and with the wind kicking around, he wasn't sure he would be able to locate the stream. Even in the daylight, it wasn't something he was able to find that easily. He could come down the mountainside, and he could track it that way, but trying to climb and find it from below was difficult. What if they had come in too high?

Scrambling along the side of the mountain, he continued searching for signs of the stream. He tried to hear the burbling water, but against the wind, there was nothing. They even had to shout to be heard, making it so it was difficult to know where the others were.

He paused. "I don't know that I'm going to be able to find it with the storm."

"We need to find it," Henry said.

"Why? We could wait another day, come in the morning when the storm has passed, and—"

"It has to be today."

Jason turned his attention to the man. "Why today? What is it that you know?"

"The dragon recognized the Dragon Souls."

"What does that mean?"

"It means the Dragon Souls are getting close. If we wait until morning, it will be too late."

Jason looked around. He didn't feel any heat, nothing that suggested the Dragon Souls approached, but he didn't

want to get caught here by them. Even though Henry—
and Sarah—might be able to use the dragon pearl and
Henry might be able to call the dragon, the idea of getting
trapped by the Dragon Souls on the mountainside troubled him.

"You knew this, didn't you?"

"I knew we had limited time. Therin wouldn't wait if
he thought something was here."

"And he was able to reach here this quickly?"

"Much like us, he would be able to call to a dragon."

Jason shivered. It had nothing to do with the cold. He
needed to find the stream, but how?

Making up his mind, he wound along the side of the
mountain. Rather than climbing, he followed the level
they were on. If nothing else, he would run into the
stream. He lost track of how long they walked, the wind
whipping around him, tearing through his bearskin,
leaving him shivering.

In a break in the wind, he heard a burbling.

It was to his left and he trudged through the snow,
racing toward what he had heard. The stream swept
around the mountainside, eventually dipping and
cascading far down the mountain.

"This is it," he said.

Henry pulled his gloves off, dipped his hands in the
water, and brought it to his face. "It's the same."

"I told you," he said.

"Interesting."

"Why?"

"Nothing." He straightened, putting his gloves back on, and looked around. "You said there was a small shelter nearby?"

Jason nodded. It was where the stream came out. He followed the stream, climbing a little while, and in the distance, the darkened shape of the mouth of the stream greeted him.

He approached carefully, listening for anything strange, wondering if perhaps Henry was right. Maybe there was some creature there. When he had been here last, he had thought he'd heard something, but he hadn't seen anything. In this part of the world, the only time he wasn't able to see a person with his dragon sight was when they were wearing dragonskin, and no creatures wore dragonskin—other than dragons.

Surprisingly, the dragons hadn't been concealed from his dragon sight. That seemed strange. Given everything else, he was expecting he should have had a harder time seeing them.

"It's just up here."

As they approached the mouth of the small cave, he felt something. Jason turned slowly, looking at Henry before turning his attention down below.

It was heat. He was certain of it.

"We need to work quickly," Henry said.

"They aren't that far away," Jason said.

"Like I said, quickly."

He locked eyes with Henry, and a flutter of fear worked through him. The Dragon Souls were coming.

They weren't far from the village. From here, it was only about two hours' climb, close enough that the Dragon Souls could harm his people. The stream itself was difficult enough to reach, but it was only difficult because it wasn't always easy to find, which was why his father had always valued it. Jason approached the cave and ducked down, staying close to the edge. A small shelf allowed him to climb inside, and he glanced at the others.

"Stay close to the wall," he said to William.

"What happens if I don't?"

"Then you fall in. You don't want to get wet out here."

William pressed himself against the wall of the cave.

"How long do we have to go like this?"

"Not long," Jason said.

The cave opened up, and he backed onto a wider shelf and peered around. He didn't see anything with his dragon sight that would suggest there would be anything here.

"That is a unique challenge," William said. "Have you ever fallen in?"

Jason shook his head. "My father always warned me that if I fell in, I probably wouldn't make it back to the village to warm up."

"Why risk it, then?" he asked as Henry and Sarah joined them.

"Because of this." He motioned overhead. In the fading light, there was a crystalline appearance to the top of the cave. It glittered, reflecting the light.

"I don't see anything," William said.

"Try this," Sarah said.

Light began to glow in her hand, and it reflected off the ceiling of the cave.

Any question that she had Dragon Soul ability was removed. There was no other way she would be able to do that.

The light reflected overhead, and Jason swept his gaze across it.

"What's in here?" William asked.

"Occasionally, we will find animals. Sometimes larger ones." He motioned to his jacket. "It's where we found the bear that made my coat."

"You caught that?"

"We didn't so much catch it as we hunted it. The meat served us for several months."

"Is that all you worry about?"

"We focus on survival in the mountains." He looked around the inside of the cave. It was the first time he'd been here when there was so much light. Most the time when he was here, there was nothing to see. With the dragon pearl glowing in Sarah's hand, he was able to make out the contours in the cave roof far better than he could otherwise. Some were made by icicles, but not all of it. Others were some sort of glittering stone.

"Do you know how much those would be worth?" William asked.

"Why?"

"They're all gems."

"Not to us."

William chuckled. "Maybe not to you, but to anyone else who doesn't live in such a terrible place."

Jason forced a smile. "It wasn't always terrible." It had been recently, but before his father had died, Jason had enjoyed living here. His father had always taught him well, showing him how to hunt, to find tracks in fresh snow, to survive. And before his father was lost, the village had been a different place. It hadn't been nearly as cold to them.

So much had changed since he was gone.

He turned his attention to the inside of the cave. "This is the only place I could imagine a dragon having been."

"There's no sign of a dragon." Sarah wandered around, scanning the ground, and looked up at him. "There are no scraps. No bones. No droppings."

"Droppings?" William asked.

"Even dragons have to relieve themselves," she said.

"Dragons poop?"

Jason grunted. They had burned quite a bit of dung in the village. What would dragon dung have done? He could imagine drying it and trying to find some way to burn it, and could imagine it would give off more heat than other kinds of dung.

"Like I said, even dragons have to void. But there's no sign of anything here."

"Over here," Henry said.

Jason followed him, looking, and as he did, he noticed a strange scraping along the stone.

"What is that?" William asked.

"Claws," Jason said. He traced his fingers through the marks. They were too large for a bear.

"Dragon claws," Henry said.

The other man stood, straightening, looking around the inside of the cave. Jason followed the direction of his gaze, looking for any other signs of markings like that.

There had been quite a few animals here. In the time he'd hunted with his father, they'd found anything from the bear to other smaller animals, creatures that would come in here for shelter from the weather. This was oftentimes the demarcation point where he would find other animals. Occasionally he would come across rabbits closer to the village, but most of the time, anything he encountered was farther downslope.

"If the dragon egg was placed here, there would be a shell," Sarah said.

"Unless it wasn't placed here," Jason said.

She met his eyes.

"I don't know. Maybe the dragon egg was somewhere else and the dragon came here."

"I don't see any signs of the shell," Henry said.

Jason looked at the ground, thinking about the last time he'd been inside the cave.

It had been a while. Long enough that he wouldn't be surprised there could be some creature here that he'd overlooked. Most of the time, he searched for tracks outside the cave, and if there were none, he didn't bother venturing inside. The danger of falling into the stream was too great.

It was easier to watch, to wait and see if there was any sign that something had come in here, but in this case, he hadn't seen anything for months and months.

"How long do you think the egg would have been here?"

"It can take as much as a year for an egg to gestate," Sarah said.

"A year?"

She nodded, looking up at him. "The dragons will lay an egg once every ten years or so."

"How is it that there are so many of them?"

"There should be more," Henry said. "It's because of the Dragon Souls. They destroy those they can't control."

"That's why there are dragonskins?"

"That and people like in your village," Henry said.

"My village suffered under dragon attacks."

"As you say."

Jason ignored him, continuing to scan the inside of the cave. Sarah stayed close to him, holding out the glowing dragon pearl, and it gave him an opportunity to look at the ground, but he didn't see anything.

"If we don't find something soon, we're going to have to leave the cave," he said.

The Dragon Souls would be getting close, and he didn't want to get caught in here when they appeared. Henry might be able to withstand an attack, and Sarah might be able to help, but how many Dragon Souls would Therin bring with him?

If it involved a dragon, he might bring quite a few.

"Keep looking." Sarah leaned down, holding the dragon pearl above the surface of the ground. She swept it in a circle, and as she spun, Jason followed her, not saying anything.

"I'm not..."

Something caught his eye.

When Sarah swept the dragon pearl in one direction, it seemed almost more reflective than other parts of the cave.

He pointed, and she followed him, crouching down on the ground.

She ran her fingers across the surface of the cave floor.

"I don't know. It could be an egg, but I'm not sure what an egg would look like in this place. The landscape will influence it. Changing it."

Jason had no idea what an egg would look like in this place, either. For that matter, he had no idea what a dragon egg would look like in general. The only thing he knew was there wasn't anything here that didn't fit with what he expected.

He searched the floor of the cave, heading over to the stream, and paused to take a drink. The water had the familiar mineral taste to it, the same as he remembered when Henry had brought him the water skin. As he leaned over the stream, taking a small sip, he stared into the water.

"Sarah?"

She swept the glowing light closer to him. As she did,

he saw what he thought he'd noticed in the bottom of the stream more clearly.

"Do you see anything here?"

She crouched down next to him, and he was aware of her warmth, aware of the way she smelled, and of her pressing up against him.

"There's something here," she said.

Jason glanced up at her, meeting her crystal blue eyes. "That's not all that helpful."

There was one thing they could do, and he decided to try.

It involved submerging part of him in the stream. Knowing what he did about water in this kind of place, the way it could freeze, he hesitated, but at the same time, he had two people with him who had control over the dragon pearls, and who might have some way of helping him if it were to come down to it.

He focused on what he saw. It was an irregularity in the stream. It was almost the way the water seemed to flow, as if it were disrupted. He couldn't tell if there was something in the bottom of the stream or whether it was simply reflections from the top of the cave.

Jason pulled up the sleeve of his jacket and dipped his hand in the water.

It was icy cold, and everything within him hurt imme-diately, but he swept his hand from side to side. At first, he didn't find anything, but he felt something on the bottom of the stream, so he grabbed it, pulling it free.

Sarah was there, the dragon pearl resting next to her,

heat radiating off it. He was appreciative of that and worried what would have happened if she hadn't brought that heat to him. Warmth rolled over his hand, his arm.

William crouched next to them. "What is it?"

Jason glanced up. "I don't know. I can't really tell what this is."

It was a curved fragment of what appeared to be rock, and it had a crystalline appearance, almost as if it had fragmented off the ceiling of the cave. Then again, as Jason studied it, it didn't look anything quite like the cave. It was different.

Sarah held the dragon pearl down toward it, and the fragment began to glow.

Her breath caught.

"It's the egg," she said.

"How certain are you?"

"There's no other way that this would do this. It has to be the egg."

Jason lifted the fragment of the egg up, holding it to the light, twisting it from side to side. As he did, he wasn't sure if he was able to detect anything else about it.

"Where would the rest be?"

"I don't know. I thought I saw part of it over there, but..." She leaned over the water, and this time, Sarah dipped her hand in. She cried out, her eyes widening, and she swept her hand around before pulling it back out and resting it near the dragon pearl. "How did you do that?"

"Do what?"

"Tolerate the stream?"

"I have some experience with cold," he said with a hint of a smile.

"It can't be that bad," William said. He stuffed his hand into the water, and as he did, he shouted.

"Quiet," Henry said.

"Gods! That *is* cold." He glanced over at Jason. "And you drank it?"

"It's not that bad," he said.

"I didn't find anything more," Sarah said.

"Is there any reason you need to find more?" Jason asked.

"The more pieces of the shell we find, the easier it will be for us to track the dragon."

Jason crawled along the stream, looking into the water, searching for anything that might be unusual. He crawled along the side but didn't come up with anything. The far side of the stream was a narrower ledge, but it would allow him an easier search. Jason got to his feet and jumped. He teetered on the edge for a moment before catching himself, and then dropped down to his knees, crawling along that side of the stream.

When he found something, he dipped his hand in, pulling it out.

This time, he had found a larger section. As before, it was curved and had a crystalline appearance. It reminded him of the ceiling, and he held it up, keeping it in place as he looked upward.

"They look quite a bit alike," he said.

"I—"

Sarah didn't have a chance to finish. An explosion of heat thundered near them.

Jason staggered and nearly fell into the stream, but managed to push himself back against the wall of the cave, anchoring his heels, keeping himself out of the water. Even though Sarah and Henry both had dragon pearls, he wasn't sure they would be able to dry him out quickly enough.

"What was that?" William asked.

"The Dragon Souls," Sarah whispered.

"Dragon Souls are here?"

"They are, and…" She cocked her head to the side. She took a deep breath, holding the section of the dragon egg up, and the dragon pearl began to glow. "I think… I think the dragon is, too."

22

H enry waited at the mouth of the cave, looking outward. Heat radiated from him and he gripped the dragon pearl, holding on to it tightly, staring into the distance. Snow swirled around the entrance of the cave, nothing but a white blanket of emptiness. The cold billowed into the cave, parting around Henry, but Jason knew it would continue to creep forward, painfully slipping into the cavern.

"I don't see anything out there," Sarah said as she approached Henry.

The other man hovered on the lip of rock that led into the cave. He glanced over his shoulder at Sarah before shaking his head. "I don't see anything, either, but in a landscape like this, I'm not sure I would be able to see anything at all." He turned his attention back out to the swirling snow, focusing outward, and the heat radiating off him continued to build.

"What are you trying to do?" William asked.

"He's probably trying to see beyond the entrance to the cave," Sarah said.

"Will his magic allow that?"

"It's not his magic," she said.

"He has that pearl. How can it be anything else?"

"The magic, as you call it, is borrowed power from the dragon."

Two types of magic...

Why did those thoughts keep coming back to him? Maybe because he didn't know *how* his father would have known about two types of magic. What reason would he have for knowing anything about magic in the first place?

He'd never left the mountain. He'd hunted outside of the village, and had travelled as far as Varmin, but not below that as far as Jason knew.

"That's what Therin said, too," Jason said.

She cocked an eyebrow at him, watching him. "How much did you talk to Therin?"

"I traveled with him for an evening." It seemed like it had been longer, but then it also seemed like it had happened long ago rather than just days earlier.

"Most who spend any time with Therin end up dead," Sarah said.

"I guess I'm lucky, then."

"You *are* lucky. Therin is..." She shook her head and her face clouded. "Awful, I suppose. He would do anything to reach Dragon Haven, and anything to destroy the dragons."

"Why does he think he can find dragons here?" Jason asked.

"There have been theories that dragons take on the traits of where they're reared."

"Rumors," Henry muttered.

"Theories," Sarah said, shooting a look at him. "We don't know if Therin believes those theories, but if anyone would, it would be him."

"But the dragons I've seen are all similar," Jason said.

"That's why they're rumors," Henry said.

Sarah shot him another look. "The dragons hatch their own. We don't know what would happen if a dragon egg were separated from other dragons—and somehow coaxed to hatch."

Henry glanced up at the ceiling of the cave. "We know they shouldn't be able to hatch."

"This would say otherwise," Sarah said.

"Fine. Either way, we won't be able to stay here for long," Henry said.

"We just need to keep away from them," Sarah said.

"If they discover this cavern, they'll find the shell."

"Why does the shell matter?" Jason asked.

"The shell allows them to track the dragon. So with that, they would be able to follow it, and if they find it, then…"

Henry didn't need to finish. Jason thought he understood. If they found the dragon, and if it did have an affinity for these lands and for the snow, then his people wouldn't be safe anymore.

"Then we need to track it."

"In that?" Henry asked, looking out toward the swirling snow that created a whiteout. Henry pulled his cloak more tightly around his shoulders.

Jason stared past him. "I've seen worse."

The other man grunted. "I'm not sure that—"

Another burst of power exploded from outside. Snow suddenly swirled, kicked up by the force of the blast. Some came down the entrance to the cave, clinging to Jason's face.

Henry leaned forward, sniffing at the air. "Let's move," he said.

William pushed up against Jason and they made their way along the edge of the stream. As Jason reached the mouth of the cave, William cried out.

He turned but wasn't fast enough; William plunged into the water.

He splashed and kicked and Jason grabbed him, helping pull him free.

William was soaked.

He glanced at the others. "He can't go out there like that," Jason said.

"I'm not sure there's much of an option," Henry said.

"You have the dragon pearl. Use it to help dry him."

Henry glanced down toward his hands. "That wouldn't work quickly enough."

"We can't bring him out there soaked. With the wind being what it is, and the snow like that, he will freeze to death in minutes."

Henry gritted his teeth.

"Move," he said to Jason.

Jason squeezed past and the other man grabbed William, pulling him back into the cave, and he pressed his hands up against William's chest. Heat began to build. It seemed almost as if William were glowing. The other man gasped and steam rose, faster and faster, swirling in the air, making it difficult for Jason to see anything else.

When it was done, William let out a shaky breath. "That was interesting."

"Can we go now?" Henry asked.

"I found something," William said.

"What did you find?"

"This," William said.

He opened his hand, and it looked to Jason like nothing more than an ice ball, but Henry leaned close to it, blocking it, holding it for a moment. He tipped it up to the light, such as it was.

Jason had seen something like it before. He remembered finding a similar stone, one that had seemed impossibly cold. This could be its twin.

"Do you know what this is?"

"No. That's why I grabbed it."

"Where was it?"

"I saw it when I fell into the stream."

"You *saw* it?" Jason asked.

"Well, when I was trying to get out, it sort of flashed in front of me."

"I think it's a dragon pearl," Henry said.

Sarah leaned toward it, frowning as she reached for it. "It looks nothing like the dragon pearls we know in Dragon Haven."

"That, I think, is the point."

"We need to study it."

Henry's eyes began to widen. "I can't hold on to it for long."

"Why?"

"It's too cold."

Jason held his hand out. "Let me take it. I can deal with cold."

"This is not just cold. It's *cold*."

Jason held his hand up, waiting, and as heat continued to build, rising around them, he didn't think they had much time before the Dragon Souls reached them. "Let me take it. We can study it when we figure this out."

Henry breathed out a frustrated sigh and handed the dragon pearl to Jason. He glanced at it, noticing how smooth it was and the way it seemed to have flickers of color in it. It surprised him that William would have been able to find it at the bottom of the stream. Something like this would look like nothing more than a rock. It would be easy enough to lose it out here. In fact, he *had* lost one out here. Maybe even this one.

He stuffed it into his pocket. It was cold, but it wasn't any colder than so many other things he'd experienced living out here.

"How did you find it?" Jason asked.

"I told you I was lucky," William said, grinning.

Another surge of heat came and Henry grabbed them, dragging them away from the stream. He turned to Sarah. "We need to track the dragon. Can you do it?"

"I think so. I'm going to try to focus on heat and use that to connect to the dragon pearl. It *should* work, but..."

"But what?"

"I've never tracked another kind of dragon before, so I don't know if it will."

The remnants of the shell glowed, casting a shimmery light.

If the Dragon Souls got too close, that shimmery light was going to be visible, and it would reveal their presence to the others. Sarah continued to hold on to the pearl and the shell, and closed her eyes.

"There's a tracing of power. I think I can follow it, but it's faint."

"Which way?"

"That way." She pointed. It seemed to Jason that she indicated upslope, and they started moving.

Every so often, they would pause and she would connect to the dragon pearl again and the egg would begin to shimmer, colors flickering off it, and then it would die back down, leaving nothing more than a faint remnant of light. Each time she did, she again pointed up the slope.

They seemed to be heading directly up the mountain-side. If that were the case, and if they were heading toward the village, he worried it meant that the dragon had gone that way.

The wind picked up, painful as it whipped past them, tearing at his clothing. He pulled his hood up, using it to keep the wind from battering his face. He glanced over at William as he hunched forward, as if trying to mask himself from the wind.

How long would he be able to hold out? It was possible that William still was damp underneath his clothes, and if so, then he wouldn't last nearly as long as the rest of them. Would the dragon respond if Henry needed to call it? If not, they would be stranded here, trapped by the Dragon Souls.

Jason didn't know if he'd be able to make it up the side of the mountain anyway. This was the kind of weather in which he would never have traveled. This was dangerous, with the snow making it difficult to know where he was going and the treacherous wind threatening to toss him backward. It was the kind of snow and wind that killed people.

Sarah stopped again, and once again the crystal began to glow.

"I think it's—"

A sense of heat exploded.

It was near. Far too close to them, so that he worried the Dragon Souls had already reached them.

Henry glanced at her. "Keep going. We can't rest."

"What about you?"

"I'm going to see if I can delay them."

"Delay?"

"Don't worry about me."

Jason glanced from Sarah to Henry. "I'm going with you," he said.

"There's nothing you can do."

"I know these lands better than you do."

"I thought you said there was no knowing these lands."

"It's not so much knowing the land as it is knowing how to navigate in the cold and the snow."

"Do I look soft to you?"

"You look like a man who was a Dragon Soul. You look like a man who might have familiarity with extreme weather, but this isn't your place. It's mine."

Henry held his gaze before nodding slightly and turning to Sarah. "Keep tracking the dragon. If you reach a village, wait on the outskirts."

The egg glowed again, the light soft and flickering in the cold. Sarah and William continued upward. Henry and Jason waited, watching as they disappeared.

"What do you propose?" Henry asked him.

Jason frowned. "Do you think that dragon pearl of yours could create an avalanche?"

"An avalanche?" Henry arched a brow at him, holding out the pearl, and heat radiated from it. It was pleasant, but all it did was melt some of the snow that whipped down, landing in Henry's palm. "I'm not sure I have enough control to create an avalanche."

"All you need to do is disrupt the snow. Do that, and we might be able to send the Dragon Souls further downslope."

"All that does is delay them. We need to do more than just delay."

Jason understood. If they continued to push back the Dragon Souls, they would run into the same issue again and again, and eventually, the Dragon Souls would be successful.

Somehow, they had to stop them. They had to prevent Therin from reaching them, and they had to either convince them that there was no dragon or…

"We have to kill it," he said.

"We have to *what?*"

"We have to make it look like the dragon was killed."

"I don't like that idea."

"It doesn't matter if you like it or not. All that matters is that Therin believes it."

"I'm not sure this will work," Henry said.

"Why, because we haven't found the dragon yet?"

"That, and the entire idea is contingent on the fact that we can convince Therin of something that isn't true. He's incredibly smart, and if he thinks he succeeded in bringing about an ice dragon, he's going to try again."

Jason pressed his lips together against the wind and looked around. The light was fading and soon it would be completely dark. It would be difficult for them to keep moving and have any hope of finding anything or anyone. "We have to try."

Henry scratched his chin before nodding. He held the dragon pearl up, and as he did, the sense of heat continued to build from it, radiating away, and something about it changed. The color began to shift, pulsating slightly, and Henry pointed.

"What did you do?"

"I asked the dragon pearl to help guide us to the others."

"The others?"

"The Dragon Souls will have dragon pearls with them. Using it like this, I can track the others."

"And they could track you."

"They could if they thought I had a dragon pearl."

An explosion thundered near them, and Henry was knocked off his feet.

Jason reached for him, but the snow began to shift under his boots. He scrambled, trying to get up, but wasn't fast enough. The snow cascaded down the side of the mountain, flowing forward. He searched for Henry, but there was no sign of the man.

Here they had wanted to be the ones to cause an avalanche. The Dragon Souls had beaten them to it.

Jason dug his heels in, trying to stop his descent. If he didn't control it, he would end up falling down the side of the mountain. The farther he went, the more the snow pulled at him. He grabbed at it, trying to lock himself in place.

If only there was some way to freeze himself.

He reached around, trying to shift his hands, and grabbed on to something.

He stopped moving.

It took a moment to realize that it was a hunk of ice.

Jason pulled himself forward, keeping himself from sliding, and looked around.

How far had he fallen?

He didn't think he'd slipped all that far, certainly not so far that he wouldn't be able to reach Henry, but now he was out here alone.

There was nothing but darkness around him. With the wind and the snow and the cold, he wasn't sure if he'd be able to find anything.

Heat exploded nearby. Was that the Dragon Souls, or was it Henry?

Jason didn't know, and because he didn't know, he hesitated to go after it.

Instead, he got to his feet and started climbing.

His boots sunk in with each step, the same as they had before, and he wished he had some way of floating above the snow as the Dragon Souls did.

Even if he didn't have some way of gliding above the snow, it would be easier if he could solidify the surface so it didn't allow him to sink. The more he went, the harder it was to keep his footing.

Jason continued to climb, thinking about his people. He thought about William, Sarah, and even Henry. All of them needed this to end. More than that, he needed to figure out what was going to take place so that he could keep the people of his village safe.

There was another sense of heat, and Jason looked into the night but didn't see anything. He scanned, searching for movement, but in the darkness it was difficult to make anything out. His dragon sight wasn't helpful at all.

That, most of all, troubled him. If they all wore dragonskin, then he wouldn't be able to see them.

But they weren't wearing dragonskin. Sarah and William weren't wearing dragonskin. If nothing else, he should be able to see them if he were able to get closer to them. Henry was going to be harder to spot.

Jason looked down, trying to catch himself, and when he glanced back up, a figure loomed in front of him.

He dropped in the snow, holding himself down.

The figure continued to loom closer.

There was no sense of heat.

He didn't see anything with his dragon sight.

That meant it was one of the Dragon Souls—or Henry.

Then again, if it were Henry, wouldn't he say something?

Jason had a sense that he would be able to find him, but it depended upon Henry knowing he was there.

He didn't want to move. He feared doing anything other than what he was already doing, and that was hiding, lying here on the snow, ready for the possibility that he would need to try and fight.

He moved one hand, getting it closer to his waist where his knife hid under his jacket, and as he did, he felt the strange icy dragon pearl.

His fingers brushed along the surface, and cold burst through him.

In the time he had carried it, there had been no sense

of cold, and it was strange it would suddenly feel cold now. Then again, maybe it was because he was lying in the snow, not moving, not exerting any energy. He was at the mercy of the wind and the snow and the environment. Everything around him was a potential threat.

He moved his hand past it, but the sense of the figure nearby loomed even closer.

Jason tensed.

As he tried to reach for his knife, something grabbed him, pulling him to his feet.

"Imagine finding you here."

Jason turned his head and came face-to-face with Therin.

23

His breath quickened and a cold sweat worked over him. It was dangerous to sweat that way out in this environment, and he tried to control his breathing, to steady his beating heart. He wanted nothing more than to get away from Therin, but the other man held him in the air easily.

Control your emotions during the hunt. You can. The creatures you hunt can't.

As he'd told Henry, this was *his* home. Not Therin's.

He had the advantage. He had to use it.

"You would have been useful," Therin said. "And yet, you chose to side with the others. It's a mistake, but unfortunately, it's one you won't have an opportunity to correct."

"You won't find the dragon."

Therin released him, tossing him back. He reached into his pocket and pulled out something. It didn't take long for Jason to realize that he held a dragon pearl in both hands. "And if you think you protect a dragon, you will fail."

"I won't fail in these lands."

Therin studied him. "Aren't you the one who said your father died because of the dragons?"

"You tried to tell me the dragons weren't responsible. I seem to remember you telling me the one who controlled them was responsible. The Dragon Souls were responsible."

"If a dragon killed your father, it's likely he got in the way."

"The dragons shouldn't have even been here," Jason said. "They don't tolerate the cold."

"Is that what Henry told you?" Jason nodded. "He's right, at least somewhat. The dragons don't particularly care for the cold, though they can tolerate it for a little while. If the dragons were here, it was likely they were here on a mission for... me."

Jason stared at Therin for a moment. Everything began to tumble together.

"It's your fault," he said.

"My fault for what?"

"My father."

Therin frowned at him. "I'm afraid you give me far too much credit. Not that I would deny getting rid of some villager if it were necessary, but—"

"You were trying to place eggs. He must've come

across you." Or Tessa, but Jason left her out of it for now. Would Therin reveal her role?

Therin watched him. "When did he die?"

"Over a year ago," he said.

Therin stared at him. "Is that right?" He cocked his head to the side and scratched his chin as if he were trying to think. "I don't really recall. All I know is that these lands will one day house dragons. The kingdom and all of Lorach will be expanded. And eventually the dragons Dragon Haven tries to hide from us will no longer remain hidden. The rebellion will finally fail."

"You won't ever find Dragon Haven."

Therin paused, studying him. A sense of power surrounded Jason, holding him in place. "You've seen it."

Had he made a mistake? Was there some way Therin would be able to force him to share what he knew? He could imagine the other man knew of torments that would compel him to speak. If anyone would have some way of doing so, it would be the Dragon Souls, wouldn't it?

Jason licked his lips and tried to back away but Therin approached, stepping closer to him, a dark grin on his face.

"I think you might be even more useful than I'd realized. And here I thought you would only be able to guide me to an ice dragon, but perhaps you can guide me to much more than that."

"I'm not going to guide you to anything."

"And you won't have much of a choice. If you refuse, everyone in that village you care so much for is going to be incinerated." He grinned at him. "Do you think the dragons fear your ballistae? They have thicker hides than any other creature, and a simple ballista will pose no threat to them."

Armor. That was what Henry had said.

The ballistae might not be of any use. The village might still be in danger from dragons. Unless he could do something to stop Therin.

"First you're going to guide me to this dragon, and then you're going to take me to Dragon Haven. Afterward, if you've served well, you can come with me to Lorach. Perhaps I will allow you to serve me."

"I'm not going to serve anyone."

"I'm afraid you're going to have to serve someone."

Jason looked around, but there was nothing and no one coming to help. Therin grinned.

"I don't know how to find the dragon."

"Perhaps not. But you *have* seen it."

"Why do you believe that?"

"Because of what you told me."

"I didn't tell you about anything."

"Ah, but you did. I heard you talking in the village. And then during our travels. You saw something. Now you just have to tell me where it was."

Jason swallowed. "Do you think it's that easy? In this place, it's impossible to find one location versus another. The only place that has any sort of permanence is—"

Jason cut himself off, realizing he'd already said too much.

"Is what?" Therin asked.

"It's nothing."

"It's something. You may not want to tell me, but you will. Oh, you will."

Therin grabbed him and lifted him to his feet.

Jason tried to fight, but the other man was strong, and Jason had to wonder if he was somehow powered by the dragon pearl, its magic giving him increased strength. As he was forced forward, he noticed heat washing away from him. Jason tried to fight, but he had no way of getting free.

"Where is this place?" Therin asked.

What harm was there in sharing the stream? It wasn't as if he was the only one to know where it was, and if he didn't reveal it to Therin, someone would.

Besides, there was nothing there that Therin would be able to find. If everything went as they intended, Sarah and William would have tracked the dragon and would have already reached it, which meant the dragon would be safe.

Why was he even concerned about that?

It wasn't that he cared about the dragon, but he wanted to do anything in his power to prevent Therin from succeeding. If that meant keeping the dragon from him, then that was his goal.

"There's a stream."

"A stream?"

324 | D.K. HOLMBERG

"I know it sounds impossible up here, but it flows fast enough that it doesn't freeze."

Therin shoved him. "Show me."

Jason looked around. There had to be other Dragon Souls, but where were they? Then again, where was Henry?

It was possible Henry was following the other Dragon Souls.

All Jason had to do was create a distraction. Out here in the bleak landscape, with the snow swirling around him, the wind whipping, there should be some way to find a chance to break free.

When disoriented, keep your wits about you. You can lose your way, but don't lose your mind.

Therin didn't know the land as well as he did.

Jason understood how to move in the snow and the cold.

The only advantage Therin had was that his connection to the dragon pearl somehow allowed him to float above the snow.

First, he needed to get closer to the stream.

As they walked, Jason thought he heard the distant sound of the burbling stream, but wasn't sure.

"How much farther is it?" Therin asked.

"It's hard to follow. Out here, distances are difficult. You've been out here long enough that you have to know that."

Therin wrinkled his nose. "I might've been out here, but I've never liked it."

The other man was a step away from him. It was his opportunity.

He kicked, separating from Therin. "It doesn't like you, either."

Jason dropped to his backside. He lifted his feet, and he slid.

It was icier than usual. He was able to glide, flowing down the snow, and as he went, he glanced back and felt a hint of heat radiating from Therin, but the other man was behind him.

The sound of the stream came upon him too fast, and he realized almost too late that he needed to slow himself.

Jason dug his feet in, jamming his heels down to the ground, and skittered to a stop.

It was almost too late. The water burbled, splashing up toward his boots, and he held his breath. A little farther, and he would've crashed into the water.

He scrambled back and looked behind him, but didn't see anything. There was a sense of heat continuing to build. The longer he was here and the more he detected that heat, the more likely Therin would find him. He didn't think he'd be able to conceal himself from the other man for too long.

It meant he was going to have to try something else.

The only thing he could think of was returning to the cave. At least within the cave, there was the hope that the structure would somehow shield him from the other man. He hurried along the edge of the stream, following the flowing water. The distant sight of the darkened cave entrance called to him.

He reached the entrance to the cave.

Once he was there, he hugged the lip of stone, barely able to see it in the darkness, and hurried along it. At one point, his foot slipped. He nearly tumbled into the stream before catching himself and throwing himself back against the wall. He paused, breathing heavily, waiting for a moment before continuing deeper into the cave.

As he remained there, he crouched down, wrapping his arms and legs around himself. A moment passed, and then another, and another.

There was no sign of the Dragon Souls at the entrance to the cave. With each passing moment, he allowed himself to think he was going to be able to survive this.

While waiting, he reached into his pocket and pulled out the icy dragon pearl. In the darkness of the cave, he couldn't really make out anything. He pulled his glove off, and he held the dragon pearl in one hand. It was strange and smooth, and it was so similar to the one he'd found the night he'd encountered the Dragon Souls.

It seemed impossible to believe he'd found another dragon pearl, but what else could it have been?

As he held on to it, he couldn't shake the sense that there was a certain hint of power within it. It was different than the other dragon pearl. That one radiated heat and gave a suggestion of something more. This was cold, but not unpleasantly so.

As Jason squeezed the dragon pearl, he breathed out.

All of this, and now he had to believe Therin was the one responsible for his father's death. For so long, Jason had blamed the dragons. While the dragon might've been responsible, it was because of Therin and his plan, his attempt to place dragon eggs in places like this so he could have new types of dragons.

And Therin wasn't even sure that it was him, but Jason felt convinced. It was the only thing that really fit. What would his father have thought about all of this?

More than anything, that question drove him. Jason knew his father was an open-minded man, and though he loved the village, and he loved their life, however simple it might be, he had also understood there was a greater world out there that they hadn't explored.

Jason breathed out as he held the dragon pearl.

"I wish you were here, Father."

Would his father have wanted to see the dragons? Would he have feared them?

The memories of conversations Jason had with his father stayed with him, making him wonder if perhaps he had known about the Dragon Souls. About the dragons and dragon pearls. About magic.

A steady rumbling built.

Jason looked up, toward the end of the cave. Was one of the Dragon Souls here? He wasn't strong enough to overpower Therin, and he certainly didn't have a connection to magic that would be of any use in stopping him.

If it were one of the other Dragon Souls, he doubted he would have any way of stopping them, either. His best bet was avoiding them altogether. Maybe he could hide in the back of the cave, keeping himself concealed so they wouldn't even know he was here.

Jason pressed himself against the wall of the cave, remaining hidden, squeezing the dragon pearl in his hand. Maybe it was nothing more than a stone, but if it was a dragon pearl, he...

The rumbling came again.

This time, Jason realized it wasn't coming from outside the cave, but inside.

Where was it?

He looked around and focused on what he could see, but there wasn't anything. The inside of the cave was completely darkened, making it difficult to make anything out. Without Sarah and her dragon pearl to give illumination, there was no way to see anything in detail.

He hesitated, squeezing the dragon pearl as he looked around, wishing he could draw power out from it.

A surge of cold worked through him.

It wasn't the first time he'd detected cold from the dragon pearl, but he was almost tempted to drop it, but this time that cold sent a surge through him, almost reverberating within him.

He remembered that from when he had held the other dragon pearl the first time.

It was a strange sensation. As he squeezed it, he felt it echoing within him.

Could he be connecting to that power?

Therin had told him he would be able to do so, and

even though he might've been lying, Henry had said the best lies had a sprinkle of truth within them.

Why would Therin have lied about that? He would've wanted to tell the truth if only to gain Jason's trust. What better way to gain his trust than by showing him a connection to a greater power?

Jason squeezed the dragon pearl, feeling that cold as it surged through him, reverberating.

That was familiar to him.

When he had held the warm dragon pearl, there had been a sense of power, but none of it had been familiar to him, not the way this was.

This reminded him of everything he'd known his entire life. The longer he held on to the dragon pearl, the more he thought he could use it.

Connect to the dragon pearl.

Wasn't that what Therin and Henry had said?

What he had to do was figure out some way of using it, and though he wasn't sure if he did have any way, he could feel that cold.

Heat built.

He was no longer alone here.

Jason didn't know if he'd be able to withstand a Dragon Soul, but if he could somehow connect to this dragon pearl, it might help him overcome whatever attack was about to occur. He continued to squeeze, holding on to the dragon pearl, using his connection to it, and thought about how he might be able to draw that power. There didn't seem to be anything he could use, and yet there had to be something.

Heat emanated from the end of the cave.

A Dragon Soul. He was certain of that.

How did he use this?

That was the key, even more than trying to conceal the dragon. He thought he needed to find some way of using the dragon pearl.

A soft rumbling came from near him again and Jason jerked his head around, but didn't see anything near him.

What was that sound?

When they had been here before, there hadn't been any creatures here. Had he interrupted a bear crawling into the cave for safety?

It would've been too dark and too windy to have made out any footprints coming into the cave, and yet, on a night like tonight, this would be a perfect place for a bear to have hunkered down, using the cave for protection from the wind and the snow.

Jason pressed his back against the wall, continuing to squeeze the dragon pearl, but what he needed was some way to see something. If only the dragon pearl would begin to glow the same way that Sarah's did.

His hand started to glow with a pale white light.

Jason's eyes widened.

That white light reflected off the crystals and illuminated a form at the end of the cave. His breath caught.

Was it Therin?

He held his hand out and tried to push out power from the pearl.

The strange white light exploded from his hand, and it shot down the length of the cave and slammed into the man. He teetered for a moment before splashing into the stream. He continued to kick, splashing, as the stream pulled him farther and farther down.

Jason shivered, unable to look away.

If it was a Dragon Soul, he might have some way of using his dragon pearl to escape, but at least he wouldn't be coming after Jason again so quickly.

He turned, using the pearl to illuminate everything inside the cave, and found nothing. Still, the sense of the rumbling continued.

Where was it coming from?

There was one place he hadn't looked, and Jason turned his attention down to the stream.

A shape moved on the bottom of the stream. From where he stood, it appeared translucent. Shimmering in the water, reflecting in a way that looked like thousands of crystals along the surface.

Jason backed away, and yet, as he did, the shape began to undulate and then broke free of the water.

A dragon.

24

The dragon was unlike any that he had seen. All of the others had spikes along their back, and they had either glowing orange or red eyes. Heat radiated from them and dark wings spread out from their bodies.

This creature was nothing like that.

The general shape was the same. There were spikes along its back, but it had flat silver eyes and scales of icy white. When it spread its wings outward, it made a noise like icicles crackling. The dragon was long and slender, its body practically translucent.

The dragon took a step toward him and ice shook free from its back.

It was like shards of needles that radiated all around, and it matched the crystals reflected off the ceiling of the cave.

Jason flicked his gaze upward.

That couldn't be coincidental, could it?

He turned his attention back to the dragon, afraid to do anything but look at the creature.

He held on to the dragon pearl, squeezing it. The dragon rumbled, watching him with those strange silver eyes. They were eyes so much like his own, and yet, the dragon's were matching. There was power in those eyes, and there was power in the way the dragon approached him, looking at him, and Jason couldn't help but hold the dragon's gaze.

"I'm Jason," he said.

The way the dragon was looking at him suggested that somehow it was aware of him. The dragons in Dragon Haven had spoken, so why wouldn't this one?

The creature was not nearly as large as the ones he'd seen in Dragon Haven. Was that because it was young, or was it because it was different?

The dragon rumbled again and Jason backed up, slamming his back into the wall of the cave. He couldn't go any farther, and he almost dropped the dragon pearl, but if he were to do that, he worried that the glow from it would extinguish and he wouldn't have any way of seeing the dragon. He thought he needed to be able to watch the dragon, that he needed to know that it was coming, and he needed to be able to react.

Then again, what would he be able to do?

It wasn't as if he had some way of fighting the creature.

"I don't want to hurt you," he said.

The dragon rumbled again, and it shook something within him.

Some part of him reverberated, echoing, and it reminded him of what he felt when he held the dragon pearl.

Jason looked down at it, frowning. That couldn't be a coincidence. There had to be something meaningful in the way the dragon pearl called to him, the power he felt within it, and it was similar to the way the dragon tried to communicate with him.

And it *was* an attempt to communicate.

More than anything, Jason was certain of that. He continued to hold on to the dragon pearl, focusing on it, feeling its power. The longer he held it, the more certain he was that there was great power within it.

What was he going to do?

The better question was, what was the dragon going to do?

There wasn't much time before Therin arrived. He didn't think it had been Therin at the entrance to the cave. He was far too savvy to have allowed Jason to use some uncontrolled power to throw him into the water. No. That was more likely to be just a regular Dragon Soul.

If there was any such thing as a regular Dragon Soul.

He looked up, and the dragon rumbled at him again.

"I don't understand," he said. He squeezed the dragon pearl, wishing there was some way to better comprehend the dragon. As he did, cold jolted through him again, and some part of him answered, a reverberation that rang through him.

The dragon rumbled. "Why are you here?"

Jason trembled.

He'd heard it.

That hadn't been his imagination. The voice had come from the dragon itself.

"That was you?"

The dragon rumbled again. "Why are you here?"

He took a deep breath, glancing down at the dragon pearl before looking back up and meeting the dragon's silver eyes. "I'm here because there are others who intend to hurt you."

How much of this would the dragon understand? If this was a young dragon, then it was possible it wouldn't understand much of anything.

"Why are you here?"

Jason frowned, cocking his head to the side and trying to look past the dragon to see if there was any movement at the entrance to the cave, but there was none.

"I'm here so that..."

Why *was* he here?

That seemed to be the real question, and strangely, it was one the dragon seemed to recognize.

At first, he had come because he had wanted to ensure the safety of his people. Then he had come because he thought it was necessary. But now that he was here, now that he had seen the dragon, and more than that, now that he had spoken to it, why was he here?

For so long, he'd blamed the dragons, and he'd attributed his father's loss to them. Yet having seen the Dragon Souls, and having met Therin and knowing the kind of person he was, he didn't know if he could continue to blame the creatures the way that he had.

He needed to let that go.

His father would've wanted him to let that go.

He took a deep breath.

"I don't know. I thought I knew. But now I don't." All that sounded foolish, and he didn't know if he was wasting the dragon's time, but at the same time, if he didn't do something now, he worried he wouldn't have enough time. "There is another who's powerful. He's going to come, and he intends to harm the dragons. He wants to control you. To train you. He wants to use you for…" Jason realized that he didn't know exactly what it was going to be, but perhaps it didn't matter. The Dragon Souls wanted to use and control the dragons for their own purposes.

The dragon rumbled, and Jason waited for the creature to ask him why he was here again. Once again, he wasn't sure that he had a good answer.

"What do you need from me?"

He lowered his hand but continued to hold the dragon pearl, and strangely, the light radiating from it no longer took his conscious thought in order to persist. He was thankful for that and wondered how much of it came from him, and how much of it was from the dragon itself.

"I need to find some way to keep you safe. I don't know how to do it."

"He cannot harm me."

"I don't know if he can or not, but I worry he has some way of—"

Heat built, and Jason cut off as he looked toward the entrance of the cave.

"He's here," he whispered.

He started forward, and he wasn't sure what the dragon might do or whether the creature might try to stop him, but the dragon merely turned.

Jason glanced over his shoulder. "You need to hide."

He thought the dragon might argue, but instead, the dragon sank back down into the water. When he was gone, there was no evidence he'd ever been there.

It amazed him that the dragon would be able to tolerate the water like that.

It was as Henry had said. The dragons adapted to their environment.

Surprisingly, this dragon had adapted to the cold, and yet, it still left him marveling at the idea that there was so much power here.

He started forward, squeezing the dragon pearl, holding on to that connection. It was cold, but it wasn't nearly as cold as when his hand was exposed like this. The reverberation echoed through him, and for the first time, he thought he understood it.

He had dragon sight.

Whatever that meant, whatever connection that gave him to the dragons, was real.

And it was one he thought he had to better understand.

He reached the part of the cave where the ground narrowed again.

"I can see you in there," Therin said.

"If you can see me, then come get me. If you dare."

"You won't be able to hide in a cave. I'm going to take you, use you to find the dragon, and then the two of us will return to Lorach."

"Not to Dragon Haven?"

"I think you have been far too troublesome. I will find Dragon Haven on my own."

The hatred in Therin's voice was so different than the man he'd met when he'd first seen him in the village. How could they even be the same person?

"Why did you kill my father?"

"What?"

Jason needed to buy some time, and he thought that pressing Therin on that matter might be the best way. In doing so, it added the benefit of getting some answers. Yet he wasn't convinced Therin would have those answers, and even if he did, he wasn't sure the other man would tell him.

"Why did you kill my father?"

Therin stepped forward, and strangely, he was illuminated by the white light, but it was almost as if Therin weren't aware of that.

It took Jason a moment to realize why that would be.

Therin held a dragon pearl in his hand, and his own orange light glowed off him, radiating away from him, and because of that, he probably didn't know that Jason held his own pearl.

"Do you know how long I've been coming to these lands?"

"No."

"Each year, I bring a few eggs to different places. Never more than that, as they are precious. I'm convinced that in the right location, we can bring about an ice dragon. Or one of earth. Or steam. Or fog. Or—"

"Why?" Jason asked.

"Because they've existed before."

Jason's heart hammered.

"Do you think I would waste eggs in a place like this if I didn't believe such a thing was possible? We've found evidence of them, and yet, there have been no ice dragons. I took it upon myself to change that."

"Why here?"

"It's not only here. I place them in other places."

"And my father?"

"Your father got in the way." Therin took a step toward him, and the light made his features clear, though shadows lined his face. "Oh, yes. I remember him. He came down the backside of the mountain, looking for trade. Came across some foolish girl who had one of my eggs."

Tessa.

Therin *had* been there.

Therin shrugged. "I can only guess she found it. It was

a mistake. He got between her and me and paid for it with his life."

Tessa had found the egg. His father had saved her.

His heart hammered. His mind started to race.

Keep your wits about you...

Jason took a deep breath, forcing himself to focus.

"She got away from me then. It took me a while to find where she'd gone off to. How could I ever have expected her to go *up*?"

"You were looking for her," Jason said. "When you came to the festival. That's what you were looking for." He took a step back, almost involuntarily, and he felt the edge of the water. His foot slipped and he caught himself, barely managing to hold on.

"As I said, it was a mistake. Had she not had the egg, I probably would've left her alone, but when he got in the way of me going after her..."

"You were looking for the egg when you came to the village." It made sense to Jason now. Tessa might not even have known what she'd had.

Therin shrugged. "I came to the village for several reasons. Mostly, I wondered if perhaps she'd brought the egg back to her home village, but something like that would draw attention. And then I thought that if she would have been successful in placing the egg, your festival would have drawn a dragon."

"You killed him for no reason. He was just protecting her!"

"That child made the mistake of getting in the way. Do

you know how hard it is to coax the few female dragons we have to lay an egg? It happens infrequently, and each egg is incredibly valuable, especially in Lorach."

"Because you bind the dragons in captivity," he said.

"You know nothing. When you come to Lorach, I will ensure that you have the necessary education, but until then..."

"I'm not going with you."

"You say that as if you have a choice. That opportunity left you long ago. Now. You will guide me to my dragon."

"There isn't a dragon. You've made a mistake."

Therin grinned at him. "I don't think so. You've seen too much. And everything you've seen suggests to me that you have seen a dragon."

"Why do you believe that?"

"Why?" He reached into his pocket and pulled out something. He held it for a moment, long enough that Jason could recognize a dragon pearl.

He slipped it back into a pouch—a dragonskin-lined pouch.

"You found a pearl. You see, I wasn't sure a dragon would be able to be born out in the wild like this, at least not without a handler to ensure its safekeeping, but when you came across the pearl, I realized one had successfully survived. No pearl could come without a dragon."

Jason squeezed the dragon pearl in his hand, worried that Therin might suddenly realize he had another one, but the other man continued to push him back, and yet, so far, the dragon had remained in the stream.

"Where is it?"

"I don't know where I found the dragon pearl," he said.

"You don't know, or you won't share?"

Jason glared at him.

"I think it's time for your people to know the power of Lorach."

Therin lunged toward him and Jason tried to fight, but the other man grabbed him. He held on to him, and heat radiated from him.

Jason stiffened, squeezing his dragon pearl. If he was going to do something, he would need to work quickly, and he didn't know how much time he had in order to act.

It would have to be perfectly timed.

If he could somehow push Therin into the stream, he might be able to buy himself some time. "What are you going to do to it?"

"I think you'd better be concerned about what I'm going to do with *you.*"

"Just take me. Don't do anything to my people."

"We are well past that point."

"We aren't. You don't have to do anything to my people. You can—"

Jason spun and pushed Therin.

The other man scrambled for a moment, grabbing at air, and then he flailed more, falling into the stream.

As he went, he swept Jason's leg out from under him.

He slipped, falling off the ledge, and went plunging into the stream too.

Cold ripped through him, and it took everything in his

being to try to withstand it. It was overwhelming, almost more than he could tolerate. As he splashed, trying to find a way free, he couldn't. The cold tore at him, and Jason cried out.

Somewhere near him, water began to steam.

Was Therin trying to burn it off with his dragon pearl?

The dragon pearl.

Jason had one, too.

He squeezed it, using his connection to the dragon pearl, that link to the power within it, and wondered if the dragon would respond.

I need your help.

He continued to splash but the current was pulling him downstream, moving quickly. As he went, he tried to scramble for the edge, knowing that if he were trapped underwater, the cold would be far more than he could withstand for very long.

Already he could feel himself getting overwhelmed by the cold and the current.

Something fluttered near him.

Was it Therin?

Jason tried to kick, but his hands didn't work the way they should. One hand was missing its glove, and he didn't know if that was a problem or not.

At least he still held the dragon pearl, but for how much longer? He didn't know if it would make any difference to his survival, anyway.

The water made him numb.

Something fluttered near him again. This time, he didn't have the strength to kick.

And then he felt it.

Something enormous. It moved beneath him and undulated, and then Jason was thrown free.

He was outside, beyond the mouth of the cave, and carried out of the water, away from the stream, and it took a moment for his cold and tired mind to realize that it was the dragon.

The creature shook, and the water went flying from Jason.

Surprisingly, with the cold radiating off the dragon, he wasn't any colder than he'd been. He was drenched, though.

Heat exploded.

Therin cackled with laughter, stalking toward him.

"You found it. And look at it. It's glorious."

Jason couldn't move. The dragon turned in place, and with it, he could feel the power radiating off Therin. The ice dragon didn't appear to be doing anything to resist.

"You have to fight," Jason said.

He could barely get the words out. His lips were numb. The cold was biting him, and there didn't seem to be anything he could do.

The dragon rumbled.

"I can't fight. I'm too... too... cold."

He shivered, trying to fight the overwhelming cold, but there was nothing in him that allowed him to struggle any longer.

The dragon rumbled. There seemed to be some words within it, but Jason wasn't able to make them out. Everything within him seemed frozen, even his hearing.

The only thing he felt was a piercing cold in his hand.

That cold began to work through him, racing up his arm, into his chest, and throughout him.

He took a gasping breath.

The cold persisted, but it was no longer intolerable.

It was almost as if the dragon had given him some sort of resistance to it.

He sat up, looking out across the landscape. Everything seemed awash in bright white light. It took him a moment to realize it radiated off the dragon, and the dragon itself was pulsing with the crystalline light, reflecting off the snow, the snowflakes, and everything all around them.

Therin stood across from him, holding his dragon pearl out. A dark smile crossed his face. "You knew about this," Therin said.

Jason sat there. The dragon was large, but not large enough to pose much of a threat to Therin. And considering the other man had experience dealing with dragons, and likely fighting them, Jason wasn't sure the ice dragon would be much of a challenge for him.

Heat continued to build, and he thought he understood what Therin was doing.

"He's calling to another dragon," Jason said.

The ice dragon rumbled, and yet, as it did, he wasn't sure it mattered.

With the power building, he didn't know if there was anything they would be able to do. If Therin was calling to a dragon, they might not be able to stop it.

Jason scrambled off the dragon's back. His boots crunched along the snow and he glanced down, realizing he wasn't sinking in.

He held his hand out, holding on to the dragon pearl.

"Leave us alone," Jason said.

"I don't think so. This is exactly what I wanted. Soon enough, I will control this dragon, and then I will train it, and—"

Jason pushed his hand out and a burst of white light streaked away, slamming into Therin.

Unlike when he had done the same with the Dragon Soul, this attack did nothing. It sent Therin staggering back, but only a step. It was barely enough to unsettle him.

His eyes narrowed and he leaned toward Jason. "You will regret that."

Therin exploded heat, and it struck Jason.

It bounced off Jason's chest.

He looked down, realizing his clothing had all been turned to ice.

Strangely, it wasn't unbearably cold. It was frozen, and he knew he shouldn't even be alive. With as much ice as now covered him, he should have died.

Therin slammed another burst of heat at him, and then another. Each one bounced off him, striking the ice and reverberating away.

Jason tried again, thrusting his hand out, and power exploded from him.

It slammed into Therin, but much like when Therin's power bounced off Jason, Jason's power bounced off Therin.

"You could be useful," Therin said. "Perhaps more useful than I had expected. Convince the dragon to work with us."

Jason hazarded a glance back. The dragon sat there, resting on the snow.

Why wasn't it taking to the air?

Unless it couldn't.

Maybe an ice dragon didn't have the ability to fly, or there was the possibility it was too small to fly. He thought about what Sarah had said about the young dragons and the time it took for them to fully develop, and he couldn't help but wonder if perhaps this dragon was too small for that yet.

"You're going to have to help," he said to it.

The dragon swiveled its head toward him and met his eyes with his deep silvery ones.

The dragon stretched its wings and Therin laughed.

"Does it think it can fly? Not yet, little one."

Heat continued to build, and it seemed as if it pressed down from above.

The dragon stretched itself out and glided forward, sliding along the surface of the snow. As it did, it shook.

The shaking was an enormous trembling, and it rumbled, reminding Jason of an avalanche. He couldn't help but wonder if perhaps the dragon had been responsible for some of the avalanches before.

As the dragon shook, as those wings fluttered, catching the snow and the wind, thousands of sharp icicles streaked out from the dragon.

None of them struck Jason.

It seemed impossible, but then, the dragon was slightly off to his side, and angled in such a way that he wouldn't be targeting him.

Therin held his hands out, a dragon pearl gripped in each one, forcing his hands to glow, and the heat continued to build, radiating off him, creating a bubble around him. The icicles slammed into him one after another, and yet, none of them damaged him.

The dragon continued to shake, but nothing it did caused Therin any harm.

The dragon rumbled again.

Jason glanced over, noticing how the dragon was growing slower.

It was getting tired.

It was still a young dragon, so any ability it had to defend itself was limited. It was going to have to be up to Jason, but he wasn't sure how he would succeed. Therin held his hands up and grinned at Jason.

Jason looked at the stream burbling near him.

There was one thing he could do, but he didn't know if the dragon's protections extended that far.

He glanced over at the dragon. "Help me."

With that, he raced forward, slamming into Therin.

The other man was strong, but the sudden movement startled him, and Jason drove him into the stream.

This time, he was ready for the cold, and surprisingly, it didn't affect him quite the same way it had the first time. He sat on top of Therin, riding him as the water flowed past, letting the stream carry him. He remained holding him. Therin tried to fight, pushing outward with heat and the power of the dragon pearls, but Jason ignored it, pushing outward with his dragon pearl. He wrapped Therin in the strange white light, and slowly, ice crystallized around Therin. The power of the stream and the cold within it gave him more connection.

After a few moments, Therin stopped moving.

The light glowing from his hands began to dim before going out entirely.

Jason held on, forcing the other man down, squeezing him into the stream, and tried to push more and more power around him, creating a larger ice ball around Therin.

That connection began to wane, and he started to feel the cold.

He shivered.

As he did, something grabbed him and pulled him free of the stream.

Jason lay on the shoreline, looking up. Everything still seemed to have that soft glow about it, although the snowflakes no longer had the sharp, needle-like quality to them. He was so cold it took his breath away, making everything difficult.

He looked up. The dragon was there, meeting his eyes with its silver ones.

"Thank you," he said.

The dragon rumbled, and he wasn't sure if there were any words in it. He couldn't tell, and then the cold began to sweep through him, and he shivered.

The dragon grabbed him and started to slide along the surface of the snow.

At some point, Jason blacked out.

25

Heat built. It swirled around him, and Jason tried to blink open his eyes, but he wasn't able to see anything. It took a moment to realize why that was. There was heat, but his eyelids were frozen shut.

"I think he's coming around," a voice said, though distantly.

"Keep working on it." This one clearly came from Henry; Jason recognized the rough gravel to his voice.

"I'm here," Jason said.

He took a deep breath and tried to move his arms, found that they did work, and brought them up to his eyes, wiping them across his face.

Icicles crackled off his eyelids and he blinked them open. A warm orange light glowed around him.

He sat up and realized he was back within the cave. His breath caught as he looked around, worried that the ice dragon might be here and that they might still be under attack, but he saw only Sarah and William and Henry.

The ice dragon was gone.

"How are you here?" Jason asked.

William laughed. "Here I thought I was lucky. From what Henry says, you shouldn't be alive."

Henry glanced over at him. He was standing near the edge of the cave, looking down. "He shouldn't be. With exposure like that, you should have died."

Jason breathed out, looking around the cave. "How did you find me?"

"We were tracking the dragon egg and the dragon, and it brought us up, but then it brought us back down and around." Sarah shook her head. "I don't know if there even *was* a dragon."

Henry locked eyes with him. "What happened?"

"Therin."

"I know Therin. What happened with Therin?"

Jason took a deep breath, drawing himself up, and looked around the cavern. The others were crouching near him, and only Henry stood. Jason resisted the urge to look toward the water, not wanting the others to know that was where the ice dragon had emerged. He wasn't sure why he hid that from them, and yet, perhaps he shouldn't.

Then again, the ice dragon was still young, developing, and he wasn't sure what they would do if they learned of it.

Probably nothing, but there was still the possibility they would try to do the same thing that Therin had done, and they might want to try to control it, to use it in their attack against Lorach.

He didn't want that for the dragon. He wanted the dragon to have the opportunity to grow, to decide what it wanted, and it wasn't going to be able to do that with others wanting to use it.

"He found me. After the attack, he came upon me, and he tried to drag me with him. He threatened my village."

"How are you here?" Henry asked.

Jason got to his knees, looking around. His jacket was still frozen, and it was a marvel that he lived. One glove was on, the other off, and he gripped the dragon pearl in his hand. It surprised him that he still held on to it, but it was probably because of the dragon pearl that he even lived.

"I... I convinced him he would find the dragon in here."

"How?" Henry asked.

"I told him we found the egg."

Henry grunted. "I'm no longer convinced it was the egg."

Jason looked down. "It's probably just from the ceiling of the cave."

Sarah sighed. "That's what we think, too. That's probably why the spell brought us back here. I thought maybe it was an egg, because it was so different, and because I was using the dragon pearl to track, but..."

354 | D.K. HOLMBERG

"I'm glad you found me," he said.

"It's good we came back here," Sarah said.

"What happened with Therin?" Henry asked.

Jason looked toward the stream. As he did, there was no sign of movement—and no sign of the dragon. Was it gone? It was possible it followed the flow of the stream, but it was also possible that it was lying there, hiding.

"When he brought me here, I pushed him into the stream."

"You *what?*" William asked.

Jason nodded. "I pushed him into the stream. I held him down. He tried to use his dragon pearls for heat, but he wasn't strong enough to overpower the cold of this place."

"It would take considerable energy to do so. It would likely drain the dragon of its own energy, and even that might not be enough," Henry said.

At least that explained why he'd managed to survive.

"I don't think the dragon pearl *was* enough. He stopped moving, and floated downstream."

"He's probably not gone," Henry said.

With Therin's connection to the dragon pearls and the dragons, it was possible that, even frozen as he was, he might be able to thaw himself. The farther he went downstream, Jason had to hope the other man would have time to figure things out. At least this way, Therin wasn't going to pose a threat for a little while.

Jason looked at the others. He needed to tell them about the dragon, didn't he?

And yet, he wasn't sure he could.

"He's probably not gone," Jason agreed. "What about the other Dragon Souls?"

"The rest of the Dragon Souls have been removed. One of them got away, but we haven't seen any evidence of them."

"He fell into the stream, too," Jason said.

"You knocked *two* Dragon Souls into the stream?" William asked.

"The first one was accidental, and it gave me the idea of what to do with Therin."

William laughed. "Like I said, *I'm* supposed to be lucky."

Henry looked up at the top of the cave before turning his attention to Jason.

"What now?" William asked.

"Now we sit out the storm. In the morning, we will summon the dragon, and then we return to Dragon Haven," Henry said.

"I'm not going with you," Jason said.

"You're not?" William turned toward him. "I can't return to my town. Not with Gary after me. Well, and because I know there are dragons." He grinned, but there was a pained look in his eyes. William wouldn't return, but Jason wondered if he wanted to. "It would be a lot better to have you with us."

Sarah watched him. Jason couldn't tell what she was thinking.

"I didn't leave my village because I wanted to leave," he said softly.

"Is there much for you there?" she asked.

Jason made his way to the edge of the stream, looking down into it. He saw his lean face reflected back up at him, the silver eye shining back at him. Different than everyone in his home village. Were he to go with them to Dragon Haven, there might be others like him. Wasn't that what he wanted? A chance to fit in, to understand what he might be able to do, and whether there was a connection between him and the dragons. What he'd seen with Therin had proven he had some power.

Memories of his father came back to him. There might be something he could learn by going with them, but there was more he needed to learn by staying.

Staring into the stream, every so often, he thought he saw movement on the bottom, but that might just be his imagination.

"Therin killed my father," he said slowly.

"How do you know?" Sarah asked.

"He told me. He said he saw him. My father found an egg Therin was trying to place, and he killed him for it."

It was a simplification, but it was enough.

"I need to return. I've been so distraught over losing my father for so long that I haven't been the person I needed to be. I need to return for my sister and my mother. I need to return for…" He took a deep breath, looking up at Sarah, meeting her eyes. There was something unreadable in them. "I think I need to return for myself."

Henry approached. "I will leave a token with you. If you ever need us, you can use it."

He handed something to him. A small piece that reminded him of the dragon pearl, though it wasn't smooth or round.

"How would you know?" Jason asked.

Henry held his gaze. "We would know."

Jason turned away from the stream. Somewhere in there was the ice dragon, and he needed to better understand his connection to it, as he was convinced that he had a connection. The longer he spent here, the more he thought he could understand it. Once he did, he could figure out if it was time to go to Dragon Haven and join the others. Until then, he would remain in the village.

It wasn't ideal. The village didn't feel quite like home to him any longer, but there were people there who cared about him.

They settled down for rest, and he had a fitful sleep, filled with dreams of cold and ice and movement underneath the water.

When he awoke, light streamed in from the opening of the cave. Henry was already up, standing there, looking out, heat radiating off him. When Jason joined him, the other man glanced back. "I've summoned the dragon."

"How long will it be?"

"Not long. We'll search for Therin."

If Therin had survived, Jason wasn't sure how long it would take for him to return. The stream would carry him far from here, and it would remain as icy cold for the entirety of the journey. It would take quite a while for Therin to come around, and even that might not be survivable.

He had to hope that the other man was gone.

It didn't make him sad at all. Therin was responsible for what happened to Jason's father. If nothing else, he thought he could let his mother and sister know, though even if he did, would they believe him? They were like he had once been, and believed the dragons were responsible for his loss.

It didn't take long before a dark shape appeared from above, and the enormous form of the dragon lowered to the ground outside. In the light, the sunlight reflected off its scales, giving it a shimmering appearance. Heat radiated from the dragon's back, and it lifted its front legs while it stood in the snow.

Henry climbed onto the dragon's back, looking down.

Jason glanced at the others.

"I hope to see you again," William said.

"I do as well."

William climbed up on the back of the dragon, sitting behind Henry.

Sarah hesitated, looking at Jason, a question filling her silver eyes. "You don't have to stay here."

He wanted to say something more to her, to explain

himself better, but he couldn't tell his sister about the dragon yet and he couldn't leave without his sister. "It's not that I have to."

"There is much that you could learn. I can see it in your eyes."

"I don't know that I'm ready."

"I hope one day you will be ready."

She held his gaze for a long moment before pulling him toward her, hugging him, and then stepping back. When she turned away, she seemed to have moisture in her eyes, and she climbed up on the dragon's back.

Jason waved, but the dragon took off quickly and circled as it went, disappearing into the air. He took a deep breath. It was time to head back.

Before doing so, he turned toward the stream, reaching his hand into it.

As he suspected, it wasn't nearly as cold as he remembered. He brought his hand out and shook off the ice that formed, and felt none of the ill effects he would've expected.

Crawling back into the cave, he crouched at the edge of the stream.

"If you're in there, know that I will come and visit."

There came a deep rumbling from somewhere, and yet, the dragon didn't appear.

Jason smiled to himself. That was okay. The dragon had helped him, and because of the dragon, he had survived.

He stuffed the dragon pearl into his pocket, pulled his glove back on, and headed out of the cave.

He looked up at the sky. It was almost blue. For the first time in as long as he remembered, there were no clouds in the sky. Wind whistled as it often did, but there wasn't any of the same bite to it as he was accustomed to feeling.

A bright sky full of hope.

Jason smiled at the thought, another quote from his father. There hadn't been many bright skies, but when they'd had them, his father had wanted to take advantage of them, believing them better days for hunting. There wouldn't be any hunting today, but that didn't mean it wasn't a good day for hunting.

Jason turned his attention up the slope, and he climbed.

From here, it wasn't a long climb. Only a few hours, and it seemed as if he made better time than he usually would have. His boots didn't sink into the snow the same way they once had, and he couldn't help but feel as if his connection to the dragon had somehow altered something for him, making it so that not only was he more impervious to the cold, but he was able to travel more easily along the surface of the snow.

As he went, he began to grow warm.

It was a strange sensation, and yet, he smiled to himself.

By the time he finally saw the edge of the village, a sheen of sweat worked over him.

He stood looking up at the village. There was movement there, and to his dragon sight, he could make out aspects of that, though he wasn't able to recognize anyone from where he stood. He breathed in the crisp air and wondered what sort of reception he would receive upon his return.

It was difficult to know how long he'd been gone. It likely had been nearly a week, possibly longer, but in that time, so much had changed for him. He had changed.

And he was thankful for that.

Taking another deep breath, he headed back to the village.

When he reached the first row of buildings, he paused. He had questions for Tessa. The egg had ended up in the cave, and he suspected she was responsible for it as she must have been the one to return with it, but those questions would come another time.

It was time to go home.

The snow was piled up outside, having not been shoveled. That was usually his job. He frowned and swept a hand across it, but as he did, the snow seemed to shimmer, freezing beneath his hand.

He stood, staring at it.

That was strange. Had his connection to the dragon changed so much for him?

Once the snow was cleared off in front of the house, he pushed open the door.

It was dimly lit, and a faint fire crackled along one

wall, the air filled with the odor of burning dung. It was a familiar scent, but not necessarily a welcome one.

There was no one here. He closed the door behind him, not wanting the heat to escape, and began to unbutton his coat, looking around for his sister or his mother.

Neither of them was here.

He checked the kitchen, thankful there was some food, and he grabbed a bit of old meat, chewing on it. The venison was oversalted, but his sister had made it tender, and it melted in his mouth. This was what he had missed while he was gone.

Now that he was back, he was going to have to hunt again, and yet, he wondered if he would find it easier. No longer would he fear descending too far down the side of the mountain.

Even if he did, he knew there was much that he could find. If he were to risk it, he could go all the way down the side of the mountain, down to the village, and perhaps find supplies.

"Kayla? Mother?"

"Hello?"

The voice was soft, muted, and Jason started toward the back room. When he reached the door, he looked inside.

"Kayla?"

His sister leaned over the bed. When she looked over, her eyes went wide. She took a step back, staggering away. "Jason?"

He nodded. "It's me."

"How are you... How are you still alive?"

"It's a long story," he said.

He took a step into the room but his sister remained stiff, watching him.

"You've been gone for so long. No one ever returns when they're gone that long. You missed Reltash's punishment for firing one of the ballistae and... where have you *been?*"

He would have loved to have seen Reltash get punished and was truly sorry that he'd missed it. "I got caught in the storm. An avalanche..." He shook his head. "It doesn't matter. I made it back."

She reached a hand forward, touching him. "Aren't you cold?"

"I'm better now."

"But your coat is frozen."

He glanced down. He hadn't realized icicles still coated him. Perhaps he should have been more careful. "I'm okay."

He looked down at the bed. Their mother lay there, resting on her side.

"What happened?"

"When you didn't return, she... I don't think she could tolerate losing another."

Jason made his way around the bed. The room had a sickly odor to it, and his heart ached at what his sister had gone through in the time he had been gone.

"Mother?"

He reached for her hands, squeezing them. Would they be too cold, as well?

He didn't think that much had changed about him.

"It's Jason. I'm back."

"Jason?" She blinked open her eyes. As she did, she searched his eyes with hers, and for a moment, he thought that he noticed silver within hers, but then they cleared. "Is it really you?"

Jason smiled. "It's me, Mother. I'm here."

"How?"

He glanced over at his sister before looking back at his mother. "It doesn't matter. I'm back."

Taking her hands, sitting next to his mother, he couldn't help but wonder how long he'd be able to stay.

He intended to remain, but would the Dragon Souls return and force him away?

Those were questions for another time. For now, he was back. He was home. And he would be here with his family. Eventually, he would have to tell them what really happened to his father. Why he seemed to know about magic and what he'd kept from them. Then Jason would have to decide what else to do. Somehow, he knew dragons would be a part of it.

The Dragon Misfits continues with book 2: Iron Dragon.

Looking for more in this world? Check out the Drag-onwalker series, staring with: Dragon Bones.

The Chaos Rises

The Elements Bond

Elemental Academy: Spirit Master

The Shape of Fire

The Cloud Warrior Saga

Chased by Fire

Bound by Fire

Changed by Fire

Fortress of Fire

Forged in Fire

Serpent of Fire

Servant of Fire

Born of Fire

Broken of Fire

Light of Fire

Cycle of Fire

The Endless War

Journey of Fire and Night

Darkness Rising

Endless Night

Summoner's Bond

Seal of Light

The Dark Ability Series

The Shadow Accords

Shadow Blessed

Shadow Cursed

Shadow Born

Shadow Lost

Shadow Cross

Shadow Found

The Collector Chronicles

Shadow Hunted

Shadow Games

Shadow Trapped

The Dark Ability

The Dark Ability

The Heartstone Blade

The Tower of Venass

Blood of the Watcher

The Shadowsteel Forge

The Guild Secret

Rise of the Elder

The Sighted Assassin

The Binders Game

The Forgotten

Assassin's End

The Elder Stones Saga

The Darkest Revenge

Shadows Within the Flame

Remnants of the Lost

The Coming Chaos

The Depth of Deceit

A Forging of Power

A Threat Revealed

The Council of Elders

The Lost Prophecy Series

The Teralin Sword

Soldier Son

Soldier Sword

Soldier Sworn

Soldier Saved

Soldier Scarred

The Lost Prophecy

The Threat of Madness

The Warrior Mage

Tower of the Gods